Hailey Edwards writes about questionable applications of otherwise perfectly good magic, the transformative power of love, the family you choose for yourself, and blowing stuff up. Not necessarily all at once. That could get messy. She lives in Alabama with her husband, their daughter, and a herd of dachshunds.

Visit her website at www.haileyedwards.net

By Hailey Edwards

The Foundling Series

Bayou Born
Bone Driven
Death Knell
Rise Against

RISE AGAINST

Hailey Edwards

piatkus

PIATKUS

First published in Great Britain in 2019 by Piatkus

1 3 5 7 9 10 8 6 4 2

A CIP catalogue record for this book
is available from the British Library.

ISBN 978-0-349-42336-4

Typeset in Goudy by M Rules
Printed and bound in Great Britain by
Clays Ltd, Elcograf S.p.A.

Papers used by Piatkus are from well-managed forests
and other responsible sources.

Piatkus
An imprint of
Little, Brown Book Group
Carmelite House
50 Victoria Embankment
London EC4Y 0DZ

An Hachette UK Company
www.hachette.co.uk

www.littlebrown.co.uk

For my readers, who always keep me on my toes. And for my husband, who still manages to sweep me off my feet.

CHAPTER ONE

———◆———

Virginia City, Nevada was a curious mix of history and touristy kitsch that left me wondering what type of charun called this place home. The location was remote, the mountains in the distance a fascination that kept my eye traveling back to them, so different from my lowland birthplace. But the boardwalk lined with shops of every kind — candy, jerky, gemstones, T-shirts, jewelry — bustled with tourists exploring the Old West town under the watchful eyes of tour guides from dueling companies.

Squinting against the sun, pretending I wasn't searching the sky for a certain dragon, I angled my chin toward Santiago. "Are you sure we'll find what we're looking for here?"

"One of our first missions on any terrene is to identify pockets of Conquest loyalists." He glared at human tourists foolish enough to stumble into his path. "This is one of the larger charun communes in this state, and they're all devoted to your glory."

A shudder tripped down my spine, and he grinned even wider. "You're an asshat," I told him.

"These people worship you. The least you can do is stop scowling at them."

"I'm not ..." Movement drew my eye to the second floor of a saloon, to the male who kissed his fingertips then pressed them to his heart while bowing his head. "They're watching." Now that I knew to look, I examined each upper window lining the boardwalk. More faces looked back. More fingers were kissed. More heads bowed in reverence, making my skin crawl. "They're everywhere."

"Told you." He sounded smug about it. "We'll meet up with them tonight, after the tourists have been bussed back to their hotels in Reno." He laughed under his breath. "Until then, smile and wave."

Campaigning for soldiers in our upcoming war made me queasy. Who was I to ask these people to follow me? To fight for me? Die for me? Because that's what war was — death. Only the number of casualties had yet to be tallied.

The air kicked up, and dust swirled around me. When I paused, the thick coils of an invisible dragon tail wrapped my ankle.

"Cole," I breathed. "You're late."

Warm breath fanned my face, and soft scales glided against my skin as he rubbed our cheeks together.

"Break it up," Santiago groused. "I didn't come here to watch you two make out."

"You can't see him," I pointed out, scratching Cole under his chin.

"Maybe not, but I can smell him." Santiago wrinkled his nose. "He's pheromone central lately, thanks to you."

Stupid charun hormones. Stupid charun sense of smell. Stupid me for not being able to control myself.

The IUD had cured the worst of the effects the coterie experienced, but Cole was my mate, and I couldn't settle around him. The heat was always there, a slow burn waiting to engulf me in flames. The others kept telling me it would get better after we had sex, after I claimed him, but the only thing that might be worse than them telling me to jump his bones and get it over with was the fact they would know the instant I did. Apparently Otillians scent-marked their mates, and I was just enough charun to want other females to smell him coming from a mile away.

"Mistress," a soft voice hissed to my right. "We have everything prepared."

I didn't have to search hard to find the source. An elderly female knelt, her forehead pressed to the planks and her arms stretched toward my feet. Taking a step out of range, much to Santiago's amusement, I did my best to remain calm in the face of adoration.

"Thank you." I stared at the back of her head. "We appreciate your hospitality."

"We live to serve," she murmured. "Our lives are yours to command."

Rubbing my face, I set a task to get her off the ground before she made an even bigger spectacle. "Can you guide us to our hotel?"

The strip was short, the town small, but she sprang to her feet with a rush of energy that startled me.

"Right this way." She hustled down the boardwalk, bowling over people who got in her way. Clearing a path for me, I realized with a groan. "We have all your rooms prepared."

Hand resting on the heaving side of the invisible beast, I murmured, "See you there?"

A soft growl of confirmation set my heart fluttering as he uncoiled his tail.

"Hurry up," Santiago called, already ahead of me. "She's old, but she's fast."

A buzz in my pocket had me fishing out my phone, my pulse skipping before the familiar number flashed across the screen. "How is she?"

"Maggie is resting." Miller kept his voice soft. "She's still dizzy, and she's drinking water as fast as I can put fresh bottles in her hand."

"Poor Mags." Having never traveled outside the Deep South, she had no clue how hard the altitude would hit her. None of us expected it to knock her, and therefore Portia, on her butt. Missing Thom, and now Portia, divided our numbers dangerously. And forced me to keep company with Santiago. "Book a flight for two back to Mississippi."

Any excuse to put off the next rally, even for a day, was a welcome break on the campaign trail for me.

"Already done," he assured me. "How are things up the mountain?"

"We met our contact." I jogged to catch up to Santiago. "We're en route to our hotel. Cole's meeting us there."

"Any trouble?"

"None so far." I knocked on a wooden beam as I ducked under a general store's awning. "We're being watched, though."

"Pay attention," Santiago growled at me then snatched the phone out of my hand and barked into the receiver, "Stop distracting her. We're surrounded. We need all eyes and ears focused on staying alive."

After ending the call, he tossed me the phone. I considered throwing it as hard as I could at the back of his skull, but I didn't want these charun to think I was a violent brute like my predecessors. Plus, impact with his hard head would shatter the cell if the drop to the ground didn't, and I couldn't afford to be incommunicado in case Dad needed me.

Dad, who I still hadn't visited, who had no idea his best friend had been murdered, and who must be getting antsy about the discharge date that wouldn't come until I was declared the victor or the permanent resident of a pine box.

Rather than spark a fight with Santiago, I pocketed the cell and daydreamed about wiping three or four of his tablets clean. I didn't know how to do that, and he kept backups out the wazoo, but imagining the expression on his face as I took a hammer to the screen made me smile nonetheless.

"Here we are," our hostess announced. "Your rooms are on the top floor of the saloon. There's a bar downstairs, and the kitchen is open until midnight."

Spry for a female her apparent age, she led us through the front door and right up the rickety staircase off to one side. She indicated three rooms available for our use. Two were neat as pins but small for the guys. The third was a honeymoon suite with an oversized bed covered in a handstitched quilt in a double wedding ring pattern. I recognized it because Granny Boudreau had left several in a trunk up in the attic.

A pang arrowed through me, reminding me the farmhouse had been listed by a realtor in Canton. All the quilts, all the dolls, all the memories from generations of Boudreaus, were boxed up in climate-controlled storage. Only the furniture remained for staging purposes.

Thinking of home circled my thoughts back to Dad and opened a pit in my stomach.

"Are the accommodations to your liking, Mistress?"

Yanked back to attention, I nodded. "These are perfect." I smiled. "Thank you."

Flushing with pleasure, she scampered down the stairs and left Santiago and me to freshen up before meeting with her clan to hit them up with pro-Conquest propaganda designed to win them to our cause.

Ugh.

Santiago lifted a finger, waiting until she passed beyond charun hearing, then shifted his hand into a thumbs-up gesture.

"They know Cole's here," I mused, eyeing the third bedroom that would sit empty tonight for security reasons instead of any fun or sweaty ones.

"You were talking to and petting thin air when our escort arrived," he replied dryly. "Not to mention the fact these aren't humans. They're charun. They would smell him, sense him. Cole is a power, and he's saturated in your scent."

A primal corner of my heart swelled with the knowledge, and it kept expanding when heavy footfalls on the stairs announced the arrival of the man in question.

The second bedroom didn't earn a spare glance from him. He spotted me standing on the threshold of mine and joined me, dwarfing the doorway. This close, I had to tilt my head back to meet his piercing blue eyes, but the view was always worth it.

The black stubble covering his head had grown longer in recent weeks, almost brushing the tips of his ears, even the one with the top curve missing. Windburn slashed his cheeks and reddened his nose, which had been broken and reset badly, multiple times. Probably by him. In the field. When it would have taken Thom minutes to patch him up as good as new.

When he brushed his scarred knuckles across my cheek, I remembered thinking once that you could play tic-tac-toe with the raised slashes crisscrossing the backs of his hands.

Leaning into his touch, I closed my eyes just for a second, relishing the contact I had been missing lately with him spending so much time in his other form for ease of travel.

Santiago snorted behind him, and Cole cut him a glare through meltwater eyes. He ground his square jaw, knuckles popping on his left hand. "Is there a problem?"

Without Portia as a buffer, Santiago's attitude got old fast. I'm talking ancient. Even Cole was losing his patience, and it took effort to rile him. Deliberate effort.

Eyebrows quirked, Santiago challenged, "Does it matter if there is?"

"Not really," I chimed in. "Why don't you make yourself useful and sweep for bugs?"

These charun might follow Conquest, but that didn't mean they would follow *me*. I was an aberration, not the warrior they expected to rise and trample this world to dust. I had to put on a show and win them over if I wanted them to come when I called and lay down their lives if that's what victory cost.

"It will be fine," Cole rumbled behind me. "They will see hope in you." He lowered his voice. "The same way I do."

Warm fuzzies bubbled up inside me, and I wrapped my arms around his waist, letting my head rest on his broad chest. I breathed him in, and my nerves settled, my worries calming. I didn't want to let go. I wanted to hold him and pretend we had a different agenda.

Tasting elk and alligator jerky. Eating apples dipped in caramel then rolled in every topping known to mankind. Maybe hitting up one of the jewelry shops and buying him a simple band. Though it would be selfish of me, human of me, since I'm the one who would get a thrill each time it glinted on his finger.

Arms closing around me, he chuckled softly. "You're growling."

"Sorry about that." I cleared my throat. "I was thinking . . . "

"Hmm?" With me in his arms, he relaxed, allowing the hours of flight to show in exhausted lines on his face.

"Would you be opposed to wearing a ring?"

Like a human couple.

I couldn't bring myself to add that part. It would hardly help my argument.

But the feral heart of me wanted this union made permanent. Symbols have power, and I had been raised to picture white dresses and diamond rings after Cupid's arrow struck. A band, visible proof of our bond, would settle me.

Tension coiled through him where my fingers joined at his spine. "Why?"

"It's a human thing," I finally admitted, daring a peek up at him. "They exchange matching rings so people can identify them as a couple."

Adorable confusion wreathed his face. "Any charun would know I belong to you."

The scent thing again. Why did everything with charun boil down to the most embarrassing of senses?

"The world is made up of more than charun." I jabbed him in the abs with my pointer finger and almost popped my knuckle on the hard ridges of muscle. "And you don't belong to me."

Sliding his wide palms up my arms, past my shoulders, he coasted over my throat, cupped my face, and brought his head down to mine. "I do." His lips brushed mine. "I always will."

"I should tell you I don't want you to say that but . . . " I captured his mouth in a hungry kiss that left him rumbling like an empty stomach, " . . . I like hearing it too much." Covering his hands with mine, I made sure I held his attention. "As long as you understand it goes both ways, we're good."

"I'm not sure which was worse," Santiago grumbled on his way past us, a whirring gizmo in his hand. "When she was an evil overlord or this PDA nightmare."

Ignoring him, which was the best revenge, I lingered in Cole's embrace until Santiago announced the room was clear and went to sweep his own.

"That's a good sign." I crossed to the bed and flopped back on the pillows. "That means they're acting in good faith."

The mattress dipped, and the box springs groaned when Cole joined me. "Many charun who survive their mistress's demise spend lifetimes waiting to be called to service, and they train their children to hold those same values."

The comfort of hearing my coterie might survive me boosted my morale, though I could never tell them so.

"I can't knock it since that might be the only thing that saves us." That didn't mean I had to like it. "It's been quiet this week."

Five days ago, we left Death behind at the bunkhouse in Canton to acclimate her coterie to this terrene. We entrusted her with the pod where Phoebe, Cole's daughter with Conquest, had slumbered for untold years. He was itching to wake her, but it was dangerous bringing a child into the hot mess our lives had become. The alternative, that he might die in the war without seeing her again, was just as awful. A decision had to be made, and soon, but he had a few days before shouldering that burden.

Cole stroked the length of my spine, his touch sparking jolts of pleasure down the *rukav*, even through the fabric of my shirt. "No word from Wu?"

"None." He hadn't made contact once since taking a White Horse SUV and leaving us behind at the bunkhouse. "We probably have him to thank for the calm waters."

Wu knew his father better than anyone, and he could predict where and how he would strike next. The destruction of The Hole might have shocked Wu with its brutality — all those lives lost in addition to Famine — but the blow had only rededicated him to our cause.

I had to believe the fact we had made it this far, had rallied followers in four towns and counting, was due to him running interference with his father.

A weak attempt at nonchalance flavored Cole's next question. "Has Death made contact?"

"Not since she texted four days ago." I twisted to peek at him over my shoulder. "Phoebe is in good hands. Death will keep her safe." I turned onto my side to see him better. "She protected her this long. Have a little faith."

A knock on the door announced Santiago's arrival seconds before he walked in. He scrunched his nose at our positions on the bed, but he joined us with a tablet in his hands.

This right here was the reason why Cole and I hadn't made any progress in cementing our mate bond. Too many eyes, ears, and noses for my comfort. Not to mention witnesses who couldn't take a pointed hint to leave even if you stabbed them between the eyes with it. But it's not like we could press pause on the world while we rented a nice hotel room away from the coterie for a long weekend of naked gymnastics.

Saving the world was more important than getting in Cole's pants.

Probably.

"What do you want?" I toed Santiago in the hip. "Didn't your mother teach you to wait until you're invited in to enter a room?"

"No." His fingers flew across the keys. "My mother ate one of my siblings because she wasn't a fan of uneven numbers."

Blinking slowly, I reminded myself that he was charun and not human. Still, it was hard not to picture a female with his features smoking a baby on the grill like a pork roast. "That's . . . horrible."

"No, that's life on the lower terrenes."

Jaw tight, Cole looked ready to thump Santiago's ear. "Is there a reason you're in here instead of in your room?"

"I planted a tracker on Wu," he said casually. "I've been mapping his path since he left."

"You — " I spluttered. "What possessed you to do that?"

"Curiosity." He shrugged. "That, and I don't trust the guy as far as I can throw him." He considered that. "Actually, I can throw him farther than I trust him. Anyway. He's made two trips to a spot near Lake Bevin. He stayed overnight both times. I'm not familiar with the area, so I tagged it." He spun the laptop toward me. "See all those red spots? They're heat signatures. Bodies."

I did a quick tally. "There are forty or more in the tree line."

"The trees are concealing them from satellite surveillance. This is the best I can do. But someone is out there, and we have no way to discover who, or what Wu's connection to them is, without taking a look-see."

"Knox kept an aerial patrol in rotation." I pushed upright and tucked my legs under me. "Could it be more of his people? He pulled everyone in, but he would have asked for volunteers to protect the civilians."

Including Thom, who was too injured to fight. He had been sent to recover at the enclave, not defend it.

"We'll scout the area on the way to our next rally." I gave up looking to Cole for support. He expected me to make the hard calls on my own. That kind of trust humbled and terrified me. I wasn't Conquest, with her centuries of experience. I was just me. Just Luce. With not even three measly decades under my belt by comparison. "We need to make sure the conclave is secure."

"Thom can take care of himself," Santiago said in a rare moment of kindness. "And if he can't, then we'll fight our way in, retrieve him, and fight out way out again."

"Good plan." I gave him two thumbs up. "I especially like the fighting parts."

"If it ain't broke," he reasoned, "don't fix it."

"Forty-five minutes until the meeting," Cole announced, giving up on our cuddle session. "Want to grab a drink downstairs?"

"Only if you let me buy the first round." I scooched off the edge of the bed and stretched out the kinks in my spine from the car ride up the mountain from Reno. Life had reached epic levels of weirdness when you preferred clinging to a dragon over a comfy rental. Cole trailed me down the stairs and claimed two stools at the bar. "What'll you have?"

"Hey," the girl behind the counter called, "that's my line."

I laughed and called back, "I'll take a rum and Coke."

Interest glimmered in her eyes. "What about your boyfriend?"

A week ago, I would have demurred, but Cole had made his feelings clear, and I didn't have a problem making mine crystal either. "He'll take a Scotch on the rocks."

The poor thing deflated when I didn't correct her, and I almost felt bad for the amount of glee in my order. There was no easy way to explain my joy came from earning his permission to stake a claim on him with his consent and not from petty girlfriendedness. Since odds were high I would never speak to the bartender again, maybe not even see her, I figured I would tip well to offset any hurt feelings.

I might be a happily mated charun, but I didn't have to be a bitch about it.

CHAPTER TWO

———◆———

I understood the reason why Cole invited me downstairs five minutes after our drinks arrived. A full quarter of the patrons stared openly at us. Another quarter cut their eyes our way. The third quarter pretended we didn't exist, but they thrummed with a sense of anticipation that prickled my hindbrain. The rest I figured must be human. They followed stares to see what all the hubbub was about, but we didn't do anything interesting or resemble anyone famous, so conversation returned to their plans for the night.

See and be seen. That's all this was about. Letting these charun acclimate to my presence while I indulged in nonthreatening behavior in front of enough humans to keep me honest. Little did they know I would hurt them long before I injured a bystander. Charun deserved to carve out their own lives and find happiness, but not at the expense of innocents, and the charun on my radar were rarely that.

"You're handling me." I nursed my drink, enjoying the warmth spreading down my throat. "You have been since we left Canton."

"I'm your consort." Cole wiped his thumb around the lip of his glass. "It's my duty."

"Are you afraid I'll tell them Conquest is a nutjob, and they're bonkers for following her?"

"They worship the title, but they can be resistant to individual incarnations."

"I'm not going to lie to them. I can't do that and be true to myself."

"I understand." He placed his cool hand over mine. "I would never ask you to compromise your beliefs." A hint of a smile tugged at his lips. "They're part of the reason why I love you."

Cole Heaton loves me.

"Yes," he said. "I do."

"I, uh, didn't mean to say that out loud." Blood rushed into my cheeks. "I don't want you to think my entire internal monologue is about you."

"Please," Santiago quipped from my other side as he claimed a stool. "All you do is gaze into each other's eyes. You two ought to have sex. Right now. On the bar if that's what it takes. This lovey-dovey crap is going to get you both killed. You can't fight if you can't take your eyes off your mate."

"My mate," I said softly, unable to hide a small thrill.

"Do you ever miss Conquest?" Santiago asked Cole over my head. "Remember the good ol' days?"

Moving with inhuman speed, Cole stretched one of his long legs behind me, hooked the lowest rung on Santiago's barstool, and yanked it out from under him. Santiago cracked his chin on the bar on his way to the floor. Blood dribbled out of the corner of his mouth when he glared up at us with a snarl on his lips.

"Mistress?"

I spun on my seat to face a young couple who stood on quivering knees with their heads lowered. "Yes?"

"We have been sent to escort you to the opera house."

"It's go time," I told the guys, leaning over to offer Santiago a hand up. "Let's do this."

We trailed our escorts out of the saloon and onto the main street. We climbed an almost vertical hill that caused me to stumble more than once before reaching a plateau and the old opera house. Two women greeted us at the door, welcoming us in, both dressed in period clothing from their day jobs.

The interior was large and open with a stage upfront. Double balconies were built off to either side, and they overlooked three chairs and a microphone. That's where our guides hustled us, but not fast enough. A commotion at my back alerted me to the fact our trio was now a duo.

I advanced on the women who had been guarding the doors, who had decided between them it was a smart idea to subdue Santiago. "What the hell do you think you're doing?"

One held him in a headlock while the other pointed a knife at his vulnerable stomach.

"We've spoken with the other clans," the shorter one accused. "You haven't made a show of power at any of these rallies your consort has organized. Why should we risk our lives for you? How do we know you are who and what you claim? You've given us no proof."

The peaceful approach had worked so far, and I had kept up the foolish hope it would continue to sway charun to my side, but it looked like I was fresh out of luck.

"Release him, or I will kill you." A bite of cold frosted my breath. "He's mine. Harm him, and you harm me."

The taller one, the one physically restraining Santiago, looked ready to bolt. The shorter one, however, had found the hill she was ready to die on, and I was willing to help a martyr out if it meant getting what we came for and getting Cole and Santiago out of here alive.

"We're loyal followers of Conquest," the shorter one snarled. "This is how you repay us?"

"Santiago is my friend," I said slowly, in case she was hard of hearing. "He's coterie. More than a friend, he's family. You're just one of the whack jobs who invited me into a meeting under false pretenses and attacked one of mine. Get the picture?"

The taller female shifted her weight, loosening her grip enough for Santiago to break her hold. Once that happened, she sprinted out the door into the oncoming night. The shorter female gave me half a second to think this might be resolved without bloodshed before she rammed her knife in his gut.

Eyes wide, he hit the floor, his knees cracking on the weathered planks. "Luce?"

Ice crystalized on my lashes, and white plumes gusted from my nostrils. The cold place rose in me, and its bitter fury was arctic. Blackness swirled behind my eyes, the void tugging on me, sucking me down as it nudged Conquest to the forefront of my consciousness. We tussled, neither of us willing to give. I fought tooth and nail to stay aware, and she fought twice as hard to smother me. In the end, we both retained some control over my body.

Pain — hot, glorious, instant — snapped through my limbs, and suddenly I was looking down at his attacker from a great height. When I fixed my glare on the shorter female, I gained layers of perspective beyond what human eyes could perceive.

I parted my lips, and a bestial rumble flowed over them. I cracked the whip of my tail at the female's feet, and she hit her knees in awe.

She submitted, it's over. That's what I was thinking.

She hurt one of ours, and she will pay in kind. That's what Conquest was thinking.

A broad palm pressed against our side, and we craned our long neck to find Cole offering support. He would back us if we taught this woman the lesson she was begging for, and he would support us if we exercised the right of mercy. The Luce he first met, so intrenched in her humanity, wouldn't have paused to consider. She would have scrambled to Santiago, got him to safety, and let the female go. But I was no longer that Luce.

I was . . . we were . . . more.

Different. Harder. Stronger.

For better or for worse, I had yet to decide.

Twisting away from Cole, we widened our jaws and roared our anger inches from the tip of her nose.

The stink of hot urine filled the air as she collapsed in her own puddle. Pity didn't factor into this equation. She wanted proof we were Conquest, at the expense of our coterie, and we were about to give it to her.

Faster than a blink, before I understood what Conquest meant for us to do, she yanked the reins from my control and struck.

No, no, no.

Our teeth snapped together in a crunch that bit clean through the hand the female had used to stab Santiago at the wrist.

Phantom laughter rolled through my mind, and chills dappled my skin.

See? she seemed to say. *I too can be merciful.*

Reeling in the urge to vanquish my enemy, I withdrew until I shrank to my human form. As I grew smaller, so did Conquest's presence in my head. I exhaled through my teeth, tasting the charun's blood, when I regained control over my entire self.

The shift into my dragon form was physical, not mental, or so Wu estimated. But I was starting to doubt his assessment. Running a finger around the collar of my shirt to loosen it didn't help as I imagined Conquest's hold over me tightening.

So much for proving I wasn't a violent brute.

"Do you need another demonstration, or are you good?" I spat on the floor near her feet then appraised the gathering, which had grown larger since I last checked. "Anyone else want to poke the dragon?"

Our guides from the saloon crawled on their hands and knees toward me.

"Apologies, Mistress," the female sobbed. "We had no idea what she had planned."

"Forgive us." The male pressed his forehead to the floor. "We are your humble servants."

Ignoring them, I knelt beside Santiago, wishing for Thom now more than ever. "How are you doing?"

"You shifted." He stared at the stain around my mouth. "You turned into a dragon at will and bit off her hand."

"What do you think Cole and I do behind closed doors?" I batted my lashes. "It's not all naked rugby."

Behind me, Cole made a choking noise.

When Santiago continued staring at me, I jabbed his shoulder with my finger. "Are you dying or what?"

"It's a clean wound." He grimaced. "I'll heal."

"Good." I helped him to his feet then gestured to Cole. "We're leaving."

"B-b-but — " the female spluttered from her position.

"I can't trust you." I rolled a shoulder. "Do you really think I would bring you into battle after this? I can't afford to risk you stabbing me in the back at the first sign of perceived weakness on your part."

"Please, Mistress." The male was crawling forward, arms outstretched. "Your will gives us purpose."

"Your purpose, as far as I can tell, is to waste my time and injure my people." I swept the room with my gaze. "Enjoy the shame of failing in your one sacred duty. I'm sure the next Conquest will be more forgiving." Who was I kidding? "Or not."

Wrapping an arm around Santiago's torso, I let Cole guard our backs as we trudged back across the street to our hotel. I would have switched establishments, but pickings were slim. This town catered to day trippers, not overnight guests.

Back in my room, where we would all be spending the night for security reasons now, I angled Santiago onto the bed I wouldn't be sharing with Cole.

Bitter? Who? Me?

"I brought a first aid kit." I yanked up his T-shirt to examine the wound. "Cole, does he need stitches?"

"No." He pressed gentle fingers alongside the puncture. "It's not that deep. Considering the location, it's doubtful she nicked anything critical."

"Antibiotic ointment and gauze it is then." Good thing too. Without our medic, our treatment options were limited. "Hold still, and I'll get it cleaned."

"I can do it myself," he griped. "Give me a rag."

"You're going to accept my help and like it." I swatted his hands. "Stop acting like a baby."

Once I had him patched up, I gave him his laptop and ordered him to stay in bed until morning. Charun healed quickly, my coterie in particular, but you could never be too careful. Poisons were popular, and we had run afoul of blades coated in them before. Better safe than sorry. I would prefer having Santiago where I could keep an eye on him than wake up in the morning to discover I had lost another member of my coterie. Even him. Probably. Best not to put it to the test.

With him settled, I joined Cole at the window overlooking the town. "Are you disappointed in me?"

"No." He watched the few human stragglers searching for adventure after dark. "They wanted a show of force, and you gave them one."

"I felt her." *She talked to me. Thought at me. Something.*

"I sensed her."

The reason for his quiet became obvious, and I took each step on this uneven conversational ground with care. "You're worried about her, not me."

"I don't care what happens to her." Turning from the window, he corrected me. "I'm worried about you, about what she might do to you if she keeps rising."

He wasn't the only one, but I couldn't burden him with my fears with his so close to the surface.

"Get out," Santiago ordered from his spot on the bed. "Go for a walk or something."

"This is *our* room," I reminded him. "You can't kick us out of our own room."

"Your anxiety is giving me a headache."

I wasn't ready to call it a night, but I wasn't willing to leave Santiago unprotected while I blew off steam.

"We're not leaving you alone and wounded."

A tearing sound jerked my head around in time to watch him peel off the bandage. "I told you I'd heal."

"You heal fast, but you don't heal this fast." I stalked over to him. "What gives?"

"The coterie draws on your power. The more amped up you get," he explained, "the bigger the boost for us. We heal faster, we're stronger, and our endurance goes off the charts."

One hope shoved every single thought out of my brain. "Does that go for Thom too?"

"Yeah." Santiago plucked at the covers beneath him. "It goes for him too."

I rubbed the heel of my palm over my heart, praying this would be enough to patch him up and bring him back to us. We needed him. *I* needed him. He was a good friend, and a valuable member of the team. "Do you guys ever think maybe you should tell me these things?"

"You have centuries of knowledge to catch up on. How are we supposed to know what you do and don't remember?"

"Hint." I sighed. "I don't remember anything. Assume if I should know it, I don't."

Santiago appeared to mull over this. "Did you know you're Cole's baby momma?"

I pivoted toward Cole. "Can I kill him?"

"Not yet." He pressed a kiss to my temple. "We might need him before this is all over."

"The cemetery ought to be quiet this time of night," I conceded. "It's a tourist attraction, so the trails should be safe."

Santiago didn't acknowledge me past that point. He dove into whatever filled his tablet screen and ignored us.

"Join me?" I touched Cole's arm. "I could use the fresh air."

He laced our fingers and held tight, even as we took the stairs.

Charun in the saloon glanced up at our entrance, but we didn't acknowledge them. We left the building and strolled the narrow main street until we reached a sprawling graveyard. The sign on the gate stated the hours were from dawn until dusk, but we had no trouble leaping the ornate fence. It was decorative, not meant to keep out trespassers with agendas.

"Do your people mark their loved ones' graves?" I wondered. "I don't know anything about your culture, but I would like to learn." I squeezed his fingers. "Maybe you can tutor Phoebe and me together."

The idea appealed to him if the rumbling purr vibrating his chest was any sign. I wasn't sure if he liked the idea of me embracing his culture or if he just liked the idea of me embracing a relationship with his daughter. He ought to know by now that I loved him too much to do anything that would hurt him, and that included holding it against Phoebe that she was his child with another female. Sort of.

"I would like that." He took in the statues and wrought-iron fences surrounding individual graves and family plots as we took a winding path down the side of the hill. "I can also tell you about Otilla, your heritage, if you want to know."

"I don't," I said too quickly. "I need to keep going forward as myself, with my own values, if I'm going to make it through this."

A vibration in my pocket brought my attention to my cell.

Miss you.

The text from Sherry, her first attempt at reaching out to me since I burned Rixton, made my heart ache.

Miss you too.

How can you godmother
from all the way over —
wherever you are? John said
you left town.

I did. I had to. For work.

I hate you guys are fighting.

A tendril of relief snaked through me. He hadn't told her the real reason why I left Canton, or what I had done. She must think he was upset about losing his partner on the force. He was, but he was pissed at me for tampering with evidence. I had my reasons, but since I couldn't share them with him, he had no way of knowing if my intentions were honorable. You'd

think he would know me better than that, but the Luce who had
been his partner for four years never would have compromised
herself — or her partner.

> I'm glad you reached out.

> Call me sometime? It's been
> so long since I've had adult
> conversation outside of visits
> to the pediatrician, I can't
> remember what it's like to
> have a convo about anything
> but Nettie's BMs.

Hating to lie to her, I typed an empty

> Sure.

Pebbles rolling downhill to our right pulled me up short, and I
glanced around. "We got company?"

Grateful for an excuse to end the conversation, I tucked my
phone back into my pocket.

"We're upwind of them." Cole flared his nostrils. "I can't tell if
we're being hunted. Yet."

"Then we walk on." I scouted the area and located a flat ter-
race several yards ahead. "Let's head for that angel. The ground
is level there. If we have to fight, we'll stand a better chance than
we do here."

"Your followers may have trailed us from the saloon." He swept
his gaze from left to right, scanning our immediate vicinity for
movement. "They might think cornering you is the only way to
get your attention after one of them attacked Santiago."

"I really don't want to shift twice in one night." I rubbed my stomach. "I ate that female's hand, and part of her wrist. That's . . ." I bit off the sentence when Cole tensed beside me, aware any stones I cast at myself would bounce off him first. We were the same, both of us biologically Convallarian, and I had no right to judge what was natural for charun until I understood the various species better. "That's a lot to digest." I stared at the front of my shirt. "Where does it all go?"

A teasing note entered his voice. "Are you sure you want to know?"

"Probably not," I decided when he started chuckling, the low sound clenching my gut for other reasons.

"I can hear them." He cocked his head. "They'll overtake us in three minutes or less."

We chose the best spot for our standoff, and then we waited. Sure enough, three minutes later, the two charun who had escorted us from the saloon to the meeting appeared with tear-streaked faces and red-rimmed eyes.

"Fancy meeting you here," I said with as much sarcasm as I could muster. "What do you want?"

"To serve you," they said in unison.

"You blew your chance when you let two members of your rebel band attack a member of my coterie."

"Angela and Helga don't speak for the clan," the female protested, drawing a knife from her belt. "They acted without warning us of their intentions."

Cole loomed beside me, he was good at that, and they cowered away from him.

"Let me sacrifice myself so that the debt can be paid," she pleaded, clutching the blade, ready to drive it straight into her heart. "Please, Mistress. Allow us to make amends. The Oncas are yours to command."

"Put the knife down," I snapped. "There's enough death coming without you throwing away your life."

The blade clattered to the ground, and she hit her knees, weeping. "I'm not worthy."

Grateful Santiago wasn't here to watch me squirm, I kept the grimace off my face. "You're worthy, and that's why your death serves no purpose. You can do more for me alive than in a grave."

"You'll give us another chance?" The hope in the male's voice gave me a migraine. "Let us prove ourselves — "

"You've done enough." I held up a hand. "Trust me. We're good here. You're in. You can join Team Conquest at the final battle."

The pair broke into hysterics, hugging and sobbing together like I'd just told them they'd won the lottery instead of handed down a death sentence.

"You're doing well," Cole said for my ears only. "You've given them purpose, redemption. They'll be more loyal to you for it."

"Assuming there aren't more malcontents in their ranks happy to sabotage us."

Guess I wasn't using my inside voice. The pair broke apart, and cold intent glazed their expressions. "We will get our clan in order. Any who no longer wish to follow the old ways will be cast out. Any who speak against you, or raise a hand against you, will pay the blood price."

A sour taste flooded my mouth. "Angela and Helga?"

"We slit their throats." The female beamed. "They will never question your right to rule again."

The dead did have a way of keeping their opinions to themselves.

"That's great." Acid churned in my stomach, that stupid hand I swallowed felt perched in the back of my throat, ready to grab me by the tonsils. "Now that we've all made amends, I'm ready for bed." Past ready. "Santiago will text you coordinates for a rendezvous when we've got them."

They almost snapped in half in their eagerness to bow and scrape.

I wondered if I had to stand there and watch or if it would be rude to step over them.

Catching the drift of my thoughts, Cole took me by the elbow and skirted the pair, leading me back up the path toward the front gate and sweet escape.

A text message had me checking my hip, and I prayed it wasn't Sherry, that she wasn't going to push me, not now, when my plate was full to overflowing, but the message wasn't from my friend. "Sariah wants to meet."

I hadn't seen her since she took over her mother's coterie after Death killed War and her father, War's mate, Thanases.

Tension coiled in his shoulders. "Does she say why?"

"Just that she has a proposition for us." I frowned. "That doesn't sound good."

Sariah still wore the rosendium bangles Cole had made for me out of the rose-gold metal Conquest used to bind the coterie to her. They forced her to obey my orders as long as she wore them, which, in essence, meant I was in control of the remaining Drosera as long as Sariah kept them on.

So much for our scouting mission. Sariah took priority, for the moment. The enclave would have to wait.

"She either wants out of her bargain, or she wants you to remove the bangles."

The promise of a headache throbbed in my temples. "That amounts to the same thing."

Freeing her meant freeing the Drosera, and Drosera as a species hadn't done much to win my trust.

Tapping my phone against my chin, I mused, "Do I respond or do I pretend I didn't see her message?"

"She'll know you're ignoring her, and she might escalate," Cole said at last.

"Fine." It was annoying, but he was right. "Guess I'll make the arrangements."

Where are you?

          I'll come to you.

You're keeping tabs on me?

         I'd be a fool not to, Auntie.

Pick a spot. Cole and I will
meet you there.

          The coffee house off
            the square.

The one where local cops, my former coworkers, tended to congregate.

You're in Canton?

She didn't reply, happy to leave me on read, and I growled under my breath. "I don't like this."

"Neither do I." A shimmering pulse of energy consumed him as he exchanged one skin for another.

Moonlight caressed his faceted scales, glittered in his leonine mane, and illuminated immense racks of branching antlers. The serpentine lines of a Chinese dragon melded with the sturdy arms and thickly-muscled thighs of a European dragon in him. His crimson eyes found mine as his gossamer wings rustled against his spine. His tail found my ankle in the next instant, and I laughed, which earned me a nuzzle and him scratches behind his rounded ears.

"Let me text Santiago, and we'll go."

About to do just that, I jolted when a tall figure stepped onto the path ahead of me.

Santiago sighed, long and loud. "Did you really think I would let you two out of my sight?"

"You've been out here the whole time?"

"You came to make out with Cole in a cemetery, away from prying eyes." He tapped his temple. "You would have been vulnerable."

"We didn't come here to make out," I argued, though I had been hoping for an unchaperoned kiss.

"Whatever." He waved his hand, dismissing me. "Are we leaving or what?"

I noticed he wore a backpack crammed with his electronics, and another bag hung from his fingertips. He tossed it to me, and I grunted from the weight. He must have combined Cole's and my things to make it easier to transport. Threading my arm through the strap, I swung it over my shoulder and secured it with a clasp that crossed over my chest in case of just such an emergency.

And then we set out for home.

CHAPTER THREE

———◆———

My darling niece was easy to pick out of the customers enjoying their coffee and treats. For one thing, she eyed the patrons with more interest than her latte. For another, she sported a purpling bruise down one side of her face.

I skipped the coffee — I was jittery enough without a caffeine hit — and sat across from her. "Who did that to you?"

"The dominant bull in what remains of Mother's coterie." She touched her cheek with gentle fingers. "Don't worry. He won't get a chance to do it again."

"You killed him."

"Yes, I did." Her posture shouted she would do it again in a heartbeat without losing sleep over it.

"Well, I'm here. You're here." Cole stood watch outside in case I needed backup, and Santiago was en route to the farmhouse, where Miller, Portia and Maggie waited for us. "What's up?"

"I want the bangles removed."

"Nope."

"That's why this happened." She pointed at her face. "They can smell you on me. They weren't suspicious at first. As far as they knew, you held me captive for weeks. Now I'm with my own kind, but I still reek of Conquest." Her lips thinned. "I can't control them unless they trust me."

"Trust is exactly the problem."

"I won't move against you."

"Without the bangles, I have no way of knowing if you're telling the truth. You betrayed your mother, and your coterie, to escape The Hole. You'd stab me in the back too if the right offer came along."

Her answering growl turned heads, but she had no easy retort prepped for that one. "All I have left is my word."

Scowl settling into place, I gave it to her straight. "Then you don't have much, do you?"

"I might as well stay with you then." She heaved a sigh. "The dominance fights will keep coming until they overpower me. I haven't stayed alive this long by being stupid. I would rather walk away now and let them kill one another than die."

One thing about Sariah — she was a survivor. But she wriggled out of danger at the expense of others. She would sacrifice anyone, anything, to stay alive. I could respect that, but I couldn't trust it. Not while we sat in a coffee shop in my hometown.

Rixton patrolled these streets. His family lived a few minutes from here. The enclave, with Thom among them, hid outside the city limits. She might not know that last part, but she knew the rest. There was a reason she chose this as our meeting place: a subtle reminder of where I came from and what mattered most to me, and that she knew both of those things.

"You took responsibility for the coterie, and that makes them your problem." The hope I could wash my hands of them, and her, was dwindling. "I don't have time to hunt them down and kill them all."

Shrewdness overshadowed her features. "You're too busy building an army, is that it?"

"I can't sit here and discuss strategy with you." I pushed my chair back, and it raked across the floor. "I can't set you free on your own recognizance, either."

"What if I offer you a trade?" Her fingers curled on the tabletop. "My freedom in exchange for Deland Bruster."

Tabling the facts she knew he existed, and that I wanted him, I asked, "You know where he is?"

"Not yet," she admitted. "I'm looking, though."

Taking a risk, I ventured, "Do you know anyone by the name of Ezra?"

"No." She crossed her legs. "Not one interesting enough for you to make me a counteroffer, anyway."

That slight hesitation, the twitchiness, made the spot between my shoulder blades itch.

"Keep your eyes and ears open." I rapped my knuckles on the table. "Bring me Ezra, and I'll remove the bangles."

"Wait. That's it?" Her eyes goggled. "Do I get any hints?"

"No." Despite setting the task, I didn't want her to succeed. "You'll know when you find him."

And, as soon as I talked to Santiago, so would we. *If* she managed to succeed where we had failed.

With all his doodads and knowhow, I was certain he could track her, make sure she didn't get into more trouble than she was worth. Giving her an impossible job to keep her out of my hair seemed like a win/win to me.

"Challenge accepted." Her eyes glittered. "I'll check in when I find a lead."

"You do that."

Behind me a plate shattered, and I twisted around like everyone else to see what had happened. They were probably thinking *butter fingers*. I was thinking more along the lines of *sneak attack*. But what I saw caused my heart to swell and pound, and my palms to go wet with sweat.

"This meeting is over." I gripped Sariah by her upper arm and hauled her out onto the sidewalk where Cole waited with a blank expression. "Make sure she leaves."

As much as I wanted to vanish with them, I had to go back in and face the music. Sherry would run after me otherwise, and it was better that Sariah not understand how much Sherry meant to me by overhearing the reaming out she owed me.

Back in the shop, Sherry remained frozen in place. Two customers who had stood behind her in line cleaned up the mess so she wouldn't have to bend with Nettie worn in a sling across her chest.

"Luce?" After thanking the people on their knees, she stepped around them to reach me and take my hands in hers. "I can't believe you're here." She swung our arms from side to side. "I would have texted you sooner if I'd known that's all it took to get you home."

Actually, a psychopathic relative had brought me here, not a desire to rekindle our friendship, but I couldn't very well tell her that.

"I'm just in town for the day." I couldn't stop the genuine smile overtaking my face. "On business."

"Oh." Understanding crowded out all those happy emotions. "You weren't coming to see me, were you?"

"No." I squeezed her hands. "I wasn't." I lowered my gaze. "I don't want to cause problems between you and your other half. He wouldn't want us talking now, let alone me in his house."

"John is a grown-ass man. He can't control who I call a friend." Her nails sank into my skin. "I'm not losing you, Luce." She thrust out her chest to get my attention, probably afraid if she let me go I would run. "Nettie needs you. You're her Auntie Luce. Look at her squishy baby face. You can't say no to squishy baby face."

Probably why I had avoided looking down at the tiny rosebud

mouth and slumberous eyes in question. "Your marriage is more important than our friendship."

"John is being a butt monkey. I got you two through worse rough patches than this one. I can do it again."

"You got us to both stop being assholes long enough to get to know each other, and I'm forever grateful for that, but I was his partner. I did an unforgiveable thing and broke his trust. He won't move past that, and I can't blame him. This is all on me."

A laugh that was half shock and half denial burst from her. "There's nothing he wouldn't forgive you."

"I have to go." I pried her hands off me then bent to kiss Nettie's baby-soft forehead. "I'm sorry I can't be there for you, Nettie, but your mom and dad love you more than enough to make up the difference."

I turned on my heel and exited the shop before she could think to come after me.

Cole was waiting by the door, and I read his sorrow. I was grateful he didn't try to tell me it was for the best, or that it would get easier. I expected him to give it to me straight, even when it hurt. Much like Santiago. Except Cole bit his lip to avoid hurting me whenever possible whereas Santiago couldn't flap his fast enough.

Since I rode a dragon here, I would have to ride a dragon back.

The wind would explain away the tears already stinging my eyes, and the trip would give me a moment to pack away what just happened among all the other things I wasn't dealing with because there was no time for me to break down the way I wanted, the way I needed, and keep functioning.

CHAPTER FOUR

————◦◉◦————

About to hop aboard Air Cole for the return trip, a text chime had me digging out my phone.

As much as I wanted to ignore it, I couldn't afford not to check with the coterie scattered all over the place.

And sure enough, the message plummeted my gut into my toes.

Heard you were in town.

Crap. Crap. Crap.

Sherry must have called Rixton the second I bolted from the coffee shop.

Just a quick visit.

Sherry bumped into you. By
accident or design?

That he would question my integrity stung. I had brought us here, but it was still so bizarre having him lash out at me, hurt me.

> I left when she arrived. What
> does that tell you?

>> She misses you.

> I miss her too.

>> Come clean, and I'll consider
>> visitation.

Yearning to go back to the way things had been, I was tempted. But I couldn't risk them. I *wouldn't* risk them.

> I have to go.

>> Damn it, Luce. What
>> have you gotten yourself
>> into? Tell me.

> I can't.

>> I saw the cat.

Pulse throbbing in my ears, I swallowed hard and attempted damage control.

> What cat? There must be
> hundreds in Canton.

It had wings. Goddamn
wings. It flew. Right off
your shoulder.

Why didn't you say anything?

I could ask you the same
thing. We're partners — were
partners — and you lied to
me. You cut me out of your
life. You backed me into a
corner I couldn't escape
without going through you.
Do you know how much that
hurt? You made my wife
cry. You know I hate it when
women leak.

A watery laugh clogged my throat, and that drew Cole's attention.

"Rixton is texting me," I explained. "He saw Thom, as a cat.
Looks like there's more damage control waiting for us in Canton."

But damn if I didn't smile the whole way back into town.

After touching base with the coterie, Cole and I went to meet
Rixton on a bench in the square across from Hannigan's. While I
couldn't blame Rixton for wanting a public spot, this put all eyes
on us. And it hurt that he thought — even for a second — that
I would harm him, that he needed insulation to protect himself from me.

"Bou-Bou," Rixton said when he spotted me. "It's good to
see you."

The endearment sparked dangerous hope, but he knew how

much it annoyed me. There was just as much chance, perhaps more, that he was being petty instead of familiar.

"Good to see you too." I measured him, top to bottom, and frowned. "You've lost weight." A lump got stuck in my throat. "So help me, if you brought me here to say you're dying, I'll kill you."

"That would defeat the purpose." He slid his gaze toward Cole. "Heaton." He stuck out his arm, shook hands with him. "I can't say I'm glad to see you since life went to hell in a handbasket the second you set foot in this town, but Luce looks happy enough. That still counts for something in my book."

"Does it?" It didn't escape my notice he hadn't touched me. It's not like I had been all that welcoming of physical contact in the past, so I tried not to take it personally. That, or the firearm visible at his hip.

"You're family." He knocked on my forehead like it was wood, like I was a blockhead. "We fight, we make up."

"You made it clear you wanted me out of your life." I heard the bite of accusation, reminded myself I had earned it, then held up my hands. "I don't blame you. At all. I understand what I did put you in a tight spot, and I never would have done that if I'd had another option."

"That's just it. I should have seen through it. You're a good cop, Luce. A damn fine cop. Just like your dad. You don't break rules. You barely bend them. What you did makes no damn sense unless there was a damn good reason."

"That's a whole lot of damns," I pointed out, and he almost smiled.

"I missed you." His voice broke. "Sherry's been telling everyone my work wife broke my heart, but it's not that. Well, okay, it might be that. Heartbreak. It's like having a little sister and witnessing her get snatched off the sidewalk right in front of you. It happens so fast, and there's nothing you can do to stop it. That's how it felt. Like we were rocking along, business as usual, and poof. You're gone. I can't make it make sense. It's been driving me insane. And when I finally broke down and went to talk to you about it, to let you explain, I saw you with that damn cat and knew I had a decision to make."

"Before or after I made Sherry cry?"

"Let's not split hairs ... " His cheek twitched, another smile attempting to break free. "The point is, I want you to tell me the truth. All of it."

"Rixton ... " I started, hating I couldn't confess all. "It's not that simple."

"You have a pet cat with wings." He swept his gaze over Cole. "Are you a kitty too?"

Cole's answering smile was toothy and sharp and made me worry about what he thought about all this.

"The more you know," I warned him, "the more dangerous it gets for you and your family."

"What about your family? Your dad is MIA, Harry was shot and killed during a home invasion, according to the report, and Aunt Nancy followed him." He exhaled through pursed lips. "You lost too much, too fast, and then you shoved me away too."

The mulish glare I turned on him was learned at his knee.

"I'm a cop. Dare I say, a detective. I've been at this a while, and I can smell a coverup from a mile away. How long do you see this working? How well did it go for Nancy? Harold?"

"That's a low blow," I said, shaken. "But you're not wrong." Cancer might have killed Nancy, but the bargain Harold struck to save her had killed him just as well. That was on me. "I kept them out of it. I thought ignorance would protect them. It didn't."

"So turn on a light." Rixton let his smile come, and its edge was honed by shared grief. "I'm tired of sitting in the dark."

One look at Cole confirmed he trusted me to make the right call. I wish I had that much faith in anything, let alone myself.

"I'm not human," I said with a hitch in my voice.

Without missing a beat, he dipped his gaze to my arms, where the rose gold bands of the *rukav* curled over my skin.

"I'm charun." I kept going, pushing out the admission. "What you would consider a demon."

"You're not evil." A hard glint came into his eyes. "Tell me that's not why you broke things off."

"How can you be sure?" I blurted out. "Most days I'm not certain who I am anymore, let alone what."

"You're a cop to the bone, Luce." He made it sound so plain, so obvious. "Evil wears many faces, but it doesn't wear yours."

Tears blurred my vision, and hiccupping sobs wracked my shoulders. The words cleansed me, absolved me in a way I hadn't known I needed to be forgiven, to be judged and found innocent by someone from my old life.

"Aww, hell. Not you too." Rixton waved his arms at Cole. "Don't just stand there. Do something. Make it stop."

Before Cole reached me to offer comfort, I flung myself at Rixton. Eyes wide, he caught me in his arms and squeezed hard enough to make up for all the years I never let him this close. The otherness of his touch prickled across my skin, but I fought through it. It was worth it to have this, to have him back.

"Let's go somewhere more private," he said when I calmed. "It was a dick move forcing you to meet me in public like some rat with a hot tip."

Wiping my face dry with the backs of my hands, I sniffled. "I would invite you to the farmhouse but ... "

Maggie was holed up with Miller there, and Rixton didn't exactly know she was still alive ... or acting as a charun host. Or even what a charun or a host was, let alone how she ended up that way.

God forbid anything in my life be simple or easy to explain.

"I saw the realtor's sign." Rixton pushed out a sigh. "How about my place then?"

Heart smashing against my ribs, I growled, "You can't — "

" — tell my wife?" He snorted. "The secret to a good marriage is never lying to your partner. I never have, and I'm not about to start. She gets a say."

"Stop doing that." He knew me so well, he could have held this conversation with himself. "A say in what?"

"I'm going to help you." He looked at me like I was crazy. "Whatever trouble you're in, I'm going to get you out of it."

"This isn't human trouble," I started. "It's dangerous."

"I'm a cop. I understand dangerous."

"Trust me on this. You don't. I'm barely holding myself together here."

"Which is why you need your friends now more than ever."

"I wish you hadn't seen that cat," I muttered.

Rixton cocked his head, and apprehension darkened his eyes. "Doesn't matter." Regret thickened his voice. "I did."

"You can pretend this conversation never happened," I offered. "You don't have to get involved."

"Explain what *this* is," he bargained, "and we'll take it from there. Deal?"

"I'll take that deal." I slanted my eyes toward Cole. "Do you think we should show him?"

The dragon was in his smile when he chuckled. "It might help put things into perspective."

"Meet us on Dale Moody Drive, and we'll give you a taste of what you're letting yourself in for."

"Done." He backed away, pointing a finger at me. "You better show, Boudreau. Don't make me hunt your ass down."

"Oh, I'll be there." I smiled a little myself. "Count on it."

*

Dale Moody Drive was a dirt track leading nowhere, an access road to various pasturelands that dead-ended in a massive turnabout large enough for the semis hauling combines and other heavy-duty farming equipment to turn around in. Teenagers liked to drive to the end and neck during the summer. I don't know what they found romantic about the surrounding cow pastures, or the fact the road was named after a football player turned roadkill when his cheerleader girlfriend caught him making out with a tuba player and backed over him, but whatever. Young love.

"Don't eat the cows." I elbowed Cole when I caught him watching a wrinkly Brahma bull plod past. "All we need is to revive the belief aliens are real by slaughtering fields of cattle across the southeast."

"I don't leave evidence behind," he argued, but there was no heat in it. "Even if I did, the teeth marks on the bone would prove an animal was responsible, not a man. Not even a green one."

When he wrapped his arms around me, I let him. When he dipped his head to mine, I let him do that too. When he pressed his warm lips to mine, I sighed into his mouth.

"I'm going to pretend my stomach's not growling," I said against his lips. "It's just too damn weird to know you've eaten entire cows, and I let you kiss me with murder breath."

"You're charun." He kissed me again, longer. "On some level, you like it."

"I'm also human on some level. I shouldn't like it at all."

We broke apart when Rixton's truck came into view. He pulled in beside us, searching for a second vehicle he wouldn't find, and got out.

"Do your worst." He flung his arms open wide. "As long as your worst doesn't include Heaton dancing around in red tights with a trident and horns. I respect a man confident enough to wear spandex, but that would require a *lot* of spandex."

"Oh, I don't know." I fluttered my lashes at Cole. "I wouldn't mind seeing you prance around in tights."

The rumbling growl of his response earned him a cocked eyebrow from Rixton. "Be horny on your own time, Luce. I'm a delicate flower. I can't handle the mental pictures you're flinging at me."

With no small amount of glee, I stepped away from Cole. "Would you like to do the honors?"

The transformation was seamless. One minute, Cole stood there. The next, a dragon loomed over us.

"What the actual fuck, Boudreau?" Rixton backed up, trying to take it all in, but his legs failed him, and he fell on his butt. "That's a dragon. You didn't say anything about *dragons*. You said *demon*. I was ready for — I don't know. Not this."

Smug, the dragon rumbled, snaking his tail over to me where he wrapped it three times around my ankle.

"Is Heaton still in there?" Rixton gave up on standing and crossed his legs in front of him like a kid ready for story time. "Or is he . . . ?"

"He's himself, more himself, actually, when he's like this." When Cole bent his head, I reached up to scratch behind his tab ears. "He's not human, remember? He just uses that form to blend in. This is who Cole really is."

"You're banging a dragon." Rixton's eyes widened. "Tell me you two don't experiment when he's like this."

"Damnit, Rixton." Heat, fast and damning, ignited in my cheeks. "Pull your mind out of the gutter."

"Is that a yes or a no?" He leaned forward. "How can you tell if a dragon is a boy or a girl? Lift their tail?"

Puffs of hot breath hit my nape as the dragon laughed . . . right up to the point Rixton looked ready to take on the job for himself.

"Cole is not showing you his dragon penis." And before he

could ask — "I haven't seen it, I don't plan on seeing it, and neither will you. Ever."

The tip of the dragon's tail caressed the length of my calf, a thoughtful gesture that made me blanch. "Do *not* encourage him, Cole."

Damn dragon. Always making mischief.

"Encourage me, Cole." Rixton bounced in place, clapping his hands. "Encourage me."

"I liked it better when you hated him," I muttered.

"It's my job to hate anyone who wants to date you. It was nothing personal. I would have been hostile and suspicious toward any guy who thought he was good enough for you."

"You're a good friend," I told him, rubbing the dragon's chin. The wing he flicked in invitation I thought might be in response to the sweet spot I hit beneath his jaw, but no such luck. "No."

The dragon rumbled in Rixton's direction and flexed his wings until he stirred a breeze.

"What is he doing?" Rixton pushed to a standing position. "Wait a minute. Is he — Can he fly?"

Rolling my eyes at his wonder, knowing once I had been just as gobsmacked, I snorted. "What was your first clue?"

"*That's* how you got here." Rixton wiped a hand over his mouth. "You rode on a dragon?"

"Yes."

"You rode . . . *on a dragon*." He slapped his thigh. "*That* dragon."

The dragon in question flapped his wings again, leaning down to put his belly closer to the ground.

"Is he . . . ?" Rixton linked his hands at his chest. "He's inviting me to climb on?" He bit his bottom lip. "I get to ride the dragon?"

"Oh God." I dropped my head into my hands. "Why did you do this?" I shoved the beast. "Why?"

He peered at me through crimson eyes that glimmered with amusement.

"Come on." Giving up on talking either of them out of this, I swung onto Cole's back. "Get on behind me."

I barely got the words out before Rixton sat flush against my spine, his hands on my hips, his knees tucked into the backs of mine.

Looping my fingers through the dragon's mane, I tried for a scolding tone. "I know how much you like showing off, but Rixton is human and —"

Wings out, Cole leapt for the sky and rocketed into the sun. That's how it felt. I was ready to cry uncle before the first barrel roll — sure, now he wanted to show off! — but the loop-de-loops, that's what had me purging over his shoulder. Bile splattered his wing, and I didn't feel bad about it at all.

"Woohoo!" Rixton crowed behind me. "Do it again. No. Wait. Can you fly upside down?"

A thoughtful sound vibrated between my legs, and I reached up to grasp Cole's antlers before he got any ideas. "Cole Heaton, you set your butt down now. No more flips, no more turns, no more dives. Bring us down gently, or I will let Rixton lift your tail so I can plant my boot up your dragon ass."

"Kinky. I *knew* you were having dragon sex," Rixton cackled in my ear. "I had no idea you were so depraved, Boudreau. All those gossip rags had it right. You're a creature of the night, a wild swamp female who — *Hey.*"

The tail so often wrapped around my ankle slid around Rixton's waist and yanked him right off.

"*Cole.*" I swung one leg over his side, then the other, until I faced down his back. "Don't kill him. He didn't mean anything by it. He was joking."

"This is awesommme." Rixton held his arms over his head like he was on a rollercoaster. "Woooohoooo!"

Scooping hair from my eyes, I drank in the sight of him acting a fool and wished Sherry was here to kick his ass for me.

"I changed my mind. Drop him." I scowled at my former partner. "Maybe impact will knock sense into him. A normal person isn't this accepting of the supernatural. They don't jump on the backs of dragons and fly off into the sunset willingly."

Talons scratched lightly at my boot to get my attention.

"I'm charun. Half charun. I don't know. I'm something not entirely human." And I hadn't adapted as well or as fast as Rixton. Though, to be fair, he hadn't also learned he was a demon, and he didn't yet know which demon I embodied. Plus, he had only glimpsed Thom, the most adorable among us, and Cole, the most majestic. Let him see Drosera, or worse — Iniid. Then we'd talk. "He's Grade A human, and he's having the time of his life."

In response to my mood, Cole dialed it down a notch. He turned us around in a slow arc and glided back to Rixton's vehicle where he landed gentler than ever. He kept Rixton aloft until the last minute then set him on his feet. Cranking his head around to see me, Cole breathed warm air in my face. I rested my forehead against his and puffed out my cheeks in a calming exhale.

All I could do was pray this was enough, that knowing the truth would satisfy Rixton. I might be recruiting, but I didn't want to draft him. Not for this. Never for this.

"Sherry is never going to believe this." Rixton jogged up to me. "She's going to think I've lost my final marble."

"You're positive you want to tell her?" I had to try to make him see reason. "Thom and Cole are the cute ones. The charun beauty scale tips after them. Fast. Trust me."

"I can handle it," he insisted. "So can she. She might look all sexy and maternal, but she's one hundred percent momma bear. She can rip and tear with the best of them. She'll want to know, and I'm going to tell her."

A fresh rush of temper had me sliding off Cole's back. I hit the ground, and he arched a ridged brow at me, sensing what I intended to do. The dragon had always known me better than I knew myself.

"Can she handle this too?" I flung out my arms. "Can *you?*"

In a burning rush fueled by my pissedoffedness, I gave myself over to my inner dragon to make a point.

Cole rumbled an intrigued sound, and it occurred to me that we had never been dragons at the same time. I was so caught up in doing that math, when he butted his head against mine, I wasn't thinking clearly, and I ... purred at him. Like a freaking cat.

Wasting no time, Cole tangled his tail with mine, knotting us together, and leaned his side against me.

"You're not going to have wild dragon sex, right?" Rixton was recovering from his shock, but he rambled as his brain fought for traction. "You said you don't have sex with him when he's a dragon, but I didn't ask if you have sex when you're both dragons. And if you did have sex, and you got pregnant, would you lay an egg? Eggs? Or would you give birth? Are dragon babies born human or dragon?"

A groan rumbled through my elongated throat that earned me a chuff of amusement from Cole. Easing back, he released his hold on his true form and became a man again. The gesture was clearly a cautionary one. Maybe he worried I would get frustrated and eat Rixton. I had, to date, always eaten someone — or part of someone — when I shifted. This would be the first time I managed to use my manners. Hopefully. Assuming I could flip the switch in the opposite direction.

After a few tense seconds, focusing on my identity, repeating my name like a mantra, did the trick.

Luce Boudreau. Luce Boudreau. Luce Boudreau.

A persistent tug in my gut twisted, turned me inside out, and my essence slid into its more compact form.

Breathing hard, I readjusted to balancing on two feet instead of four, shaking off Cole when he offered to steady me until the acidic churn in my stomach eased to a bearable level.

Apparently shifting caused indigestion. No wonder the dragon always wanted a snack between changes.

"Sorry." I crossed my arms over my chest. "That was uncalled for."

"Do you eat people?" Rixton was bright-eyed and fully recovered by the time I adjusted to the limitations of being human. "Do we taste like chicken?" His brow puckered. "Hmm. Is it still cannibalism since you're not technically human?"

"I have eaten people," I admitted, "but they deserved it."

I chose not to dwell on the flavor.

"Humans don't taste like chicken," Cole added, still amused. "Chicken is a lean meat. Humans are fattier. The taste is richer, but not gamey."

A surprised laugh shot out of me, and I met his gaze. "You're not serious."

"I've eaten more humans than you, and I made the conscious decision to do so." His lips quirked up at the corners, his smiles coming easier these days. "Plus, I have a more refined palate than you, considering the variety of meats I've consumed over the years."

"I'll award the point." God knows his dietary options hadn't been limited to pork, chicken, fish, or human until this world. "Rixton, you see what I mean? You want this? Not just for you, but for your family?"

As if remembering his wild ride, he swept his gaze over Cole. "What little boy doesn't want a pet dragon?"

The snarl that ripped out of Cole wiped the happy right off Rixton's face.

Conquest had enslaved Cole, and many other races and

species. A human joking about leashing him was bound to be triggering.

"He was joking." I joined Cole and stroked a hand up and down his back until he calmed. "No one owns you, and no one ever will again."

Whatever ownership rights I had inherited from Conquest, I would find a way to forfeit once the small matter of surviving Ezra was behind us. Going forward? Assuming there was a future for us, he would always be free to make his own choices. I owed him that much, and I would pay it out of my own hide if that was the cost.

A hard glint crushed the boyish excitement on Rixton's face from a moment earlier. "What asshole thought they should own a dragon?"

"Me," I said softly, and I was grateful when his human ears didn't catch the admission.

CHAPTER FIVE

———◆◆◆———

Farhan drummed his fingers on his battered desktop. No matter how hard he stared at the phone, it didn't ring. It didn't do a damn thing but sit on the blotter and mock him. The same as it had every one of the last seven days.

Adam wasn't going to call and set up a meeting between himself, Luce, and his father. He wasn't an idiot.

When his father had strolled into Farhan's office last week and demanded just that, he knew the shit was about to hit the fan. When Ezra spouted the location of the enclave, the outpost where Wu's bloodline lived in secrecy, he retracted his previous thought.

The shit wasn't about to hit, it already had. They were just in too deep for the blades to spin.

Adam had known this day would come, and it had finally arrived. Only his centuries of prep work had kept the enclave one step ahead of his father, but the guy had long strides. It wouldn't take him long to catch up once he got mad enough, and discovering the enclave had evacuated their warehouse before he got

there was just the kind of insult that would nudge him to pick
up the pace.

His thumb was swiping the green circle, the screen pressed
against his cheek, before he registered the phone had rung.
"Kapoor."

Adam came across cool as a cucumber, but then he hadn't been
in the same room with Ezra in memory. "Has Father contacted
you again?"

"Yeah. He's called twice for status reports. Rumors of Luce's little
army are running rampant, and he wants them squashed. Both the
rumors, and the army." Farhan's chewed-ragged fingernails tapered
into claws and left fresh pinpricks among a sea of others nicking
the finish. That was the problem in a nutshell. *Luce's* army. Not
Conquest's. Not an ancient idol resurfacing, but a new icon rising.
"I've put him off as long as I can. He expects you to meet with him,
in person, with Luce as your plus one."

"He'll kill her."

"I know." Better her than him, or them for that matter.

"She's our one chance to end this. I can't waste her life."

"He's not going to keep taking no for an answer. He's already
pissed the enclave evaded him." Farhan sighed. "Does he know?
About you and Luce?"

"I'm not dead, am I?"

"No," he allowed, "but I doubt Ezra lets you off the hook that
easy. He's going to want you to wish you were dead, not reward you
with a peaceful send off. That means he's going to keep hounding
the enclave, even if you manage to get them out of this scrape, and
he won't rest until he wipes them off the map."

The door swung open, and the blood drained from Farhan's
cheeks in a stinging rush.

One in-person visit from Ezra was ... not good, but survivable.
It told you that you were in trouble. *Big* trouble. But if you still had

a pulse afterward, you had some value to him. Two visits? That meant your trouble outweighed your worth, and he had come to rectify his previous lapse in judgement with something a little more final than a slap on the wrist.

"I have to go." He ended the call before Adam got a preview of coming attractions. He might not be able to buy his friend much time, but he could make it a few days. Maybe. In all the years he'd spent testing others' resistance to his methods, he had never had them turned on himself. Perhaps this was karma.

"Adam refuses your invitation to a meeting." Farhan linked his hands on top of his desk, pleased when they didn't tremble. "He won't be persuaded otherwise."

"We'll see."

Ezra walked into the room like he didn't have a care in the world, hands in his pockets, gait long and easy. A lock of blond hair fell across his forehead, and Farhan was helpless to stop his fingers from curling with the urge to smooth it back for him, to trace the flawless skin that luminesced with power and drew people to Ezra like iron filings to a magnet.

"I'm quite skilled at convincing people to do what I want." He produced a dagger that gleamed with white light. "All you need is the correct leverage. The enclave is proving harder to stamp out than anticipated. They scattered like cockroaches before my legion." He thumbed the hilt. "A father's love can only spread so thin. My son must have favorites. You can tell me who they are, and I'll make your death quick."

Knox. Kimora. Lira.

Which of them would Farhan sacrifice to save his own hide?

"Fuck you." He exhaled with the relief of surrendering his burden. The double agent gig was up. "Luce will end you."

"Not if I end her first." Those same easy, gliding steps brought him within arm's reach of Farhan. All that separated them was his battered desk, and particle board wasn't much of a deterrent. "I regret you made me resort to such crude measures."

Easy as sliding the blade into its sheath, Ezra took his time sinking the razor-sharp metal to the hilt in Farhan's gut.

He gritted his teeth to keep his groan from escaping. It was too early for him to cry uncle. He had to make this last and greatest sacrifice count.

"That the best you got?" he panted through the cresting waves of agony. "I expected something more original from *The* Original."

Ezra smiled then, and it was full of warmth, so beautiful Farhan blamed the tears in his eyes on witnessing the joy his execution brought Ezra.

"Child." His eyes twinkled with delight. "All I've done is introduce a toxin to your bloodstream that will make transporting you simpler." He twisted the blade without flinching. "You and I will have a civilized discussion about my son and his ... indiscretions. You can cooperate, or you can be coerced. You will tell me all you know either way. The choice is yours. I'll leave you to it."

The poison swam through his blood like molasses. Eyes heavy, he tipped his head forward, chin resting on his chest. He sagged on the dagger, and the blade ripped through him. Ezra was allowing him to eviscerate himself.

"Adam inherited my charisma." Ezra kept his wrist firm, his arm an iron bar. "Your loyalty is misplaced, unearned. Adam isn't worth this. Don't let a sentimental attachment, one that isn't real, cost you your life."

The rest of the speech drifted in one ear and out the other. The haze of pain clouded Farhan's brain, made his eyelids too heavy to lift. His knees buckled, and thanks to his chin hitting the desk, he fell back and off the dagger.

Ezra had one thing right. Adam wasn't worth this. But it had never been about him.

Farhan had killed too often for empathy to be more than an afterthought, an emotion he ought to experience that prompted him to say and do the appropriate thing. His job as a janitor had broken a vital part of him, and the only way he saw to fix it was to patch up the world that had churned him out so no other kid got the same raw deal. Starting with taking out the dick who helped shape this world in his own image.

Black edged Farhan's vision, and the pain twisting through his gut chased him into the dark.

CHAPTER SIX

—◈—

The Rixtons' home looked exactly how I remembered it. Welcoming. Spotless. Lived-in. A place any cop would roll up to after a long shift and exhale *thank God I'm home* after parking in the driveway. It radiated comfort and peace, a bastion in the life of a detective who never took his work home with him when he could help it.

Sherry was sitting in a rocker on the front porch when we arrived, Nettie bouncing on her knee. She scooped the baby against her chest and leapt to her feet when she spotted us. "Luce."

"Hey, Sherry." I tried for a smile, but it wouldn't gel. "Rixton Jr. is looking happy and healthy."

"Don't call her that." Sherry recoiled in mock horror. "The last thing she needs is to grow up like her daddy."

"A cop?" I wondered, aware she wasn't a big fan of law enforcement careers.

"No." She slanted her husband an exasperated look. "A sailor-mouthed man-child who thinks ice cream for dinner is perfectly reasonable as long as it complements the cookies he ate for lunch."

"I have a bossy stomach," Rixton protested, pausing to drop a kiss on her lips. "I have to do what it tells me to do, or it makes me pay."

"All the grease and sugar, that's what makes you pay. Your stomach is the victim here."

A smile warmed me down to my toes to hear their familiar bickering, but it came to an abrupt end when Sherry registered how close Cole stood to me, that he was there at all.

"We need to talk, Sher-bear." Rixton kissed her again. "All of us."

Gone was the wild-eyed joy of riding a dragon. This was Rixton the husband, the father, and he wouldn't make this easy for me when it came to airing my dirty laundry in front of his wife.

Turning on hostess mode, she asked, "Would you like to come in?"

Unruffled by her scrutiny, Cole took my hand. "Yes, thank you."

"Well." She beamed at me. "Well, well, well. How the mighty have fallen."

"You have no room to talk," I grumbled, falling into old patterns with ease. "Look what you married."

"Hey, we all have to live with the consequences of our decisions."

"I'm not a consequence," Rixton huffed. "I'm a prize, like the kind you find in the bottom of a cereal box."

"Cheap?" I winged up an eyebrow. "Made out of plastic?"

"I'm not cheap." He sniffed. "You've seen the bills I run up at diners."

"No one believes you're cheap." Sherry patted his arm then guided him inside. "Take a seat and then you can all explain to me why you're here. Together." She settled Nettie in a bouncy seat she placed at my feet with instructions on how to keep it jogging the baby, a mildly terrifying proposition, then clasped her hands. "Anyone want a drink? Water? Milk? Wait, no. All I have is breastmilk. Sweet tea?"

"Tea would be great," I said, and Cole agreed.

"Alas, I only have two hands." Sherry admired her manicure. "Luce, join me in the kitchen?"

"Happy to help." I grimaced, aware I couldn't escape the trap she had set.

About two steps into the kitchen, she pounced. "You're with the mountain man?"

"Yep." My own personal mantain. "I am."

"With him, with him?" she whisper-screamed. "He's so tall and muscular and ..." She made hand gestures that, I assumed, meant she wondered if he wrestled anacondas in his spare time. "Know what I mean?"

"Mmm-hmm." Not a clue. "We should hurry up and get back in there."

"John isn't going to grill your *boyfriend*." She all but sang the last word. "He's going to be happy you've found someone who gets you."

Tilting my head, I asked, "How can you tell Cole gets me?"

"Oh, he gets you all right. Probably every day and twice on Sundays. He watched your butt as you walked away like some guys watch the Super Bowl."

"The relationship is new." Eons old, but fresh to me. "We haven't even had sex yet."

"Aww." She made a heart with her hands. "I'm so happy for you. You never date, but you brought this one home. He must be special." Switching gears, she poured sweet tea in enough glasses to go around. "So what's with the cloak and dagger? You were ... harsh ... at the coffee shop. I didn't expect to see you again, at least not for a while. You lectured me on going behind John's back and then you show up with the man in question. What gives?"

"We really need to do this with the guys present." I helped

her carry glasses. "And Sherry? I'm sorry about the coffee shop. Rixton texted me after, asked if we could meet up. We did, and we worked out a few things. Maybe not enough to make us okay, but it's a start."

Nodding as if that's what she figured, looking a little proud of herself for ratting me out, which prompted the call from him in the first place, she led the way back into the living room where the men chatted away like old friends. And, much to my disgust, there was a new light in Rixton's eyes when he looked at Cole. Dare I say it was admiration? Adoration? Hero worship?

Geeze. Let a guy ride your dragon, and all of a sudden you're back in his good graces.

After we all sat and did the small talk thing for a few seconds, Rixton reached the end of his patience.

"I rode a dragon today," he said proudly, not the smoothest segue ever.

"You did drugs? When? Where? *Why?*" Sherry's eyes popped wide. "Luce is FBI now. She'll take you in for testing. Maybe charge you with possession. What is wrong with you, blabbing in front of her like that? Putting her in this situation?"

"You're thinking of chasing the dragon," I cut in. "He means he literally rode on the back of a dragon."

Edging the baby to her side of the room, Sherry glared at me. "Did he share his drugs with you?"

"This is not going well," I told Rixton. "You shouldn't have led with the dragon."

"That's the best part," he protested. "Okay, we'll rewind. Sherry, love of my life, lust in my loins, hot momma of my angel baby, divine goddess of — "

"Cut the crap." I slapped the back of his head. "Get to the point."

For the first time in memory, the family man slipped behind the cop mask in his own home, and Rixton fixed calm, clear eyes on his wife, ready to pace her through questioning. "You've heard the shit people talk about Luce."

"Yes." Sherry darted her gaze between us. "I frequent the coffee shop and read the papers."

Meaning she grasped the fine line between gossip and what got printed.

"They weren't all wrong about her." Rixton reached for his wife's hands, gathered them in his. "Luce isn't human. She's a dragon."

"*She's* the dragon you rode?" Puzzlement turned to righteous fury. "Are you trying to tell me you're having an affair? With *Luce?*"

"What?" He reared back, stunned. "No. I would never cheat on you."

"Then what are you talking about with the drugs and the riding dragons?" Tears sprang to her eyes. "Johnny, I don't understand. You're making less sense than usual, and that's really saying something."

Before he somehow made it worse by implying Cole had been involved in a threesome with us while we were all high on narcotics, I clamped a hand over his mouth. "Shut up, Rixton, and let me handle this."

And then I told Sherry my story, in my words, and waited to see if I still had a friend at the end of it all.

CHAPTER SEVEN

The glazed eyes told me Sherry was struggling to process long before I finished my story. I wasn't known for lying. I was considered an honest cop, a straight arrow, but the story I was peddling threw her as much as her husband nodding along with the high points.

Voice soft and tentative, she turned to her husband. "You knew about this?"

He brought her hands to his mouth and kissed the backs. "I found out today."

Sherry searched his face. "You believe her?"

"I saw Cole," he said calmly, electing to edit me out for the moment. "He's a dragon. An actual dragon. With wings. Like a flying dinosaur but less extinct."

"I don't understand." She faced me. "How long have you known?"

"Luce was ignorant of her heritage until the night she helped Harold Trudeau pull Jane Doe from the swamp," Cole said, speaking to her for the first time. "After that, I had no choice but to meet with her and warn her about the dangers of a world she had no idea existed."

"This is a lot to process." Sherry stroked her daughter's cheek. "I can't … " She shook her head. "I can tell you all believe what you're saying is true, but how can I believe it too? Luce as a demon is … impossible. She's one of the best people I've ever known. She has a good heart. She was a cop, for pity's sake. A damn good one. How can she be evil?"

Explaining how Ezra had slanted public opinion against us from the dawn of time would only cause more smoke to pour out of her ears, so I kept it simple. "We're not evil. Not all of us anyway. We're just different."

Cole measured her reaction to that news. "Would you feel better if you saw proof?"

"No." She covered her mouth with her hand. "Sorry, but no. I need time. I don't need … " She raked her gaze down Cole. "Thank you, but no. I can't … " Her bottom lip wobbled. "Luce?"

"I'm still me." I crossed to her and sank to my knees in front of her. "I'm still Edward Boudreau's daughter. I'm still the same woman who pinned on a badge and rode Canton's streets each night. That's me. That's who I am. The rest of this … I'm still figuring it out too."

Head loose on her neck, she nodded and stood. "I'm going to lie down."

"Sherry … " I bit my lip, but she gathered Nettie and escaped to her bedroom.

"She'll dissect what she's learned, absorb it, then shelve the information where it belongs." Rixton linked his hands in his lap, his cop face still on. "Have a seat." He exhaled. "I can tell there's more. Something happened. Cole didn't decide to initiate you on a whim. It was too risky for you, and him, if it went bad. You mentioned Jane Doe. She kicked this off, right? She had the same bands as you do. What's the connection?"

Ah, Rixton. Using one of his best investigative techniques. Letting a suspect think they were off the hook before he yanked the line taut. "She was, technically, my sister."

Given all he was risking, I had no choice but to tell him the rest. Conquest. War. Famine. Death. I explained who I was, or had been, to the best of my ability. He peppered me with questions, pressing until sweat broke along my spine. Then, just when I caught my breath, he gave Cole the third degree.

He wanted to know it all. Everything. Down to who Cole was to me, why he should trust him, let alone the rest of the coterie, and a hundred other things I had never thought to question the night I learned all this.

And I hated, absolutely loathed, how parts came across sounding like the recruitment spiels I had been giving — should still be giving, if I wanted world-saving numbers on my side — when I meant the exact opposite.

We hit a snag in a predictable spot, and I hated filling in those blanks more than all the others combined.

"There's one more thing you should know." I swallowed past the lump in my throat, the remembered pain of the moment, the guilt still brimming beneath the surface of every interaction. "Maggie is alive."

"I'm sorry." Rixton mimed cleaning out his right ear. "It sounded like you said Mags was alive."

"She is," I forced out. "She's not ... " I cleared my throat. "She's not the same."

"Why didn't you lead with that?" he demanded, his temper sparking. "Does her family know? Of course they don't. Stupid question. God, Luce. She's alive? Really? I thought ... It's been so long ... "

Explaining what really happened to her, and how she survived it, drained the color from his face. The awe and wonder from earlier had been erased by the horror of her near death and the circumstances of her rebirth.

I told myself this was what I wanted, for him to grasp my life wasn't just riding dragons through the sky and scratching winged cats. There was an ugly side to this world, my world, and I wished he never had to see it. But turning a blind eye didn't mean it wasn't still there, only that it caught you unawares when you glimpsed it on the edge of your vision. He was a cop. He understood the actions of a few weren't a barometer to indicate the worthiness of the many. But he was also Maggie's friend, and he was hurt that she had been alive all this time, that I had known that, and we kept it from him.

"She had to make a clean break. It was best for everyone." The excuse sounded weak, even to me. "She's okay. All things considered. She's adapting."

"I'm going to talk to Sherry," he said, rising, "and then I would like you to take me to see Maggie."

"We can do that." I waited until he left then sagged against Cole. "That sucked."

Sighing into my hair, he wrapped his arms around me. "Not everyone's good opinion can be bought with a dragon ride."

"She's my friend. She's been my friend for a long time. She was my friend when Rixton hated my guts."

"She's also a new mother, struggling with raising a child in a violent and terrifying age for any parent, and she's just learned that monsters under the bed are real."

"I guess," I grumbled, still wounded. "It was stupid to think I would get two free passes."

"Sherry knows Luce the woman. Rixton knows Luce the cop. She's going to judge you based on the person she believes you to be. He's going to judge you based on the judgement calls you made over the years and their outcomes. It's not a fair measuring stick, so give her time to absorb it all."

Happy to cuddle him, I kept my position while we waited on Rixton to rejoin us.

"Ready." He walked past ten minutes later and held open the door for us. "Your ride or mine?"

"Really?" I glanced down the hall to the master bedroom. "She going to be okay?"

"Pretty sure she convinced herself the FBI had kidnapped you and was holding you against your will. She's got a thing about the FBI. Maybe she watched one too many Men in Black movies, or maybe it's because of her Area 51 fixation, I don't know. She doesn't trust suits. When you joined, she wanted to be happy for you, but then you dropped off the face of the planet. That's why I confessed to our . . . difference of opinion. She didn't believe you had gone dirty for a hot minute, but I tried."

Sherry, the closet conspiracy theorist. "I had no idea she had a thing for aliens."

"She was careful not to geek out on you." He winced to admit, "She worried you would think she sought you out, befriended you, because of your origins and not for my sake."

A cynical part of me accepted it as a real possibility, but even Mags had approached me to play the role of a lion in her pretend circus when we were kids. Our friendship grew from there, so even if curiosity or opportunity had brought Sherry into my life, I had no doubts she stuck around because she cared for me.

"Tell her not to sweat it." I shrugged. "Whatever made her reach out, I'm grateful for it."

Relief swept through him, easing his tight shoulders. "You're good people, Bou-Bou."

"I will eat you if you call me that again," I threatened, but it only made him smile.

*

Rixton got his wish. We flew Air Cole to the farmhouse. He didn't whoop or holler this time, but he did grin from ear to ear until I worried his face might split in half. Maybe he hadn't been kidding about his childhood obsession with dragons.

Cole landed with a thud that brought Miller to the front door with a wave for us.

Home.

I was home.

That's what my eyes kept telling me, but my heart had other ideas.

Without Dad, the farmhouse was just a bunch of wood nailed into a familiar shape, not my safe place.

I didn't have one of those anymore.

"Hey . . . " The greeting died on his tongue when he spotted my plus one. "You brought a guest."

Rixton slid off Cole like a pro then offered me a hand down I didn't take. The prolonged contact with him jangled my nerves, making me twitchy. I disguised it as bravado, jumping to the ground with a bare flex of my knees to absorb impact then cocking a daring eyebrow at him that ensured his next dismount would blow mine out of the water.

"You remember Miller." I clasped Miller's shoulder, the touch grounding me after prolonged contact with Rixton. "Rixton saw Thom. He had questions."

"Ah." He flicked a glance at Cole as he strode up behind me. "That explains a few things."

"A few," Rixton agreed, "but not all."

Miller's nod acknowledged Rixton, but he didn't offer more.

The question I had wanted to ask first popped out next. "How is Maggie?"

"Better. She's not at one hundred percent yet, but she's getting there. With Portia boosting her immune system, and her back to a familiar altitude, she ought to normalize within the next twenty-four hours."

Canton's two hundred and thirty-three feet was a huge drop from the six thousand, one hundred and forty-eight feet in Virginia City. Hopefully reacclimating was less painful for them than the initial shock of such high elevation.

Scanning the area, Rixton asked, "Where is Maggie?"

Tension coiled in Miller's shoulders, and his voice lowered a register. "Why are you interested in Maggie?"

"She's my friend." Rixton eyed Miller with suspicion. "Who is she to you?"

"Miller." I slid my hand down his arm. "Tell Mags that Rixton is here. Let her make the call to see him or not."

Anger and hurt twisted Rixton's expression when he swung his head toward me, but I exhaled. "She needed time after ... everything. She's made peace with her situation, and she's accepted her old life is behind her. At least for now. You're a blast from her past, and I'm not sure how she'll handle it. She may not want to see you. She avoided me for a long time."

"I'll respect whatever decision she makes," Rixton said, and that must have been the right thing. Miller walked off to relay the message while my old partner looked on. "Are they a thing? What about Justin?"

"Justin can't know about Maggie. She has to let him go." I worried my bottom lip with my teeth. "Miller is her friend, for now. They mesh well. But she's also half charun at the moment. When her bargain with Portia expires, I don't know what will happen between them, if anything, and they don't either."

"Justin is a good guy." Rixton massaged his wrist. "I hate for Maggie to lose him, to lose her old life."

"Me too." I would never forgive myself for the decisions I had made, or the fact I would make them all over again under the same conditions.

"You two are the reason she's alive." He repeated what the others had told me a hundred times, but hearing it one hundred and one didn't alleviate the guilt. "That's got to count for something."

"*Rixton.*"

Maggie's joyous shout carried from the porch where she emerged with Miller on her heels. "I can't believe you're here." She flung herself into his arms, and we all ignored the momentary stiffness on his part. "I missed you. How's Sherry? The baby? Everyone?"

"Damn, it's good to see you, Magpie." Rixton's voice strained. "I thought we'd lost you."

"I'm still here," she said, and I couldn't tell if she was reassuring her or him or both of them.

"How are they treating you?" He released her after pressing a kiss to her forehead. "Luce cracking the whip on you?"

"Maggie isn't coterie." Miller shoved past him, bumping Rixton with his shoulder. "Conquest doesn't own her."

"And Luce wouldn't whip me." She aimed that last bit at Miller. "It's a figure of speech. Luce is always thinking up things to keep me occupied. She's driven, and she drives me to be my best. That's all he meant."

Miller grumbled what might have been an apology just to earn a smile from Maggie.

"Coterie dynamics are complicated," I said in response to Rixton's frown. "There's a balance I have to maintain between who I was and who I am. I'm learning them, and they're relearning me."

He made a thoughtful sound, one I knew from years of working with him. It meant he was intrigued, and that he would be keeping his eyes and ears open. Nothing eluded him when he was fully engaged in the pursuit of the answer to a puzzling question, and that's what my life had become to him.

The pair wandered off together, aiming for the bench under the old oak tree, and I watched them go, happy Mags got one reunion at least.

Sniffing the air, Cole wandered toward the woods with a crinkled brow while Miller walked with me to the kitchen so I could snag a bottle of the water I kept chilled for the realtor to hand out to prospective buyers.

"It's okay to be happy," he said quietly. "I know how much Rixton means to you. Having him back in your life could be a good thing."

"He told his wife." I gripped the fridge handle until the old plastic protested. "Sherry knows as much as he does."

"What happened to Harold and Nancy isn't your fault."

"They were my family, and the cadre targeted them because of that, because I loved them."

"Death won't cross that line. You have a solid truce."

"For now."

Death always came for you in the end.

And that's why we needed every willing body on the final battlefield, whatever form it took. We had to end this, and I couldn't help picturing this war as a giant, bloody meat grinder. I kept feeding it, and it kept chewing them up, spitting out the pulp.

We needed more. Fighters. Time. Strategy. Time. Hope. *Time.*

But unless I had a fairy godmother I didn't know about, the odds of any of those landing in my lap were slim.

Through the window, I spotted Cole disappearing through the trees. "Where's he going?"

"I don't know," Miller said, a smile in his voice, "but it would be a shame if he went there alone."

Immediately suspicious, I narrowed my eyes at him. "What, exactly, were you and Mags up to while you were waiting on us to arrive?"

"I can't see Cole anymore." Ignoring the question, he leaned around me. "I hope he's okay out there. All alone. With danger closing in on all sides. Just a lone dragon in the wilderness. In the coming dark."

Despite the fact the backyard was hardly wilderness, a lone dragon could do a hellacious amount of damage, and it was barely twilight, a tremor of anxiety was getting the best of me. "What about Rixton?"

"After he and Maggie finish visiting, I'll drop him off at his house."

"We're going to talk about this when I get back, mister." I drilled a finger into his chest. "All four of us."

Whatever Maggie and Miller had gotten up to, I had no doubt Portia had encouraged with manic glee.

"You can thank us later." He gave me a nudge. "For now, you better hurry."

"Don't eat my partner," I warned.

"Former partner," he corrected.

"Miller . . . "

"I won't eat your friend. I will deliver him to his wife in the same condition as he arrived in."

"You better." I gave him one last jab. "Hurt him, and you hurt more than me. You hurt Mags."

The jab landed, and I don't mean my finger. Miller would never hurt Mags if he could help it, and that meant Rixton was safe. Cole, on the other hand . . . Unable to shake the nagging sense of urgency spreading through my limbs, I left Miller to chaperone and went in search of my mate.

CHAPTER EIGHT

———◈———

Soft light glowed through the dense foliage ahead, and I kept swatting aside limbs until I stumbled into a small clearing we once used for feeding deer. A ring of stumpy wax pillars flickered, their repellent scent reminding me of the emergency candles we kept in the kitchen cabinet for power outages.

"That's a fire hazard," I said, but I heard the wonder in my tone. "And is that ... a tent?"

Blankets spread across the pine needles I recognized from Granny Boudreau's collection in the attic.

Lured by the sound of my voice, Cole stepped into the clearing with me.

At a loss for words, I waved a hand to indicate the romantic tableau. "Did you plan this?"

"No." He tugged on his ear, the ragged one. "This is all Miller, Maggie, and Portia."

"How did they get you out here?" It was obvious how I had been tricked. I would follow Cole anywhere.

"I smelled the smoke from extinguished matches and came to investigate."

Given Famine's affinity for fire, I couldn't blame him for that smell making him antsy.

"How long have they been planning this?" I wandered over to the sun-faded tent and spied a mountain of pillows stuffing its interior. "This is ridiculous." I laughed. "Magical, but — "

Cole slid his palms over my hips and turned me in his arms until we faced each other.

Music clicked on from somewhere nearby, and I heard retreating footsteps.

"Damn limb," Maggie cursed. "Who leaves sticks lying around for people to trip over?"

"We're in the woods," Miller answered dryly. "Sticks are kind of a thing out here."

"I can hear you," I called. "I thought you were talking to Rixton?"

"He's waiting for me at the farmhouse," Maggie said after a rumble from Miller prompted her to answer.

Amused despite myself, I tossed out, "Are you guys staying for the show?"

"*No,*" they shouted in unison as leaves rustled during their sprint out of hearing range.

"We're going to have to have a talk with them about boundaries."

Meltwater eyes blazing, Cole palmed my cheek. He slid his thumb over my bottom lip, his own parted to expel his shortened breaths.

"We might not get this chance again," he said gently. "I'm not going to force you to — "

Laughter exploded out of me. "Force me? Are you serious?" I pressed a kiss into his palm. "I spend a portion of every day succeeding in not climbing in your pants while failing to imagine what it would be like to have you want me."

A frown scrunched up his face. "I do want you."

"Are you sure?" I asked in a small voice. "I don't want to take advantage of you."

"Are you sure?" The troubled expression smoothed away to delight. "I was hoping you would."

At some point, I had to accept he loved me, wanted me, and not her. Sex wouldn't prove that, but the act of Cole giving himself to me did. I wasn't strong enough to resist him. I didn't want to resist him. I wanted him. Period.

Sometimes it felt like I always had, that he was the itch beneath my skin I could never quite scratch.

Though it looked like I was about to get my chance to try.

"Dance with me?" I tucked in against his chest, and Cole wrapped his arms around me. We swayed together, heat building between us, as the music played on. "You move well for a mantain."

Cole blinked, and I realized my mistake. I hadn't meant to give away my nickname for him.

"Thank you." He hesitated. "I think."

These woods had introduced me to his dragon, and he had hunted me through these trees as a man when the edge of need rode him all those months ago. Just thinking about it got me all hot and bothered.

All coy-like, I traced my fingers down his shirtfront. "You know what would be more fun than dancing?"

Molten heat sparked in his eyes as he raked them down my body. "I have a few ideas."

Taking his hand, I led him to the tent. Spinning him so his back faced the open flap, I leaned in for a kiss — then shoved him as hard as I could before pivoting on my heel and running as if the hounds of hell nipped at my heels.

A roar split the air when he landed on the pillows, but I was too busy laughing to be properly frightened.

Cole would never hurt me. Not in a million years. Not for anything.

That knowledge gave me the courage to flee from the predator crashing through the underbrush on my heels. Unable to chuckle thanks to the stitch in my side, I wheezed out my amusement as he snarled in pursuit behind me.

"First one to the ravine wins." The wind snatched the words and flung them at him. "Move it, Heaton."

Tree limbs slapped me, and leaves got stuck in my hair. Brambles tugged on my clothes, which gave me the brilliant idea to distract the competition by yanking my shirt over my head and hurling it at his face. It hit him, blinded him, and he lost precious seconds regaining his lost momentum.

Since that worked, I unfastened my bra and tried hurling it at him next.

Chalk that one up to a tactical error. True, it was the only piece of clothing left I could remove without stopping, but I had underestimated what a glimpse of side-boob would do to him.

Hot fingertips brushed down the length of my spine as he grasped for me.

Unwilling to get caught just yet, I put on an extra burst of speed, zigzagging through the trees to cost him time. The crumbling edge of a ravine loomed ahead, and victory sang in my veins. I knew these woods like the back of my hand, had played in them all my remembered life. He couldn't beat me unless I slipped up . . . or let him. But where would be the fun in that?

Grinning like a maniac, I yelled over my shoulder, "Hurry up, slowpoke!"

That's when his breath hit my cheek, his arms went around my middle, and we hit the ground in a hard roll that carried us over the ledge. We plummeted straight down into the water and hit with a splash that soaked the banks of the small spring-fed pond where I used to spend hot summer days swimming with Maggie.

"*Cole,*" I howled as I shot up from the icy depths, but he silenced me by sealing his mouth over mine.

His large body was hot and hard against mine as he hauled me into the shallows.

"How am I going to get these jeans off now?" I managed through chattering teeth. "What are you — ?"

Gulping air, he sank down until water closed over his head and started to work on my pants. I braced my hands on his shoulders, toes sinking in squishy mud each time he yanked on the fabric, dunking me in the process. I came up laughing each time, louder and louder, until I couldn't breathe.

The universe really did not want me to have sex with this man.

About the time I was ready to claw my way onto the bank, he achieved his goal, yanking my underwear free with the same hard pull.

"I'm impressed, Mr. Heaton," I told him when he surfaced, but he filled his lungs and ducked again. "I'm as naked as I'm getting. What are you ... ?" His mouth found my core in an open-mouth kiss that crossed my eyes. "Oh." I dug my nails into his shoulders. "*Oh.*"

Pleasure coiled in my middle, winding tighter, burning hotter, and I forgot how to breathe. Writhing in his grip, I clawed at him, at the water, at thin air, desperate for traction, something to send me falling off the ledge where he kept me balanced with masterful strokes of his tongue.

Two broad fingers speared my core, and I convulsed around them with his name caught in my throat.

Cole surfaced, and this time there was no clothing between us when he drew the quivering mass of flesh that used to be Luce Boudreau to him. He gripped the backs of my thighs, opening me to him, and slid home with one hard thrust.

The water had stolen my chance to explore his body, but the

way he filled me left me no doubt I had been right. Cole was proportionate. In all ways.

"Gods, you're tight," he breathed in my ear. "Am I hurting you?"

I answered him by nipping his throat hard enough to draw blood and linking my ankles at his spine.

Permission granted, he pistoned his hips into mine, his hands tight on my waist, until the force of our lovemaking broke his grip. Growling at my slick skin, Cole walked us to the bank then pinned me to the silty ground without missing a beat, giving me the leverage to give as good as I got.

Cole roared my name when he came, and the steady rumbling purr in his chest where our bodies stuck together shoved me over the edge again.

An earthy scent rose from his skin, and I filled my lungs with the intoxicating fragrance.

"You marked me," he growled softly, his lips blazing a trail down my throat. "I wasn't sure you could."

"That's me?" I lifted my arm to my nose, inhaled, and shrugged. "I don't smell half bad, honestly."

Rocking his body into mine, his length hardening with each breath, Cole groaned helplessly against my shoulder.

Smoothing my hands down his back, I had to swallow a moan to ask, "Again?"

"Yes." He quickened his strokes, the vibration in his chest deepening. "Your scent . . . "

"I know." I smelled it on him now, and it caused my gut to clench, my nipples to tighten. I wanted to bite him, to mark him with my teeth, but this claiming would have to do. "Take what you need."

"You," he whispered, his voice guttural. "Only you."

And he spent the next few hours proving it true.

CHAPTER NINE

———◈———

Adam woke in his Jackson, Mississippi hotel room to an acute pinching sensation in his chest. He rubbed his tired eyes with his fingertips and blamed the tightness on the grim news he was about to deliver.

The peculiar ache plagued him as he dressed, as he checked out of his room, as he made his way to the roof and then covered the distance to Canton.

Landing at the farmhouse where Luce grew up brought him no ease, the opposite in fact, when his arrival failed to bring her running with a demand for how he found her.

No curtains rustled in the living room. No one came to the door. No one called out a hello.

But the tracker he had secreted in the lining of her NSB-issued boots told him she was here.

Rubbing the skin over his heart, he turned on his heel and set out through the woods.

A whiff of extinguished candles, the cheap kind that smelled about as much like their intended fragrance as burnt tires, drew him into a scene right out of one of the romance novels Luce had left stacked on her nightstand at the bunkhouse.

Blankets were scattered over the dirt. A tent had been pitched under the cover of limbs to make aerial surveillance difficult. Pillows overflowed its interior. And music played. Soft country ballads that broke him out in a feverish sweat.

This was a carefully planned seduction, but where had the seducer or the seductress gone?

Inhaling deeply, he drew in the distinct scents of Luce and Cole. Both were hours old.

Peculiar.

No blood tingled in his nose. No fear burned his sinuses. No signs of interlopers, either.

Before he could second-guess his motives, Adam set out down a path trampled by two sets of boots. The tread on one was familiar, the Lucchese logo an imprint in the soft dirt. The other boasted thick treads, the style Cole favored.

The farther he ventured, the stronger the trail, until his gut clenched in response to the tantalizing perfume of Luce's arousal that coated the back of his throat until he was swallowing her taste.

Desire thrummed in his veins, beat in his head, made it hard to think beyond the want turning his blood molten.

He heard their murmured conversation before he crested the drop-off leading straight down into a deep pool. Despite the fact he had trouble breathing when he spotted them, he couldn't tear his gaze away from Luce. She lay curled against Cole's side, both of them naked, their legs tangled. Cole reclined on the bank, covered in mud and oozing satisfaction. He kept stroking his hand down her side, tracing her curves like he couldn't believe she was his to touch.

The scent hit him then, knocked the breath right out of him.

Luce had marked Cole.

Several times.

The steady downward trajectory of her hand made him think she planned on doing it again.

They no longer carried individual scents. They smelled like a meld of the same person, with the balance tipping toward Luce the way it always did with Otillian matings.

Luce was strumming his hipbone like the strings on a guitar, and she gazed at him with so much love in her eyes that Wu recoiled from his voyeuristic perch as she closed her hand over Cole's stirring interest.

A gasp rang in his ears. His. Shocking him like a slap to the face.

This wasn't part of the plan. None of this. He shouldn't care. It shouldn't bother him. He'd had a mate, a woman he'd loved, and she was dust and memory now. Luce was ... an experiment. A test. A creation.

His father saw himself as a god, and perhaps the apple hadn't fallen so far from the tree.

Adam had forged Luce Boudreau, and the primitive core of him wanted to keep her for himself. But she deserved to live, while she could, and love for as long as any of them had left. He had already tasted his happiness, and it had died on lips gone cold centuries ago. What he felt for Luce was chemical, biological.

He might like her. He might even imagine her as a friend. But he couldn't love her.

Forcing his fingers down before they worried bruises on his skin, Wu jerked back, hiding, but water splashed, and a possessive growl from Cole carried to him.

"It was just a bird," Luce teased. "Or a deer. Maybe a bunny."

"We should go." The snarl didn't leave his voice. "We should return to the farmhouse."

"Relax, nothing will get past Miller or Portia." A soft laugh escaped her. "Besides, you destroyed our clothes. I'm not walking back there naked. At least if we hit the campsite first, we can lift some blankets."

"All right," Cole said, caving under the kiss Adam heard Luce bestow on him. "We'll stay until dawn."

A teasing note entered her voice that explained how they ended up here. "Race you back?"

"I won last time," Cole said, smug. "You won't beat me."

"I don't have to." Luce splashed, either exiting the water or provoking Cole. "I win either way."

The hungry growl Cole emitted filled the basin, startling a thrilled squeak out of Luce. The joy in the sound gave Adam heartburn, and he wasn't sure why. He couldn't feel romantic love for her or any other female.

Too bad the bond stretching between them, taut as a wire, hummed disagreement.

Unable to watch her streak past with Cole in pursuit, two lovers reveling in the discovery of one another, he shut his eyes. For her, all of this was new. The powerful physical connection with her own kind, with her own mate. For all that Cole had bedded Conquest throughout their tumultuous relationship, Luce was a fresh experience for him too.

She had given Cole her heart, and a woman like Luce was loyal to a fault. Even if she had feelings for Adam beyond attraction, she would never give up Cole for him, and that was before she learned the truth.

Once she realized who she was to him, what he had done, he might wish his father had killed him before she got ahold of him.

CHAPTER TEN

───◦◎◦───

Though our boots squished when we walked, Cole and I were otherwise dry and ready to face the day. We didn't make it far before the first nose wrinkled in our direction. Being that it belonged to Portia, and was on Maggie's face, I couldn't say I minded too much.

"You two had sex." She leaned in closer. "A *lot* of sex." She gave herself a high five. "Way to go, Mags. We're brilliant."

Santiago, who must have arrived during the night, walked up behind Portia and shoved her aside to look at Cole and me.

"He stinks to high heaven." He gagged a little. "How are we going to hide with the two of you smelling up the place? Any decent tracker will be able to latch onto your marking."

Ever the peacemaker, Miller joined us to defuse the situation as much as any situation involving Santiago could be defused without knocking him unconscious and thus removing him from the situation completely.

"Portia and Maggie dreamed up the laidcation idea while they were sick in Reno," he told us. "Portia left herself notes that Maggie would read over and add to so they could both contribute. They were just waiting on an opportunity to spring one of their plans into action."

"Laidcation," I repeated.

Santiago rolled his eyes at me. "It's like a staycation but with sex."

Cocking an eyebrow, I had to wonder if Portia hadn't bounced ideas off him too. "How do you know?"

"Gods, that stench." Santiago made a production of pulling his tee up over his nose, a copout if I ever saw one. "It's worse than ever."

"Aww. Thanks." I wrapped my arms around Cole's middle. "We had extra sex just for you, Santiago." I made kissy sounds at Cole while he chuckled at me. "Pretty sure I could go again."

More gagging noises erupted from Santiago, and he clutched his stomach as he staggered backward.

"Drama queen," Portia called as he retreated. "What a wimp."

A low rumble escaped Cole before I spotted the enormous shadow sailing over us.

On mammoth wings, three sets of them, Wu landed with grace that ought to be impossible with so many moving parts.

"Luce," Wu said, rustling his feathers in an agitated fashion.

"I thought you'd flown the coop." I cocked an eyebrow at him when he refused to look me in the eye. "You haven't called once."

His gaze, when it lifted to mine, shone golden. "I came to warn you."

Breaking away from Cole, I squared up with him. "What now?"

"My father has located the enclave. His forces are surrounding it as we speak. If we don't get there, and fast, he will hammer at its defenses until they crack, and then he will kill them all."

"Thom," I breathed as my morning-after glow extinguished in a cold rush of guilt for not prioritizing Santiago's intel and letting Sariah sidetrack me by luring me home to deal with . . . everything. "Cole?"

Always a step ahead of me, he let the dragon claim his skin then angled a shoulder to make climbing on his back easier.

"I'm going with you," Santiago said. "Portia isn't one hundred percent yet — "

" — the hell I'm not," she protested.

"She and Miller can hold down the fort until we get back," he continued on as if she hadn't spoken. "I've already given the Oncas these coordinates. That means someone has to stay behind and play hostess."

What it really meant was Maggie's sickness directly affecting Portia had shaken him worse than he wanted to let on.

"As much as I hate to say it, he's got a point." I was lucky her eyeballs couldn't shoot lasers. "Our allies need a safe place to gather, and this one is as good as any."

"Scoot along now." Santiago shooed her toward the house. "Go dust something."

The right hook she smashed into his jaw staggered him, but it put a smile on her face, and he seemed to feel better too. Who was I to stand in the way of true — if twisted beyond recognition — friendship at work?

"I call shotgun." I swung up onto Cole's back and fisted his silky mane. "You riding with us, or . . . ?"

"Cuddling bird boy for however many hours it's going to take us to get there ain't happening."

Without another word, he climbed up behind me. He didn't hold onto me. He counted on his thighs and charun reflexes to keep his seat as Cole launched us into the skies.

As much as I wanted to quiz Wu on how his father had located the enclave, I had a sneaking suspicion I already knew thanks to Santiago's intel. He told us Wu had flown there twice, and he spent the night both times. That meant anyone following Wu, like his father, would have stumbled across the enclave too.

Knox warned me when the enclave went dark, it couldn't be found. But I was willing to bet the loophole was you could if you followed someone in who already knew the way.

Damn it, Wu.

The news about his father imploding The Hole must have rocked him harder than I thought if his knee-jerk reaction was to run straight to the enclave to make sure it was still standing.

An inquisitive rumble vibrated between my legs, Cole checking to make sure I was all right.

"I'm worried about Thom." I resumed finger-combing his downy hair. "That's all."

"He'll be fine," Santiago gritted out. Softer, his words blown behind us, he added, "He has to be."

We arrived near the enclave and set down about ten miles away. We avoided the lake, choosing the cover of the forest to conceal us from flyovers. Under the limbs of an old growth pine, we cornered Wu, whose tucked-in wings meant he couldn't escape without giving us answers first.

I advanced on him, Cole and Santiago at my back. "You led them straight to Thom."

"What? No." He startled. "I would never endanger my family."

"Your father isn't your family?" Santiago pointed out without missing a beat. "Who's to say where your true loyalties lie?"

"Luce." Wu held my gaze. "You know I would never harm the enclave or allow anyone else to harm them."

"I want to believe that, but we have proof you've spent two nights in the area on separate occasions. What were you doing? Why go there at all? You're more aware of the risk than any of us."

"How did you . . . ?" His gaze snagged on Santiago. "You tracked me. How?"

"Your leg had a nice, big gash it in before we patched you up. I might have left you a present."

"That's how you did it?" I swung my head toward him. "Are you serious?"

Wu had almost bled to death helping us raid one of War's nests and rescue Thom. This was a poor repayment.

"It didn't hurt him. He didn't even know it was there." Clearly disgusted with me, he snarled up his lip. "P.S. Thanks for blabbing. Now he'll want to cut it out."

Wu glared at his thigh, the wheels in his head turning, but he only shook his head. "Later."

I wasn't certain if he meant he would square up with Santiago later, or if he would cut it out of his thigh after we handled this.

"I came here the first time because Knox sent an SOS. I didn't spend the night with them, I stayed out here, walking the land, trying to determine what spooked him into making contact." A frown gathered across his brow. "When the enclave goes dark, it cuts ties with the outside world. It's the only way to remain untraceable in the digital age. I couldn't contact him. His message was a one-time transmission."

"Knox sent you here? Not Kapoor?" A cold lump settled in my gut, a weight that promised bad news was on its way. "I emailed him a report a few days ago from one of Santiago's secure tablets. He didn't reply, but that's not unusual. He tends to follow up twenty-four to forty-eight hours later to clarify things." But he hadn't touched base yet. "When was the last time you spoke to him?"

Wu's eyelids crashed shut, and he reached up to rub them. "He was testing me."

"Kapoor?"

"No," Wu rasped. "My father. He wanted to see how much I would risk for the enclave. He requested a meeting, using the enclave as leverage, but he wouldn't have lowered himself to using those exact words. Threats are beneath him. He's a male of action."

"He told Kapoor just enough to guarantee he would get in touch with you." I pieced it all together. "And then your father sat back to see what, exactly, he would say and how you would react to it."

Wu jerked his chin in a tight nod. "As I said, testing me."

"He wanted to be certain the enclave was the right place to apply pressure," I surmised. "Kapoor proved him right." And proved his loyalty to Wu, an unforgiveable offense. "Do you think he's still alive?"

While he wasn't my favorite person, and I would always associate him with the end of my human life as I knew it, he was a good guy. He tried to be, anyway. That counted for something.

"Perhaps," he said, but I could tell he didn't believe it.

Irritated with myself as much as him, I snapped, "You didn't think to extract him sooner?"

"Farhan is smart enough to remove himself from the equation. He must have gone underground."

Farhan, not *Kapoor*.

Must be easier thinking of him the other way around. Less personal. Less . . . like a friend.

"Threats to family have a way of eclipsing everything else." I rested my hand on his shoulder. "But friends are a kind of family too. We have to look out for each other."

Gaze distant, he stared at the point where I touched him. "Am I your friend, Luce?"

"I like to think so, yeah." I rolled a shoulder and dropped my arm. "You're a rung below Santiago if you want rankings."

On my periphery, Santiago puffed up like a peacock ready to strut, as if his previous ranking of dead last was something to be proud of.

"Find Kapoor," I bargained with him, "and I'll demote you again. Rock bottom."

Pleased as punch, he grinned. "Consider it done."

With that handled, I turned back to Wu. "What's out there waiting on us?"

"Two platoons. Fifty charun." He dipped his chin. "Malakhim. They're what you would consider angels."

"One set of wings instead of three." Santiago swept his gaze down Wu. "I'm guessing that means they're not as fast, strong, or smart as you."

"Nothing is," Wu said, and for once he wasn't bragging. "The cadre come closest, but ... "

"Famine had to resort to poison to incapacitate you." The knife wound might have been painful, but the venom on the blade had begun systematically shutting down his body. "The fact remains, even if he's ten times the birdman they are, they've got numbers on their side."

"Who knows about the enclave?" No, that was the wrong question. Someone would have to know who the enclave was to know how to use them as leverage, who to leverage them against. "Who knows what they are to you?"

"You," Wu said simply then panned his gaze to Cole. "And I assume your coterie, or at least your mate."

"We're not the leak." I dared him to contradict me with a look. "Exposing the enclave exposes Thom, and I would never do that. Neither would the others."

Accepting this as truth, Wu inclined his head. "We can figure out the how later. For now, we need to get our people to safety."

Cole rubbed his chin, thoughtful. "How many civilians?"

"Four dozen."

The grim cast to his expression made it clear how doubtful he was we could get all of them to safety.

Frustrated, I wheeled on him. "This still doesn't explain how your father located them in the first place."

"Luce." Anguish filled his eyes, the gold in them burning. "Father captured a scout. That's how he found them."

"Who?" There had to be worse news to put that look on his face. "Who's missing?"

"Kimora."

"Knox's daughter." I crushed my eyes shut. "No wonder he was willing to risk getting a message to you."

Even Santiago grimaced at that. The male who held Thom's life in the palm of his hand was getting ready to squeeze. He had sent a plea to Wu. That broke protocol. Already, he was putting his daughter's life above his own, ahead of his people. All Wu's father had to do was offer to make a trade, a quick lie to get the front door open. And then he would kill them all, Thom included. If we didn't stop them first.

This was a major complication none of us needed, one that put me in the unenviable position of weighing the girl's life against Thom's. For me, there was no question. But I wasn't going to condemn her if there was any possible way for them both to walk away from this. "Any idea where she's being held?"

"The front lines." The edges of his mouth crimped. "That's how I know she's still alive."

"What do we do?" As their fearless leader, I probably wasn't supposed to ask. But as someone who wanted to avoid more casualties on our side if at all possible, it would be foolish not to lean on their centuries of combined warfare experience. "How do we protect the enclave and Kimora?"

"If we strike first, we give away our advantage." The set to Cole's jaw was grim, and I knew he was thinking of the impossible choice between daughter and duty. "They might kill her to punish us, or they might throw caution aside and attack the enclave."

"We have to prioritize the enclave." Wu couldn't meet my eyes. "It's what she would want."

"There's a chance they won't kill her." Someone who didn't know Santiago better might mistake the remark for empathy, but it was ruthless practicality. "They need a way in. She must be resisting if they haven't breached the sanctuary yet."

Wu shut his eyes, but I knew from experience it did nothing to block out the barrage of mental images. Resistance was good for us, but it might prove a death sentence for her.

"If they captured her in the air," Cole said, aware she was an aerial scout, "they have a general area, not a precise location."

"If you're right, we could evacuate the enclave before they locate it." I chewed on my lower lip. "That takes time, though. And where would we put them?"

The silence on his end left me to fill in the blank for myself.

"Fine." I blew out a sigh. "We stash them at the farmhouse, but when this is over, if we all survive, you're cutting me a check big enough to cover Dad's retirement in whatever senior living community he chooses."

The tightness around his eyes lessened. "Done."

Cole palmed the base of my neck, his fingers digging in to massage away the tension. "You don't have to sacrifice your home. We can find other accommodations for them."

Sacrifice was the word for sure. The farmhouse had already weathered so much, and sheltering the enclave would be the final blow. Of that I had no doubt.

A battle was coming, and this was as good as choosing Canton as the battlefield. With the breach site in Cypress Swamp, maybe I was giving myself too much credit. Maybe it had always been meant to happen there.

"Dad has already said his goodbyes to the place. If he knew what we had planned, he would approve." After all, he had opened his home, and heart, to me when I had nowhere else to go. "It's a good plan. There's enough land that we can shelter some of our new recruits there too. That will give the enclave an extra layer of protection."

Gratitude shone in Wu's eyes, mingling with the grimness so often present in his gaze when he looked at me.

"Once we get the civilians to safety, we can circle back for Kimora." I risked checking with Cole, almost certain he would demur, but wanting backup from some quarter. "Sound good?"

"Trust your instincts." He kissed me softly on the mouth. "Wu, show us the way in."

Instincts got me into trouble every day. Mostly the territorial urges that convinced me climbing Mt. Heaton daily for recreational exercise was a great idea, even with Daddy Wu breathing down our necks. And then there were the instincts that roared at me to maim or kill all those who injured my friends and family.

Well, okay, so I had to admit those had always been there.

Wu dissolved the wings from his back, hid them away wherever they went when not in use. "All right." He rolled his shoulders. "Follow me."

Then he set off at a sprint through the trees, so fast he almost blurred and left me gaping after him.

"Tag." Santiago grunted then shoved me so hard I fell on my butt. "You're it."

Growling, I leapt to my feet and shot after him, Cole at my heels. I risked a glance over at him, and he was smiling, wide and fierce. I wondered if adrenaline was to blame, or if he found Santiago amusing. I preferred the former to the latter, but he could side with the frenemy all day long if it kept that look on his face. Cole hadn't had enough to smile about in his life, and one day I aimed to fix that. If we survived.

Wu was a wraith ahead of us all, his movements quick and sure from familiarity. Santiago was likewise silent, if a touch slower. Even Cole, the heaviest of us, was quiet. Especially compared to me. I had to choose speed or stealth.

"Let go." Cole wasn't even winded. "Reach for your instincts."

Easy for him to say. Each time I let go, I let her in. So far, I could push her back out, but what if that wasn't always the case? Letting her wear a path to the forefront of my brain couldn't be good news long-term. Then again, we had no clue how many hours or days we had left. I had to be prepared to give it all if I wanted to protect the ones I loved from what was coming.

Breathing as deeply as the constriction in my lungs allowed, I summoned the cold place. It rose around me in a chilly embrace that turned my breaths into white plumes. Cole noticed and nodded for me to dig in, dig deeper, so I did. Frost obscured my vision between blinks, and then the layer of numbness that separated me from my humanity settled over me.

The landscape snapped into sharp relief, each scent a distinct flag in my mind as my senses heightened. A fluidity crept into my movements, until I pulled ahead of Cole, ahead of Santiago, to run alongside Wu.

A frown puckered his brow, as if he could never truly decide if he wanted Conquest to rise or fall.

We beat the others to a huge boulder sheltered beneath thick evergreens, and Wu turned to me.

"Let go," he echoed Cole's earlier advice, his tinged with warning. "Reserve her power for when you need it most."

A long moment passed where I stared out at him, ice glazing my skin, and wondered why I should listen.

"This isn't you, Luce." He braced his hands on my shoulders. "You're not her."

Warmth spread through his palms, down my arms, into my

tingling hands, and the cold place thawed enough I could shake off the chill.

Cole reached us and nudged Wu aside with an elbow to the ribs, clearing space to frame my face with his wide palms.

"You'll get the hang of it." His fingers tangled in my hair. "All it takes is practice."

"Bringing Conquest forward is dangerous." Wu examined the rock. "All it takes is Luce getting stuck in that mindset, and she'll burn herself out. It's reckless to let her practice when we're in the field."

"Yeah, Cole." Santiago swaggered up to us. "Luce ought to confine her practice to all that free time she's got. Between building an army and running for her life, she's got boatloads. Far better she test herself in all that downtime than when she's surrounded by people who can defuse her if her inner bomb starts ticking."

Chuckling, I punched his shoulder. "Sometimes I almost like you."

"Give it five minutes," he advised. "It'll wear off."

Knowing he was right, I turned my attention back to Wu. "Where are we?"

This wasn't the way Wu had brought me in last time. Then, the enclave had been housed in a warehouse, and we had landed on a roof I christened with my lunch. Either that wasn't their main living space, as I had assumed, or this was for end-of-world emergencies.

"This is the bunker. The exit, which we're about to make use of, is about five miles from the warehouse. It's all connected through underground tunnels."

Dismissing the image of sardines in a can that popped into mind, I pressed, "How do we get in?"

"The password changes every twenty-four hours. There are fifty in play each quarter." He rubbed his jaw. "Just give me a minute."

A mossy slab of rock slid beneath his palm, kicking off a chain reaction of shuffling stones and creating a giant Rubik's Cube for him to solve.

"That's not magic." Santiago leaned forward, energy buzzing around him. "That's mechanics."

"Humans live at the enclave as well. We had to take their limitations into consideration."

Limitations. The word burned my biscuits. I hated the way charun dismissed an entire species out of hand. This was their world, their home, their —

Damn it.

It was *my* home.

I might have been born charun, but I had been reborn human, and the raising Dad had given me was all that kept me hanging on most days.

A low hiss brought my head up in time to watch a jagged panel slide open to reveal a tunnel bathed in fluorescent light. Elbowing Santiago aside, I reached Wu. "How do you want to do this?"

"We separate." Wu ushered us down a sharp incline. "Each of us takes eight to twelve civilians, depending on the size of their family group. We meet up in Canton, at your house."

"No." Cole left no room for argument. "It's too dangerous to leave Luce unprotected."

"He's right." Santiago kept pace with us. "We can split into thirds, but not quarters."

While they argued logistics, I searched the building for occupants.

A lone figure approached, his shoulders curved under a heavy weight, and his expression grim.

"Knox." Wu approached him, and Knox embraced him, sobbing onto his shirt like a child seeking solace from a parent. "I'm so sorry."

"She's all I have left of her mother." His fists clenched in the fabric of Wu's shirt. "I can't lose her, Adam."

"We'll do what we can," he soothed, "after we get the rest of you to safety."

Knox took a moment to compose himself before facing us. The puffy skin around his eyes told me this wasn't his first breakdown. I could only imagine how he must feel, torn between his people and his only child. As hard as I fought for my dad, I understood how strong the parent-child bond could be, and the fact it went both ways was the only reason the enclave was still secure.

"She's sacrificing herself for you, and for her people." I hated to be the one to tell him, but I was being thrust into leadership roles left and right. "You can't let it be for nothing."

Knox leaned on Adam until I was amazed the leaner man didn't buckle under the weight.

"I can't see how we can extract her without giving up your location," I said, hating to drive my point home. "We'll have to get these people to safety then circle back for her."

"I'll stay," he rasped. "I'll keep an eye on her."

Wu visibly jolted. "Who will lead the enclave if you fall?"

"I put the enclave first when the NSB murdered my mate." His glare drilled into Wu. "My human mate, who couldn't take me with her when she died." Hissing out a breath through metal teeth, he regained control. "I didn't seek vengeance. I let it go. I did what I had to do, what you told me to do, to protect my daughter." A hard thread wove through his resolve. "Kimora is all I have left. I've sacrificed enough for this cause. I won't give up my little girl too."

"We need someone to stay behind and keep tabs on their movements." Cole's sympathy made it hard to look at him. "It might as well be Knox."

"Do not engage," Wu snarled. "Keep your phone on. We'll text when the enclave is settled, and again when we've returned. Keep to the west end, stay downwind, and don't die."

Knox didn't make any promises, but he did gather himself enough to lead us into an area identical to the one I had visited earlier. A few of the amenities were positioned in different locations, but it was otherwise identical to the layout of the warehouse.

All that faded into the background when a whipcord-thin shadow coalesced into a familiar outline.

"*Thom.*" Heedless of his injuries, I tackled him in the tightest hug I had ever given another person. "How are you?"

"Recovering." He rubbed his cheek against mine, a soft purr spreading through his chest at the contact. "It's good to see you."

"It's good to see you too." I squeezed him one last time then let go, giving Cole room to clap him on the back and Santiago to make a biting comment to cover the relief in his eyes. "I feel better about this mission already."

Thom smiled at me, his cat's smile, all sharp teeth and feline cunning.

"Needless to say, you're on my team." I ruffled his hair and couldn't stop the pressure welling up in me. "It's so damn good to see you. I know I said that already, but damn. It's really, really good to have you back."

While I caught up with Thom, whose daily texts had stopped when the enclave went dark, Knox divided the civilians into three groups. We didn't have to waste time waiting for them to pack. They had go-bags on hand thanks to the emergency protocols they were under stuffed with clothes, food, and weapons.

Once everyone was assembled, we met at the base of the ramp. Knox introduced us to each group. I expected protests or demands for explanations. These people had children, and they were sending a third of their numbers out with Conquest of all people. But one look at Wu silenced them. No, it reassured them. On their faces, you could see the ironclad belief he would never let any harm come to them.

That, more than anything, solidified his claim that whoever had ratted out the enclave had done so without his knowledge or permission. A troubling thought for later reflection.

"I'm with Luce."

Santiago let the statement hang, glaring at me, daring me to choose Cole over him. But, even though I much preferred Cole's company, I was the weak link. It made sense to pair me with someone else. The announcement set Thom's lip curling in the promise of an argument, but the expression vanished in a blink. I turned back to Santiago in time to catch the remorse on his face, and I understood.

Grief was a binding force that tugged on my heartstrings every time I thought of Uncle Harold or Aunt Nancy. They were family, I loved them, and I hadn't saved them. I barely rescued Dad, and I still hadn't been fast enough to keep Famine from poisoning him.

Learning Santiago hadn't volunteered to go with me out of the goodness of his heart, or because he enjoyed my company, wasn't a shocker. He knew I wouldn't let Thom out of my sight, and he wanted to make amends for the brutality Thom had experienced when members of War's coterie pulled off his wings.

Who was I to throw up a roadblock when he was following in my footsteps? Trying his damndest not to repeat past mistakes. Hoping this time, he would be quicker, smarter, better. That no one would pay for his miscalculation in blood.

Cole, whose casual affection came easier since our swim, wrapped an arm around my waist. "Are you good with that?"

"Yeah, yeah." I leaned into him. "I guess I can stomach a few more hours of his company."

A flash of relief crossed Santiago's features before he schooled them into their usual, ornery lines.

After that, there was nothing left to do but claim our groups and line up in preparation for our turn. It was decided we would follow the enclave's evacuation protocol, which meant we gave each group a head start of thirty minutes before releasing the next to better our chances by keeping our numbers low and spread out.

The strongest among us, Cole departed with his group first. He glanced back only once, but there was no mistaking the message for me. *Be safe. Be careful. Be vigilant.*

I will I promised with a curve of my lips and mouthed, *I love you.*

The breath punched from his chest, the words a jolt to his system I was smug enough to enjoy inflicting on him. *I love you too.*

And then he was gone, and I was left with Santiago scrunching up his nose like love had a particular smell that offended him. For all I knew, maybe it did.

"Can I have a moment with Luce?" Wu stood to one side. "In private?"

Santiago narrowed his eyes, but he took a few steps back that would do nothing to keep him from overhearing whatever Wu had to say.

"I'm going to circle back for Knox after we get the enclave settled at the farmhouse. I need you to stay with my people until backup arrives. I can't leave them unprotected."

Against my will, my gaze slid to Thom, who had grown thin and pale during his recovery. "I'll keep them safe until you return."

"Thank you." A shudder that must have been relief rippled through him. "You give me strength, Luce."

Unsure what to say to that, I patted him on the shoulder. "Don't get dead."

Withdrawing, Wu shot me a rare smile. "I'm hard to kill."

Maybe, but being hard to kill didn't make him unkillable. Most immortal beings stayed alive by avoiding confrontation, but we were running headlong into one. Given Wu's familiarity with the terrain, and the people, he was bringing up the rear with the largest group.

While I counted down the time remaining, Wu conversed with Knox in low tones. Watching them, it was easy to see the familial relationship. They might not look alike, too many generations had passed for that, but they were close. I hoped that Knox would take Wu's advice to not engage, but I had no doubt if they raised a hand against Kimora that he would act.

This might very well be the last time the two spoke, and it was obvious in the earnestness of their expressions that both of them were aware of the grim possibilities unfurling around us.

"Time to go." Santiago took stock of our group, lingering over Thom, then gave them a tight nod and raised his voice. "Stay close, be quiet, and follow orders. Do that, and we'll get you all out of here alive."

Trembling lips and wet eyes met his pronouncement, but there were set jaws and jutting chins too.

These people might be afraid, but they were prepared. They wouldn't hold us up or ask unnecessary questions. They believed in Wu, and they trusted Knox to put them in safe hands. This was the moment they had trained for, and they were as ready as they would ever be.

"That goes double for you." He poked me in the cheek. "I'm not explaining to Cole how you got dead."

The sobering reminder that Daddy Wu had given up on his catch and release program where I was concerned was unwelcome. He wanted me six feet under, but I was going to make him fight for every inch. The others could scatter, but he would never let me escape. He wanted me dead, and he wanted Death to embrace her namesake, so that things could go back to normal.

Cadres rise, cadres fall. Rinse and repeat every century as needed.

Too bad for him, I had no intention of falling on my sword. He would have to run it through me. No, I was a shield, and I would protect my family and friends, the people of this world, until my dying breath.

We made it to the farmhouse thanks to cool heads, two vans we rented after reaching the nearest town, and a whole lot of luck. Cole was waiting for us, his group already settling in on the second floor. There were only two beds, but we had plenty of quilts and pillows to make pallets on the floor. Plus the couch and Dad's recliner. Space was already at a premium with only two-thirds of the refugees present, and it was about to get downright cramped.

Cole swept his gaze over me, his wide shoulders loosening when he verified I was whole. "There's talk about roosting in the trees."

I returned the evaluation, relieved a scratch on his cheek was the only damage on him. "It would give them room to spread out."

"It would also make security a nightmare," Santiago groused. "They need to stay inside."

Thom lingered at my side while the others filed into the house to carve out what space they could find, but he watched them with a twitch of his fingers, like he wanted to snag a spot before they were all gone.

"Don't be a hero." I tugged on his arm to get his attention. "Run if you have to."

"I'm not a coward." He kissed my cheek. "I won't leave these people undefended."

"We can help with that," a new voice promised.

"Mateo Vega." I smiled as the leader of our first recruits emerged from the woods. "Did Santiago text you?"

For an antisocial grump like him to spearhead our recruitment efforts of his own free will, the world really must be ending.

"About an hour ago." Mateo jerked his chin over his shoulder.

"I brought fifty of my best, but I have more if you need them. The Cuprina are a strong people."

Tall and lean, Mateo was easy on the eyes. The ethereal wings extending from his back didn't hurt either. Though I would never tell him so, the antennae arching over his head reminded me of the headbands that come with children's Halloween costumes.

The delicate appendages were exactly the kind of thing that would have tempted Thom into his boxy housecat form so he could divebomb him while batting them around. The fact he didn't bat an eye, let alone a paw, at Mateo carved a divot in my chest.

"That's the best news I've heard all day." His mothlike clan was laidback and kind. How they ended up supporting Conquest of all people, I had no idea. "We appreciate all the help you can give us."

Crossing the space between us, he took my hand and kissed its back. "All in service to you, Luce."

"Luce," I mused, retrieving my fingers. "Not Conquest?"

"We're not disciples of hers. We're here for *you*." His antennae twitched. "I thought you realized. We don't support her agenda. We crave an end to the cycle of violence on this world. It's our home now, and we want to live in peace." A fierce grin broke across his features. "We're willing to go to war to do it."

Turning on Santiago, I had to ask, "How did you … ?"

"Find them?" He snorted. "They're finding me."

A frown knit my brow, and I hauled him away from Mateo for a chat. "I thought all the clans we visited were Conquest's supporters."

Trying for innocent, he batted his lashes. "I never said that."

"Worship makes you uncomfortable." Thom came to his rescue. "He must have been trying to put you at ease. The task was already outside your realm of comfort."

Ungrateful for the save, Santiago shrugged. "What he said."

Nape prickling, I demanded, "Does Cole know?"

Santiago squinted, debating, making me doubt whatever he said next would be true. "No."

"Liar."

"Cole is on a transparency kick where you're concerned." He cut me a flat look. "He doesn't tell you the whole truth. You seem fine with him editing your life. Why not me?"

"Cole is my mate. We have to be as honest as we can be with each other if we want a shot at making our relationship work. You're my friend. The rules are . . . " I considered him. "Actually, they're the same."

"Fine," he grumbled. "I'll stop manipulating you into building an army who worships the ground you walk on."

Not believing him for a minute, I did a mental calculation of the stops on my campaign tour. "Virginia City was the first true believer city, wasn't it?"

The vibe had been weird from the time we arrived, and they had been the only clan who demanded proof I was who I claimed to be. Even though all the members weren't to blame, it was clear on their faces when I shifted that the evidence put their reservations to bed.

All it cost was a female's hand. And then her life. And the life of her co-conspirator. No big.

"Yeah." He rubbed the base of his neck. "That could have gone better." Sheepish, he admitted, "I started you off easy to build your confidence. I thought you were ready for the big leagues, but those people were hardcore. I should have chosen an easier target first, but we needed their numbers."

"Huh."

He dropped his arm. "What now?"

"You did something nice for me."

"Whatever." He pivoted on his heel and left, and I returned to the gathering.

"I feel so loved," I told Thom, and he chuckled, a raspy sound that reminded me of a cat's tongue.

"The worse he hazes you," Thom agreed, "the more he cares."

"No one's heart is *that* big."

Eyes dancing, he didn't contradict me.

"I need to get back to my people." Mateo flexed his wings, and the filmy skin caught the light. "We'll keep an eye on the house. We have your numbers. We'll call if we have any trouble."

"Thank you." I saw him off then checked on Thom, who was drooping. "You need to rest."

"I haven't done more than walk the length of the enclave's tunnel until today."

"Let me help you get settled." I took his arm and guided him in the house. The recliner he preferred as a cat remained where Dad always sat, causing my heart to pinch with missing him. "I'm not sure if it will be as comfortable for you on two legs as it is on four, but Dad fell asleep in it watching TV all the time. It can't be that uncomfortable."

The funny thing was, the chair was prime real estate. I expected to shoo someone out of it to make room for Thom. Yes, it was preferential treatment, but he was my friend. The enclave must have realized that since they had gone out of their way to leave him a comfortable spot. One that probably smelled like him from all the time he had spent dozing there.

"Be back soon." I eased him onto the seat and kissed his forehead. "Call if you need anything."

"I will," he whispered, eyelids sinking as I looked on.

A tiny hand slid into mine, and I jerked at the contact. "Oh. Hey."

Lira, the child I met on my visit to the enclave, stood beside me in a frilly dress she'd paired with kid-sized combat boots.

"I'll protect him." She reached out and patted his cheek.

"Sometimes, when no one is looking, he turns into a *cat*." Glee sparked in her eyes. "Daddy said not to touch his wings, but Thom lets me scratch his ears."

Confirmation Thom had been shifting, even in semi-private, eased a weight on my chest I hadn't noticed bogging me down since I first set eyes on my friend again.

"Do you think, when I get to go back home, that he could live with me for always?" She stared up at me, eyes hopeful. "He's a good kitty, and I would take very good care of him."

A snort escaped me before I could stop from hurting her feelings, and her face crumpled.

"I'm sorry. I didn't mean to laugh." I gave her sticky fingers an apologetic squeeze. "Thom isn't a real kitty. He's a man who can turn into one. You can keep a kitty for a pet, but you can't keep a man as a pet."

After careful consideration, she decided. "Dad wouldn't like that."

"Between you and me . . . " I leaned down to whisper in her ear. "Kitties are *much* better than men. I'll see if I can talk your parents into getting you a real cat when this is over. How about that?"

"Really?" She jumped up and clamped onto me at hip level. "You mean it?"

"Really." I laughed, easing her down. "I mean it."

No guarantees, but it couldn't hurt to ask, right?

With Lira on Thom guard duty, I went in search of Cole. "Any sign of Wu yet?"

"No." He glanced up from his phone. "He ought to be here within the next ten minutes."

"You texting Death?" I jabbed him in the ribs with my elbow then rubbed the tender spot. I had fallen on concrete softer than him. "Should I be jealous?"

"Janardan," he corrected me. "Even if I didn't have a mate I loved, I would never steal one from a friend."

Surreal to think he had struck up a friendship with one of his brothers-in-law. After dealing with War, and her homicidal counterpart — Thanases — I wasn't sure what I had expected from Death. The title alone was foreboding, but the female herself was subdued, and totally in love with her mate.

Out of all my siblings, I was glad she was the last one standing. Even I had to admit, "They are disgustingly cute for a corpse and his animator."

And what else could they be? Just like Conquest, Death had a type. But whereas my alter ego preferred a good purr in a man, Death appeared to find a pulse optional.

"Janardan lived a single lifetime, but it wasn't enough." Cole pocketed his phone, giving me his full attention. "Death couldn't bear to be parted from him, so she got his permission to reanimate him after his natural death."

And since he was her mate, a conduit of her power, he could stand separation from her for long periods of time whereas the rest of her coterie would drop like marionettes with their strings cut if they got out of range. That's why Janardan had been forced to brave this terrene to negotiate a truce with us alone. No one else would have survived the transition without Death to anchor them.

Worry my own coterie was just as susceptible without me around squeezed my heart in an iron fist. But, I reminded myself for the hundredth time, other coteries had survived the cadre. Otherwise, there would be no charun from the lower terrenes on this one.

A commotion at the house drew our attention, and adrenaline spiked, but the happy faces surrounding me made it clear Wu had arrived with the last of the enclave in tow. Families rushed down the lane to embrace one another, and Wu shook hands and accepted pats on the back like he had carried each of them individually to safety.

Once he escaped his adoring fans, he strolled right up to me. "We have a problem."

"Many of them, in fact." I took his proclamation in stride. "To which are you referring?"

"The Malakhim have captured Knox."

I cursed under my breath. "Kimora?"

"A sentry crossed our path, and a cry went up before we could silence him. Knox sacrificed himself to save us from detection."

A selfish act or a selfless one?

After capturing Knox, they would escort him straight to his daughter, right where he wanted to go.

Wu, despite his best intentions, might not have done the enclave any favors by hiding and protecting them all this time. The enclave, Knox included, viewed him as their own sort of avenging angel. But he answered prayers with about as much dependability as any divine being. The sooner they realized that, the sooner they would start looking to each other for salvation.

"They don't need two guides to show them the way into the enclave." Cole exhaled. "Knox is the more valuable prisoner. He'll know where the other outposts are and how to access them. He'll also know where the enclave would have gone after it's discovered they've escaped."

"True." I hated admitting he had a point. "But you have to keep in mind that Knox is also seasoned, and a leader. They'll know he won't give up his people for nothing. They'll need leverage to get him to cooperate. That's Kimora. They'll keep her alive until they don't need him any longer."

"And then they'll kill them both," Wu finished, eyes sparking gold.

"Mateo has agreed to watch over the farmhouse. The enclave — " and Thom " — will be safe here while we figure out how to extract Knox and Kimora."

Singling out Santiago, the one guaranteed to know, I asked, "Where are Portia and Miller?"

"Purchasing supplies for your guests now that they have backup on site." He glanced up from his phone. "Do you want them to report back here, or do you want them to meet us at Lake Bevin?"

"Tell them to meet us there." We would need all the extra hands we had available to pull this off. "We ought to arrive about the same time."

Without the enclave in tow, we could cover more ground faster.

Creases gathered across his forehead, worry for Portia he would die before acknowledging. "All right."

Strolling up to Wu, I crossed my arms over my chest. "Feel like giving me a lift?"

Cole tensed behind me, but he didn't interfere, and I could have knocked Wu over with a feather.

"Yes?" He made it sound like a question. "If you like."

"I like." That was the easy part. Convincing Cole . . . that might not go as smoothly. Playing dirty, I sauntered up to him, planted my palms on his chest, then claimed his lips until mine tingled. "I want to talk to Wu alone." Best to give it to him straight. "He's like a peacock with his tailfeathers fanned when he's around you. I need him to open up without all the posturing."

"I don't trust his intentions." Cole searched my face. "The enclave matters to him. He's made that clear. They're innocents, so I have no problem using our resources to defend them in exchange for them sheltering Thom."

Sensing he had more to say, I prompted him. "Okay."

"Wu is risking his life, and the lives of those he loves, to rise against his father. We need to understand what his vision of the world after is, and if there's a place for us in it. The Malakhim won't retreat unless we defeat their leader. Maybe not even then. The upper terrenes may let this play out, let us weaken ourselves against their earthbound forces, and then attack when we're at our lowest."

The subtle hint gave me chills. "Unless someone of equal strength steps in to fill the void."

"This might be a power bid for Wu. You might be a means of overthrowing his father and claiming his position as a leader for his people. I'm not saying Wu isn't the better option, but I am saying we need to determine his goals and motivations before we align more closely with him."

"I agree." After all, his father had been a better option to someone once upon a time too, and we saw how that had panned out. "Also? I really, really don't want to fly."

Never in a million years would I admit that Wu's flights were smoother than Cole's as a dragon, but even with Wu I was left with jelly legs and quivering thighs from holding on for dear life.

I was the only winged member of my coterie terrified of flying. Good grief. How could I complete my transformation into a badass dragoness if I couldn't control my own gag reflex?

Cole tipped my head back with a finger placed beneath my chin. "You'll get used to it."

"That's not as comforting as you must think it is." I sighed. "How can I learn to fly if being flown makes me airsick?"

"It's different when you have control." Mischief sparkled in his eyes. "I'll show you one day. Soon."

"Soon," I squeaked. "I mean, yeah. I can't wait."

"Here." He reached in a pocket. "Take these." He tossed me a tube of chewable Dramamine, and my heart fluttered. "That ought to help with the worst of it."

"You're an angel." I blew him a kiss and returned to Wu, resigned to facing the awkwardness of clinging to him for the next few hours. At least this time he was wearing a shirt. "Ready?"

Wu frowned after Cole. "He's no angel."

"Neither are you."

"Hmm."

"Don't get your feathers in a twist. It's just a thing people say. I hate to tell you this, but dragons beat angels any day. They're cooler by a factor of ten."

"They're giant lizards with wings."

"They're as close to a living dinosaur as I'm ever going to get." Rixton had that part right. "How is that not awesome to you? Do you know how many documentaries I've watched on them? At least a thousand. Cole is a living fossil record."

"I'm a living symbol of Christian faith."

"A few months ago, I would have awarded points for that." Sorrow ebbed through me. "Faith isn't as easy when you've lost so much family in such a short time." Aunt Nancy. Uncle Harold. Even though Rixton, Nettie, and Sherry were alive, our friendship had been a casualty of this war that might or might not survive. "Plus, you kind of debunked God as I know him when you admitted your dad basically seeded rumors of his own almightiness."

"I didn't say your god doesn't exist. Just that he isn't a being I have encountered."

"Mmm-hmm." I looked him up and down, already plotting the best handholds. "Give it up, Wu. You lost fair and square. Dragons rule and angels drool."

Laughing softly, he opened his arms to me and bent his knees. I wrapped my arms around his neck and latched my ankles at his spine. As it turns out, he was right about this being the safest way to travel with him. Even if it was the most awkward.

With a wave to the coterie, I held on tight as Wu launched us skyward.

CHAPTER ELEVEN

———◦◉◦———

Wu broke the silence after we pulled ahead of the others, a curious glint in his eyes that made me wary. "I assume there's a reason why you chose to travel with me and not your mate."

My *mate*.

Cole was my mate.

The title hummed through my bones, just like Wu had promised me it would with the right person.

Shaking off the warm fuzzies before they turned infectious, I pressed, "Any luck finding Ezra?"

"Arranging a meeting between the two of you is proving more difficult than originally anticipated."

"I'm confused." Vague answers had that effect on me. "Is that a *yes* or a *no*?"

"I will update you when a time and date are set."

Emotions churned my gut when I envisioned meeting the male who had made all those calls on my birthdays. He had held me together with his presence over the line whenever my body burned, itching to release what prowled beneath my skin.

How had he remained as much of a mystery as what he was doing to me all this time? Had he provoked those crippling episodes? Prevented them? I wasn't sure, and that made him dangerous. As much as I hoped he could help us, that he *would* help us, I had as much reason to suspect he would do the opposite. Anyone with altruistic motives would have revealed themselves to me after I rejoined the coterie and learned of my birthright, but he hadn't. That didn't award him any points in his favor.

Writing that topic off as a temporary loss, I plowed ahead. "How about Deland Bruster?"

"He heard rumors you're recruiting, and he's gone underground."

Bruster had the uncanny ability to look into a person's soul, and he was the only charun on Earth who could peer that deep. He would prove invaluable in interrogating Ezra and learning what he stood to gain from all this. But it cost. Not money, but secrets, and only the ones held tightest to your chest.

Running low on those, I had no doubt he would dream up something else he wanted in trade.

"We need him. Both of them."

Wu didn't have anything to add, so I settled in for the flight, expecting him to go quiet on me.

"You've done something no other cadre member has ever done in the history of ascensions." He studied me. "You've united unaligned clans against my father. You've won them to your cause. Do you understand how remarkable that makes you? That they would risk themselves, their families, their secrecy, to stand beside you to end this when they've only ever cowered in shadows until now?"

"Don't give me too much credit. I thought I was winning over Conquest loyalists. I didn't realize there was more to it until Mateo showed up at the farmhouse."

"Santiago was right to keep the truth from you."

Irked at how often I was kept in the dark, at how often I preferred it, I growled, "Santiago is an ass."

"He cares about you. They all do. I envy that."

"Why?" It was my turn to study him. "You have the enclave."

"Knox is the closest relationship I've dared with them in generations. I risk exposing them each time I visit. My friendship endangers their lives."

"I hear you." The wind whisked the sigh off my lips. "It's the same for me, with Rixton and Sherry."

Fear that knowledge wasn't enough, that he would want to help, made me grateful Wu was supporting me, otherwise I might have wobbled on my legs imaging Rixton squaring off against charun like War and Famine. He would do it too, for the same reasons as me.

His family. His friends. His home.

Funny how many of those things used to overlap for us.

"How do you want to play this?" I pushed out those fears to clear my head. "You know the parties involved better than the rest of us. You can anticipate their strategies."

"They will use Kimora as leverage to force Knox to reveal the location of the enclave," he confirmed, "but how long that lasts is anyone's guess. Knox is aware we've evacuated his people. All he's surrendering is an empty building. Once the Malakhim learn we've thwarted them, they will retaliate. They'll kill Kimora unless Knox reveals the enclave's present location. Father won't stop with rousting them. He doesn't do things by half. He moved against them, and that means he wants them dead."

Basically, he was reinforcing my supposition. Except his speculation was backed by experience with this breed and familial knowledge. "Do you think Knox has given up the bunker yet?"

"He'll draw it out as long as he can," Wu said darkly, "but he can only last so long before he breaks."

"Then we cross our fingers and hope for the best."

Because that's ever helped in the history of ever.

"If more than the one sentry observed our group, we'll be too late. They'll dismiss the bunker and press for the enclave's location." His gaze went distant. "Once they put hands on Kimora, Knox will cave. She's his only child, and her mother was his mate. He won't lose her. He would die to protect her."

Thinking back to the decimation of The Hole, I wondered, "Are there any fail-safes in the bunker?"

"Yes." Wu zeroed back in on me. "Why?"

"The enclave can never use that location again," I said, thinking it through. "They'll have to cut their losses and hole up in another one of their homes after this blows over." *This* meaning the war, and possibly our lives. "There's no way to get back in to collect keepsakes or material belongings — "

"Those are tucked away elsewhere. Only necessities are allowed in the bunker."

"Even better." I settled in for the ride. "In that case, I have an idea."

We touched down in a different area than before, just to muddy our scent trails. That's one thing you don't have to consider when you're on the street. Lifelong criminals develop a sixth sense where cops are concerned, but they couldn't literally sniff us out. No matter how many times they called us pigs, we didn't smell like bacon.

Cole and Santiago joined us just as I got my land legs back, but I was happy to fake a case of the wobbles if it gave me an excuse to lean against Cole for support.

Santiago, not fooled for a minute, rolled his eyes. "What's the plan?"

Wu deferred to me — big surprise — and I got ready to sound crazy.

"We're going to give the Malakhim what they want." And make them regret it. "We're going to lead them straight to the bunker, and we're going to let them in."

Santiago arched his brows. "And?"

"Wu is going to trigger its doomsday protocol and blow them all sky high." I smiled in response to his spreading grin. "You down with that?"

Rubbing his hands together, he bounced on the balls of his feet. "Boom, baby."

"Cole?" I glanced over my shoulder. "What do you think?"

"It won't stop the Malakhim from coming for the enclave, but it will announce loud and clear that they're under our protection. It might make the Malakhim think twice before attacking again."

"Or it might light a fire under them." I sighed. "Whatever we do, we're going to take a loss. Hopefully, just property-wise. At least this way, we take some of them out too."

"We time this right," Santiago said, "and we'll get more than *some of them*."

However many we took out, we couldn't get them all. That meant retaliation was all but guaranteed.

"We go our separate ways," I announced. "That gives us four chances to locate Knox and Kimora and set our trap. Everyone remember where to go?" They gave me blank stares that halted just shy of asking if *I* was sure *I* knew where to go. "I may not have a super snoofer, but I have a decent memory. I can find my way back to the boulder. As long as I'm not expected to open it, we're good."

"I'll handle that." Wu grimaced. "Just get them there. I'll do the rest."

The edge in his tone made me wary. "Can you remote detonate?"

"It's meant to be activated from the inside, as a last resort. I can set a countdown. There's a thirty second delay to give the most people the best chance of escaping."

"Can you beat the clock?" I gripped his arm, forced him to look at me. "This is not your fault. You get that, right? Don't turn yourself into a roast duck for atonement's sake."

"The enclave is my family. They wouldn't exist if not for me." Remorse darkened his eyes. "I allowed them to flourish knowing this would happen one day."

"And you took every precaution. They have multiple bunkers and multiple aboveground refuges, right?" With Wu's analytical mind and who knows how many generations to prepare for this, he wouldn't have stopped with one escape route. He would have mapped several. "You did your best by them."

The tightness of his lips when he bent them into a smile told me he wasn't convinced but appreciated my effort.

"You still have Ezra and Bruster to find," I reminded him. "You can't do that from a roasting pan."

"It's good to know you've got your priorities straight," he teased, and I sensed his outlook brightening.

"You want to win?" I didn't wait for him to answer. "Then we have to set all our pieces on the board. No one gets to sit out this round."

"Be careful, Luce." He cupped my cheek in his palm. "The only things the Malakhim want more than what they already possess are you and me."

"Back at you." I withdrew before Cole started grumbling, but he didn't make a peep. Wisps of his truce with Wu held firm, which still puzzled me. "Don't make me come in there after you."

When he left, Santiago held my gaze for the length of two heartbeats, but whatever his message, I couldn't interpret it. "I'll text Miller and Portia with an update."

He was gone before I could thank him.

That left Cole and me, and we had to get moving. The most I could offer him was a kiss that scorched my lips when he returned it with equal hunger and a whispered "I love you" that earned me a genuine smile.

Yep. I was a goner. Good thing I wasn't prone to swooning, or I would be swaying on my feet after that lip lock.

Each glimpse into Cole's heart reaffirmed my commitment that one day, when this was all over, I was going to spoil him until we both forgot how he looked wearing a frown. I couldn't make amends for what Conquest had done to him, but I could give him the life he deserved. I could give him a home, a safe place to raise his daughter — technically, our daughter — and a lifetime of love with no strings attached.

We just had to get through this rough patch first. If you considered suffering the wrath of a godlike being hellbent on our destruction a rough patch.

Air whistled through my lungs as I sprinted through the trees in search of the Malakhim. With two hostages, they must have quit sweeping the area looking for their way in. They had one now. They just needed to see which of their keys to the kingdom turned first.

I almost stumbled over the first Malakhim, which was not a great sign. That meant I had pulled on the cold place to silence my footfalls without making a conscious decision to do so. It also meant I had my hands around his throat, snapping his neck, before my brain registered I had made the call on instinct.

Too bad the instinct wasn't mine.

Scanning the area for signs of a partner, I found none. I was alone with the corpse.

A layer of ice kept me numb, insulated from what I had done with stone-cold resolve. Hunting and killing Drosera alongside Thom was one thing. This was ... next level. Cold, precise, and nothing I could have pictured doing six months ago.

While I stood over the cooling body, I took a moment to measure what we were up against. What I saw didn't reassure. The Malakhim were the embodiment of the angelic ideal. They might not be sporting halos, gold sandals, or togas, but this one had blond hair and dreamy blue eyes that were hazing over. He was built lean but tough, and his wings … Tears sprang to my eyes at how they crumpled under him, twisted and dirty.

That surge of emotion was all it took to catapult me out of the cold place and back into my own skin. I fretted over what exactly I was feeling, why this death had affected me so powerfully, and I pinned it down to a lifetime of Sundays spent in church gazing up at paintings of angelic hosts charging into battle.

They were supposed to be the good guys. They were supposed to be righteous and just. They were supposed to exemplify the best human qualities. Or us theirs.

The pang in my chest was a budding identity crisis I didn't have time to indulge.

Angels were the bad guys. Full stop. I had to believe that, or else I had to accept *we* were the bad guys. And I couldn't keep putting one foot in front of the other if I didn't trust the path I had taken.

Edward Boudreau had raised me right. That much I knew without question. All I had to do was rely on my upbringing, and I would be fine.

Exhaling, I eased around the fallen angel. I had killed this one too fast for a warning call to go out thanks to the fact I hadn't realized how cold I had gone until it was too late. I was burned out and grateful for it. Walking at a mostly human speed, with all the noise that came along with it, I figured it was the next best thing to shouting *I'm over here, come and get me*. Just a tad subtler so they didn't suspect I was bait for the trap Wu was busy setting.

I didn't have to wait long for a Malakhim to hear me lumbering and come investigate. This one was on foot too, a must considering the limbs overhead, but he flared his wings when our gazes clashed like he wanted nothing more than to rocket into the sky to report.

An almost silver aura surrounded him, and when he flared them a second time, tears sprang to my eyes.

Now, I had been raised Southern Baptist. Dad might prefer communing with God on open waters, usually with a fishing pole in his hand, but I had gotten my dose of religion on the weekends when I stayed with my aunt and uncle. Especially during the summers when they needed extra hands to help babysit as well as run the bible school camp.

But even then, I had never experienced such overwhelming awe, in church or out, that I was unable to raise a hand to protect myself when he took aim with his golden bow and sighted an arrow at my heart. Not until this very moment.

That's when it hit me. Thankfully before an arrow got the chance.

Charun are all gifted in some way. They all possess some form of magic, for lack of a better explanation. This was his.

The urge to raise my arms, cry tears of joy, shout to the heavens. It was a manufactured effect, a manipulation. One Wu should have warned us about before letting us challenge the Malakhim.

Drawing on the cold place again so soon caused me to break out in a sweat, but finally, after salty beads of perspiration rolled into my eyes, I doused myself in frigid clarity. The shock to my system woke me from his thrall, and sensation flooded my limbs. My tears dried on my cheeks as I spun aside, hissing when the arrowhead grazed my forearm.

"That wasn't very nice," I snarled, weaving through trees faster than he could take aim.

"You're a blight on this world," he said, and even his voice held layers of compulsion. "It's my duty to end the threat you pose to the good people who call this terrene home."

Calling me a blight was harsh, and another time it might have triggered more navel gazing about my innate goodness. Thankfully, what with all the running for my life and all, I had no time to dwell. Plus, the fact he was cued in to charun lingo, calling this world a *terrene*, gave me a foothold. These flighty bastards might think we're their evil cousins, but that didn't make them right. It made them victims of the same propaganda I fell prey to at times like these.

Believing you're flawed, broken, or wrong was ten times easier than trusting you were perfect just the way you were or whole or right. Bad things always stick with us longer than the good. I don't know if that's a self-esteem problem or a human problem, but it's true. The fact I hesitated, that I wondered, assured me I wasn't the mindless monster this wannabe angel believed me to be.

"What about the threat you pose?" I challenged, snapping off a limb the length of my arm. "Do you really care whether humans live or die?"

Without hesitation, he kept the flurry of arrows coming. "Our duty is to protect them from the likes of you."

That . . . was not an answer. Apparently he only came with preprogrammed responses.

"The likes of me? Really? That's the playbook you're reading from?" I kept pushing, diving deeper into the cold, letting the frostbite numb me to the nicks and scratches down my arms when he hit too close. Still, he didn't call for reinforcements. He must want this kill as a feather in his cap. While arrogance was leading him by the nose, I had to push harder. "Who taught you to shoot? Ralphie Parker?"

"Who is this Ralphie Parker?"

"You're posing as an angel, but you've never watched *A Christmas Story*?" I circled behind him using a burst of speed I never would have believed myself capable of and rammed the stick through his right eye, barely resisting the urge to quote the famous line about shooting your eye out. "You lose serious Christmas cheer points for that one."

His gut-wrenching scream was music to my ears, and I leaned in to listen until his voice broke. That was how the next Malakhim scouts found me. Hunched over their comrade as he slid from my embrace, my fist clenching the stick gouging out his eye. The horror on their faces registered in a distant way, but I was too deep to swim to the surface.

From the rear, a Malakhim gleaming with power stepped forward. "You will die for this, foul creature."

Foul creature? *Ouch.* "Now you're just being mean."

I shoved the male in my arms forward, all but throwing him at them, and ran.

This lost to my charun side, I didn't have to wait on my brain to process feedback from my eyes to point me in the right direction. Vision didn't come into play, neither did memory. I wouldn't even call it scent recognition as much as a *knowing*, like a compass pointing in my head, and all I had to do was follow.

Listening to my instincts, I led the Malakhim on a chase through the forest, careful not to run in a straight line. As much as I wanted this done, I didn't want them to shy away from what we had planned. Halfway there, I spotted Cole several yards away, a contingent on his heels. On my other side, I spied Santiago with more than both of our numbers put together. He had a talent for pissing people off, so I wasn't surprised, honestly.

Ahead of us, the rendezvous point was made distinguishable by the gaping hole in its side. Wu had done his job. Now we had to hope the Malakhim would assume they were herding us and not the other way around.

Santiago pulled ahead and sprinted for the darkness. I slowed to give him enough time, but it was going to get ugly. The stragglers on his tail would soon notice me, and the Malakhim hot on my heels, and understand they had been played. We just had to pray we had all gotten out by then.

I plunged down the sloped tunnel mouth, cursing under my breath when I had no choice but to run into the back of the Malakhim ahead of me. He turned, gilded dagger raised, and aimed for my heart. I spun aside, hitting the nearest wall and cracking the back of my skull, but then Cole was there.

"Miller and Portia are keeping the Malakhim confined to the tunnel."

There was no time to check my phone to see if I had missed any texts or calls. "They're here?"

"Yes." He gripped my arm and dragged me behind him. "We have to get out."

"How are we going to get through that?" Dozens of Malakhim clogged the entrance. "They're not going to shuffle aside and let us pass."

"Luce," Wu hissed from across the room.

There was no time for second guesses. I used Cole's grip on me to haul him in that direction. Santiago, who had skewered the Malakhim who tried to stab me, paused to steal the golden weapon then sprinted after us.

"Hurry." Wu led us into a narrow tunnel that sealed with a metallic clang, alerting the Malakhim to our escape. "We have twenty-five seconds."

Heart thundering in my ears, I held onto Cole for all I was worth and stuck to Wu's heels like sheer will could save us all. I would have grabbed for Santiago too if there had been room. Coterie bonds were tight, and the fear of losing even one of the guys, let alone Maggie and Portia, constricted my chest.

Through the rough-hewn maze, we twisted and turned on an

upward incline that ended in another steel door with a complicated mechanism sealing it closed from the outside.

Just like in the movies, an electronic voice began counting
down behind us.

Five.

"Wu." I pounded on his back. "Get us out of here."

Four.

The locks clicked, and the partition glided open.

Three.

Sunlight streamed in, hitting my face, and I rushed forward
blindly, dragging all three males with me toward the trees in the
hopes that putting enough trunks between us and the blast might
protect us.

Two.

Shadows closed over our heads, tree limbs stretching over us.

"Please be okay," I panted out a plea to the universe to protect
Miller, Maggie, and Portia. "Please be okay, please be okay."

The explosion juddered the ground beneath us, and we fell
in a heap of limbs. Cole crawled over me, using his muscular
body to shield me from the blast. Santiago was thrown wide. I
couldn't see where he landed. Wu crawled to me on knees and
forearms and curled against us, his arms protecting my head,
his face inches from mine. I was staring into his eyes when the
first tree broke across Cole's back, when one of the limbs pierced
Wu through the chest, pinning him to the ground. Blood
frothed on his lips, but he didn't budge. He had kept me safe,
they both had, and it made me queasy how quick they were to
sacrifice for me.

"Cole?" I had an eyeful of his chest when I turned my head, but
that was it. "Speak to me. *Cole?*"

"I can't . . . move."

Grateful tears sprang to my eyes. "You're alive." I kissed every bit of skin I could reach. "Thank God." And anyone else who was listening.

"Santiago is twitching." He cut his eyes to the left. "He hasn't opened his eyes yet, but he's breathing."

"He's too big of an asshat to die." I prayed that was true. Portia would kill him if he kicked the bucket.

Wet rasps at my elbow punctured my bubble of relief as I focused on my partner.

"Hold on, Adam." I wriggled until I got an arm free then stroked his hair. "The others will be here soon." Unless they were trapped under hundreds of pounds of debris too. "Did you get Knox and Kimora to safety?"

Wu parted his lips, but no sound escaped them.

"Adam." I wiped my thumb across his cheek. "Stay with me. It's going to be okay."

"Foreign matter slows the healing process," Cole rasped. "We need to get the wood out of him."

"How are we going to do that?" It was all I could do to reach him for comfort.

"This is going to hurt." Cole lowered a portion of his weight onto me. "Can you handle it?"

"Save him." I could deal with the pain. Plus, there were worse ways to go than being squished beneath Cole. "Ready when you are."

In my head, the press of Cole's body against mine was sexy. The reality was he was a *lot* of male, and there were at least two fallen trees crossed at his spine, adding their weight to his bulk. I hadn't realized until he shifted his efforts elsewhere how much he had been shielding me.

Groaning, I did my best not to thrash as my lungs squished flatter than pancakes. Think crepes.

Planting his palms on the ground, he leveraged the trees off him long enough for me to suck in a breath. Switching all that strain onto his left arm, he reached across with his right and gripped the limb protruding from Wu's back.

Wu and I sucked in matching breaths, and when Cole's elbow buckled, and he slammed into me, driving the wood deeper into Wu's body, we both screamed.

Several minutes later, after we had all caught our breath, I had to shoulder being the bearer of bad news. "We have to try again."

Wu blinked slowly, a sign I took as agreement.

"Oh no, Mistress."

The buzzing in my head must be getting bad if I was hearing words interspersed in the noise.

"The tree," the same distant voice cried. "Move it."

Cole shuddered above me, the press of his body lightening.

"Now the other," a female ordered with a cat's scream in her voice. "Lift it off him."

This time when Cole rocked forward, he kept going, rising over me, allowing me to suck down air.

"Luce," he rasped. "Can you move?"

"Gimme a ... minute." I gulped oxygen until my lungs burned. "Just ... need to ... catch ... my breath."

"Wu is injured," he called to our rescuers. "He needs emergency medical treatment."

Shifting the trees off Cole meant Wu was no longer staked to the ground. But whereas Cole and I were attempting to get to our feet, he continued lying there in a spreading stain that wet the pine needles beneath him.

Pretty sure I had a fractured rib or two, I gingerly picked my way to him. "You can't go around claiming you're hard to kill if you let one measly tree defeat you."

Eyes gone brown and dull without a hint of gold, he whispered, "Not ... dead ... yet."

"Keep it that way." I patted his cheek then shouted, "I need a medic or transport to one." I stared him down. "You have to live so I can kick your ass for not warning me the Malakhim could awe me to death."

"Only works . . . " his eyes slid closed, " . . . on humans."

Poor guy must be gone if he was giving me credit for humanity.

Desperate to keep him lucid, I nudged him for details. "Knox and Kimora?"

"Safe." He sucked in a breath. "Meet us . . . at . . . the farmhouse."

"Good." I rested my hand on his shoulder. "I know how much they mean to you."

Cranking my head around, I got my first look at what I had recruited in Virginia City.

Gone were the unassuming visages the Oncas had used when they greeted us. Now their skin was burnt orange, and dusky fur mottled with spots covered their bodies. Wings the color of bruises held them aloft until they landed on dainty paws. Their smiles of reassurance weren't all that comforting after you noticed how their wide jaws had elongated to make room for their many, many teeth, but their nubby little tails made up for it in spades.

Forget flying monkeys. Conquest had flying, otherworldly bobcats.

Fierce shrieks erupted from their maws, the cries of hunting cats, and I had to admit I was impressed. Slightly terrified, but impressed. And not at all surprised to learn their charun aspects were feline.

Conquest really had been a crazy cat lady.

They were running in full beast mode with their wings tucked to their spines and their whiskers quivering on their muzzles.

The female tipped back her head and yowled, calling six males to her side who lifted Wu into the air.

Clutching my side, I sank to a seated position. "What about Santiago?"

"He's the one who called us. He's already been evacuated," she assured me. "You three were the last."

The ringing in my head ought to worry me, but I was fresh out of braincells to devote to yet another issue. "Where are they taking him?"

"Our healers are gathered not far from here," she said. "Fifty miles or so."

As a crow flies, that might not be much, but it was still a long trip for Wu.

"You said we were the last." Heart a lump in my throat, I searched for signs of our missing coterie members. "Did you encounter more of our people?"

"A male and female. His injuries were severe. Hers were minor. We took them to the healers as well."

A surge of relief that Miller, Portia, and Maggie were en route to help swept through me so fast my head spun. "Thank you."

"They are yours, as we are yours." She lifted her chin. "We only did our duty."

"Still, I appreciate all you've done for us."

A familiar shadow loomed over me, and I cranked my head around to get a better look at Cole.

"We're in your debt," he said to them, and they flushed with pleasure.

"There is no debt between us," they rushed to assure us, but the glow remained on their faces.

I noticed the female awaiting further commands and recalled my manners at last.

"We weren't formally introduced." I lifted a hand. "I'm Luce Boudreau. This is Cole Heaton, my mate."

Soft laughter huffed behind me, but I didn't care. He was mine. All mine. He was lucky I didn't have my name tattooed on his butt. Sadly, that felt like a Conquest thing to do, so no stamps of ownership from me.

"I'm Noel, and this is Franklin, my mate." Her fingers linked and twisted in front of her. "We have purified our clan. Only the faithful are among us now."

That was code for they had killed anyone who didn't want to side with me, and that everyone here was prepared to die on my command.

I wasn't sure which was worse, and I hated that it didn't matter, that I couldn't let it touch me.

That pesky human part of my brain was still screaming. It never shut up. Not for a second. It just kept going and going and going. You'd think it would go numb or go hoarse or — I don't know. Whatever your conscience did when you flat-out ignored it for months on end. But nope. I must be more human than anyone gave me credit for since I couldn't smother that piteous wail fueled by the atrocities I was committing left and right.

Luce Boudreau wasn't the same female who helped fish a body out of the swamp where she had been found fifteen years earlier. She wasn't even the same person who picked up a falchion and slaughtered her way through an abandoned mall's worth of Drosera to reach Thom. I wasn't sure who she was anymore. She had so much blood on her hands, she had no recognizable fingerprints.

"Thank you for all you've done." I stuck out my arm and clasped hands with her, forcing myself to hold still while she wrapped her furry fingers around mine. "You might have saved our lives."

We had no way of knowing if our plan had worked. The risk of Malakhim letting us bleed out until we were too weak to fight them was a distinct possibility if we had left behind any stragglers.

Franklin surveyed the utter destruction. "How did this happen?"

"We blew up some Malakhim." No need to explain about the enclave. They would learn about them soon enough. "I don't suppose you spotted any on your way in?"

"The skies were clear," Noel informed us. "We saw only the swath of destruction."

Swath of Destruction should be my new middle name.

"Take us to Wu." I pulled a broken twig out of my hair. "We need to secure him as soon as possible."

Until we knew his endgame, it was in our best interest to keep an eye on him. The fact he was his father's only son, as far as I knew, made him leverage.

What a very Conquest thing to think.

Ugh.

Daddy Wu seemed like the kind to torture and punish his offspring, not outright kill them. Otherwise, with his revolutionary tendencies, I got the feeling Wu wouldn't have survived this long. That meant if Wu double-crossed us, we could return the favor.

Cole rested his wide palm on my shoulder, its weight a comfort. "You're frowning."

"I hate when Conquest leaks her strategy into my head." I covered his hand with mine. "I hate weighing a person's worth by what another person is willing to do or give up for them. I hate that part of me agrees with her assessment."

"Are you sure those aren't your instincts you're listening to, not hers?"

"Is there a difference?" I hadn't meant the question to come out quite so barbed.

"Yes." He awarded me his full attention. "She wouldn't have fretted over those calculations. She would have made them, gotten what she wanted, and been done with it. She never would have given the transaction another thought. The fact you're sick over doing what wouldn't cost her a single night of lost sleep is one of the reasons why I love you."

"You're good at pulling me out of my head." And my head out of my ass, but I wasn't going to puff up his ego too much. "Let's get moving."

The shift into his dragon happened between blinks, and he wasted no time winding his tail around my ankle four times.

"How can I ride like this?" I lifted my leg, which weighed a ton thanks to my anklet. "Can you fly without your tail? Isn't it a rudder or something?"

Grumbling under his breath, the dragon released me. He twitched a wing, urging me to get on with it, and I didn't imagine the sparkle in his eyes. On his back, I was at his mercy. I had no control over what he did or how fast he did it. All I could do was clutch his mane and try not to vomit down the back of his neck. Trust me. You do *not* want to wash barf out of dragon hair. It's a nightmare. The stuff is like feather down. Dragon hair, not barf.

Heaving a sigh, I swung onboard in a practiced move I had perfected while living at the bunkhouse. By the time I knotted my fingers in his mane, Noel and Franklin were airborne. Cole let me settle then joined them in the sky.

From up here the view was utter devastation. I marveled that any of us — let alone all of us — had survived the blast.

Considering Wu's injuries, I could only hope Miller's weren't as severe or worse. It sounded like Maggie, and therefore Portia, had come through unscathed like me. Thanks to the guys prioritizing our safety over theirs.

Idiots.

Leaning forward, I buried my face in Cole's mane and let his steady presence soothe me. The pain in my ribs and back were easing, probably thanks to that power boost Santiago had mentioned. I healed fast, but ribs were tricky and painful.

A rumble shook me as the dragon gave me permission I hadn't realized I was asking through my body language.

Eyes too heavy to keep open, I fell asleep and trusted him not to let me fall.

CHAPTER TWELVE

———◈———

Dwelling in the cold place for so long had wiped me out, and I slept like a baby. I'm not sure of the logistics, but I woke in Cole's arms, his steady gait familiar as he carried me into the tent where the healers worked on Wu. A single chair sat next to Miller's cot, and Maggie slumped over in it, her hand covering his on the thin mattress.

It didn't have to mean anything beyond Portia comforting an old friend, but the set of her shoulders screamed Maggie to me.

Cole and I exchanged a look as he set me down, but we didn't have a leg to stand on when it came to schooling people on relationships.

I crossed to them and wrapped my arms around Mags from behind. "Hey, you."

She jolted awake, snapped upright, and almost busted my lip in the process.

"Luce." She spun on the seat and linked her arms at my spine. "Thank God you're all right."

"How's Miller?"

"He's got a nasty lump on his head and a broken shoulder." Her complexion paled, and her hands tightened in my shirt. "Portia got knocked out. I'm not sure how. I was ... resting ... then I came aware with blood dripping into my eyes. Miller was running, and I must have been too. I stumbled and fell." Her gaze found him on the bed. "He knew what happened before I did. He came back for me, threw us both to the ground, and covered me as best he could."

"Don't blame yourself for his heroics." I hooked a thumb in Cole's direction. "He did the same thing. So did Wu." Turning my attention to my partner, I frowned. "It didn't work out well for any of them."

"Cole." She peered around me. "I didn't see you there. I'm glad you're okay."

Cole was a mountain of a male. He was impossible not to see. Unless you couldn't look away from a certain bedridden charun who had just earned hero status in her eyes. Oy. She would be mother-henning him for weeks, and he would be eating it up with a spoon.

"Thanks, Maggie." Cole gentled his tone. "I'm glad you're all right too."

"Can you sense Portia?" I drew back to look at her face. "What did the healers say?"

"They said our bond is holding strong. She ought to wake soon." Maggie shrugged. "Miller is still out too, so I'm not worried yet. I can sense her, she's just more distant than usual. I can't switch places with her." She laughed under her breath. "I never thought having absolute control over my body and mind would be weird one day."

"Tell me about it." Conquest and I were less symbiotic than Maggie and Portia, but we overlapped in places. The more I pulled on my instincts, the stronger the hold she had on me. "We're not in Canton anymore, Toto."

Mags rolled her eyes and covered a yawn that made me wonder if hogging the pilot's seat was exhausting after so long splitting the difference with Portia.

"I need to go check on the others." I extricated myself from her grip so she could relax again. "Keep an eye on Miller for me, okay?"

Nodding earnestly, she got comfy in her seat, eyes on Miller.

Heart heavy, I rejoined Cole and put my fear into words. "Could their connection be charun biology?"

"Miller has known Portia for centuries, and he's never shown any interest in her."

"He told me it was a combination of the two." I rubbed my arms. "I'm starting to wonder if it's not that the coterie bond made him more accepting of Maggie as a human, that he's seeing her — a human — in a light that he can't understand without the context of Portia's cohabitation."

"Let's hope they get the chance to figure it out," he said, and I heard an echo of the same wish for us in his tone.

Leaving Maggie to her vigil, we located Santiago. He was propped up in bed with a phone large enough to be a tablet, a phablet I think he called them, tapping away on the screen. I had to clear my throat before it registered he had company.

"You seem to be recovering well," I said dryly. "The screen didn't crack?"

Smirking, he held up an identical phone with spiderwebs veining its glass. "I always carry a spare."

"Of course you do."

Lowering his electronics, he stared across the room. "How is she?"

"Mags is good." I left out mention of Portia altogether. "Miller protected her from the blast."

Yes, it was mean to play his usual tricks on him, but I might never get another chance.

"Portia," he growled. "How is Portia?"

"We don't know," I admitted. "Portia sustained a head injury, and it woke Maggie instead of knocking her — the body? — unconscious. That's what triggered Miller's protective instincts. Mags has been in control since they arrived. She can sense Portia, but she's not surfacing."

Genuine worry leaked into his voice. "That's never happened before."

"She's never timeshared with a host before, either." I patted his shoulder and repeated what Maggie told me. "Miller isn't awake yet. Let's not get too worried about Portia until then."

Mouth tight, he nodded then waved us on while he started back doing whatever it was we had interrupted.

Our last stop was calculated to give the healers time to disperse. They had been in the thick of treating Wu when we first arrived, but only a few remained around his cot, and all but one left to give us privacy. The last one watched him like a hawk, and I was grateful for it considering the severity of his wounds.

"You're still kicking, I see." I jabbed him in the shoulder with my pointer, earning a frown from the healer. Well, the closest thing they would give Conquest to a frown. "Guess the next tree will have to try harder."

A smile graced his mouth, helped along by the drugs in his system. "I'm sure you'll take notes and pass them along."

"We did it." I swept my gaze around the tent. "And we all survived."

"We did," he agreed, groggily. "What next?"

"We go home and regroup." I smoothed the hairs away from his forehead, the slight touch singing down my arm with a resonance that spoke of potential for a relationship that would never go beyond partnership for us. "Cole and I will handle the logistics. You rest."

"I'm sorry, Luce," he murmured, eyelids drooping. "So ... damn ... sorry."

A chill swept down the length of my spine, and Cole wore a matching frown at the apology.

"Maybe it's the drugs talking." I touched Cole's arm. "Or a possible head injury."

I looked to the healer for backup, but she shook her head once, and Cole's mood darkened.

Leaving the tent behind, we sought out Noel and Franklin. "How long will it take your people to pack up and move?"

"We can be ready in six hours." Franklin took her hand. "Just tell us where to go."

I gave them directions to the farmhouse and promised to meet them there.

Unable to hold still, I paced a track around Cole until I flattened the grass underfoot.

Though it hadn't done me much good up to this point, I drafted a quick report to let Kapoor know the particulars about the explosion at Lake Bevin, but it didn't feel like enough.

And that was before I spotted a missed call from Rixton, and then a text, demanding what the hell I was doing blowing up mountainsides without him. A guess on his part, but a right one. There was no point in lying to cover it up at this point. He was already in too deep, and I had to stop him before he bottomed out.

"You're making me dizzy." He caught my arm when I veered too close and pulled me to a stop. "What's wrong?"

"All roads lead to Canton." I shook my head. "The last place I wanted this showdown is in the streets of my hometown, but we keep getting nudged in that direction."

"Breach sites have a magnetic quality. They lure cadre to them, you in particular."

"The Rixtons are in Canton, so are a lot of familiar faces I don't want to see hurt."

"We'll establish more than one base. We can stay at the farm-house until the others recover and then set out again. Noel and Franklin can establish a second outpost, maybe in Jackson. We can send two or three other clans to rendezvous with them while we keep building our numbers."

"When do we know it's enough?" I searched his face. "How can you tell when you've done all you can do?"

"It's never enough." His smile was sad. "All you can do is your best, until you run out of time."

"You need to work on your motivational speeches."

"This will be the first time you've seen the atrocities that occur in battle. This will be the first time you grasp the scope of your heritage, and I wish I could protect you from all of it."

"Me too." I rested my forehead against his chest. "I wish I could hole up with Dad and wait for it to blow over, but I can't. Without me, it won't."

"You could try," he said softly, his arms coming around me.

Shock snapped my head up, and I scowled at him. "You're not getting rid of me that easily."

"I know."

"If it was that simple, I would lock up all my loved ones and only let them out once this is done."

He read my intent too easily. "You're not getting rid of me that easily either."

"I know," I parroted. "Can't blame a girl for wishing, though."

In the uncanny way he had, Thom sat in the field beside the house, waiting like he had been expecting us. Cole touched down, and I hopped off in the grass. Thom smiled at me, the corners of his eyes crinkling, and prowled to us.

"How's it going?" I kept it casual right up to th
pounced, wrapping his frail shoulders in a hug that i
ling breathily. "Tell me if I'm invading your *me* space too muc.

"Never." He rubbed our cheeks together. "It's an instinctive response to an injured coterie member." He withdrew and started leading us toward the house. "Your presence gives me strength, and your touch anchors me."

"What I'm hearing is you should stick with me." I winked at him. "Clearly, I'm good for your health."

Minus the part where aligning with me had cost him his wing in the first place.

"Luce." He slowed until I caught up to him. "I made my choice to join this coterie long before you arrived, and I don't regret my decision. What happened to me . . . " His shoulder twitched at the reminder. "It wasn't your fault." Satisfaction lent his voice an edge when he growled, "You avenged me."

A stomach full of Drosera was a small price to pay for how proud he was of me. "You would have done the same for me."

"Yes," he said, gaze sweeping my face. "I would have."

Rustling leaves betrayed Mateo's arrival. "You're back."

"I am." I gestured for them to follow then circled the house to sit on the weathered picnic bench beneath the old oak tree. "We're expecting company. A clan of Oncas will arrive in a few hours carrying wounded. They have tents, so they'll be camping around the property. They won't be sharing with the enclave, and they shouldn't bother you. I just want you to be aware of them."

Cole shook hands with Mateo. "We'll introduce you once their leaders arrive."

"Our people have lived in isolation to avoid conflict for so long, we've lost touch with our charun brethren." He smiled like he meant it. "I look forward to renewing old acquaintances, and alliances."

With that, he shot off to rejoin his people and spread the word about the guests who ought to be arriving shortly.

"I'm going to nap," Thom announced. "I spent too long outside today, enjoying the sun."

A hint of suspicion had me examining him for signs of fatigue. "Are you sure you don't want to hang out with us for a bit?"

"You have a few hours," he said pointedly. "I'm sure you can think of a constructive way to spend them."

When I glanced over my shoulder at Cole, who had fallen behind while checking his phone, I got the hint.

We had time for a trip out to Cypress Swamp. We might as well since we were back in the area. It would put his mind at ease and give me a chance to update Death on our progress and see if she had made any.

Death had retained her knockoff movie star guise, right down to the mole high on her cheek. Dressed in jersey knit shorts and a tank top salvaged from one of our drawers, she gave the impression of a Hollywood starlet researching an upcoming role about the lives of swampers. She also wore socks but no shoes and . . . Were those oven mitts on her hands?

"Hey, sis." I stepped onto the pier, wary of what we might have interrupted. "What are you up to?"

"Janardan is teaching me how to microwave frozen dinners for the children." Neat furrows gathered across her brow. "They prefer to catch their meals, but we agreed humans are off limits, and local wildlife is scarce."

Between the Drosera churning up the swamp, and the ever-present smell of decomposition that trailed her children like perfume, I couldn't blame the deer or gators for making themselves scarce. Fish had been plentiful, but the ones her coterie hadn't already devoured had relocated before entire schools got digested.

"Nicodemus." Janardan beamed. "I didn't expect a visit for another week at least."

"We were in the area." I nudged Cole toward his friend. "You guys catch up, and us girls will chat out here."

While they retreated to where Phoebe was being kept, I claimed a chair at the wrought-iron table near the water and indicated Death should join me.

As she removed the mitts, her dark eyes found mine. "You don't wish to see the child?"

There was no good answer for my reluctance, so I went with, "Cole will appreciate time alone with her."

"You no longer feel the bond between mother and daughter." Her slender fingers rose to her throat. "I can't imagine the magnitude of such a loss."

"I don't remember her to miss her," I admitted. "I'm sure we'll bond once she hatches — revives? — but I'm not sure we'll ever have the same connection she shared with her mother. How's that going, anyway?"

Cole might not have told me in as many words that he planned on waking Phoebe, but he and Miller had built an incubation chamber to jumpstart the process, which was proof enough of his intentions. He might not be ready to admit it — even to himself — but he wouldn't rest easy until he saw her again.

Tomorrow wasn't guaranteed for any of us, so I wouldn't stand in the way of him claiming what happiness he could grasp, however fleeting. Even if a sliver of me regretted sharing his attention with a wooden obelisk when our time together was limited enough without this latest complication.

"Phoebe will emerge within another week if we go on as we are now."

I swallowed hard. "A week?"

Seven days until I learned if I had it in me to mother Conquest's child. No, *Cole's* child. Conquest might have given birth to her, but Cole had named her Phoebe. *Sweet one.* He was the one willing to sacrifice it all to spare her from embracing her heritage and claiming her mother's title as her own by secreting her away into Death's care.

"It will come back to you," she decided. "Your bonds with your coterie are too strong for you not to embrace the girl as one of you. She is your mate's offspring, after all. Even if you couldn't love her for herself, you would open your heart for his sake."

"I don't know how much you know about my life," I started, "but I was adopted by the man who found me when I was a child. He raised me as his daughter, and I see him as my father." I absorbed her surprise with a grin. "He showed me every day that it's possible to love a child who's not a blood relation. Phoebe and I are complicated, but we'll figure it out. Not for Cole's sake, but for hers."

"Well said." She smiled, and there was genuine warmth there. "Tell me more of your life among humans. I'm interested to learn how they shaped you into this ... " She gestured to me, and I braced for her to call me a shell, " ... person. You remind me a little of Conquest, when she was a child, but even then she was ambitious. She was bred for her title, and she never stopped to enjoy what was in front of her. Her eyes were always turned skyward, her thoughts a world away."

Unhappy to find myself intrigued by memories of a childlike Conquest, I told Death my story instead. Each word cemented my identity and reminded me of who I was — Luce Boudreau, daughter, friend, godmother, cop. And by the end of the hour we spent there, I was tempted to add sister to the list and mean it.

Out of my siblings, I had feared Death's title most of all. Not for what it might mean for me, but for those around me. Dad was no spring chicken, and Uncle Harold hadn't been either. But instead of an enemy, I had found an ally, maybe even a friend. Death held a reverence for life that mirrored mine. And wasn't life funny like that? When what scares the pants off you is actually what's best for you?

Now all I could do is hope life knew what the heck it was doing.

That would make one of us.

The Oncas beat us to the farmhouse, but not by much. Several enclave members greeted them to help move the wounded indoors until tents could be erected. Santiago ditched his cot and rejoined us, but Miller was still out cold and so was Wu. Portia hadn't surfaced yet, either. We had no choice but to spend the night and hope for the best come tomorrow.

"I'll stay here and keep an eye on the others." Santiago stared off into the distance. "You two can go stay in your tent in the woods, far away from the rest of us. We really don't want to smell what you get up to tonight. You'll be doing us all a favor."

A flutter twitched through my lower stomach, but I held firm. "You're kicking us out?"

"I already have a cot with my name on it. We should keep the last one open in case we need it."

Cole hadn't spoken much since we left the bunkhouse. The inner battle over whether waking his daughter was a selfish act or a merciful one crowded his mind, and I didn't want to add my two cents when it should be his call. But that didn't stop me from admiring the view as the gears in his mind gained traction.

As if surfacing from a deep pool, Cole sucked in a breath that cranked his head toward me.

Rubbing my thighs together, I got the impression I was the reason a flush was darkening his cheekbones.

"We'll take the tent." Cole watched for my reaction when he said it. "This might be the last chance we get to be alone for a while."

"On that note, I'm out." Santiago made a beeline for Maggie, who smiled hesitantly as he stared down his nose at her like he might will Portia to the surface. "Need a break? I can wait here if you need to pee or something."

"Oh." She rose slowly. "Okay. Sure."

On her way past us, she shot me a *what do I do* look, but I was just as stumped by his behavior.

Nice Santiago was … disturbing. No wonder she powerwalked back to the house to avoid him.

"I would offer to race you to the tent," I said once we were alone, "but I'm beat."

The tender look he shot me almost made me feel bad when I pivoted away and sprinted for the woods.

"Sucker," I called over my shoulder and laughed when his roar scared birds — and Cuprina — from the trees.

CHAPTER THIRTEEN

———◆———

The next morning, Thom delivered us a hearty breakfast of two freshly killed lizards, one missing its tail, and an update on our wounded before leaving us to eat and dress while he stretched his legs on a walk. Thankfully, his absence meant I could toss the limp bodies into the nearby underbrush without offending his feline sensibilities.

Confinement with the enclave had clearly worn on him. Winged charun weren't meant to spend so much time below-ground, but I suspected the real problem wasn't confinement to a particular area but to a particular shape. His inability to fly meant he had all but abandoned his natural form, and I missed his ratty ears and stubby tail. Most of all, I missed his mischief. No, that's not right either. Plain and simple, I just missed my friend.

On the upside, Thom had brought us good news, and I was eager to see for myself.

Back at the farmhouse, we approached the medical tent in time to watch Portia step through the flaps.

"I'll go check on Miller." Cole pressed a kiss to my temple. "Meet me later?"

"Sure."

Portia hesitated when we split up, like maybe she had wanted to talk to both of us, but she elected to visit me first.

"Hey." I touched her arm, hoping the contact gave her a boost. "How are you feeling?"

"Rested." She tried on a smile, but it wobbled. "For me, it was no different than falling asleep. Maggie had to endure the healing. I woke up, and our body was good to go."

"I'm glad to hear it. We were all worried about you."

"You weren't hoping Maggie might stay in control?" Lips trembling, she folded her arms across her chest. "I get it if you did. She's your best friend. It must have been nice having unrestricted access to her again, getting to talk without fear of being overheard. That kind of thing."

"Portia." I gripped her shoulders. "You're the only reason she's still here. I can never repay you for what you did for me, for *us*. She's my best friend, but you're my friend too. I'm not choosing one of you over the other. That's not how this works."

"I don't worry for myself," she said, mouth firming, "but I'm the only friend Santiago's got. I don't want him to lose that."

"He won't." I gave her a hug, and even the way she returned it spoke of her own personality. "And you're not his only friend. He might not want me to be, but I am."

"I'm glad." She released me. "He never had that with Conquest. Believe it or not, he's been in a better mood since you joined the team."

"If this is Santiago in a good mood . . . " I locked my jaw to keep from insulting her bestie. "Glad I could help." I set out toward the tent, and she fell in step with me. "How is Miller?"

"Good as new." She smirked at the bright sky overhead. "He hasn't gotten out of bed yet, though."

"Why?" I glanced around at the hustle and bustle of charun overrunning the farmhouse.

"You can't guess?" Laughter danced in her eyes. "He woke up to Nurse Maggie clutching his hand and holding his straw while he sipped water with ice chips. Miller isn't stupid. He's willing to walk with a limp if it means she offers him her arm for support."

"What are we going to do about that?" I wondered aloud, more to myself than anything else.

"We let them figure it out on their own." She shrugged. "You might be responsible for everyone on Earth, but you're not responsible for their happiness."

My laugh came out sounding more like a wheeze. "No pressure."

As I pushed through the flaps on my way to see Miller, I noticed the empty cot and remembered who had occupied it last.

Wrapped up in memories of last night and reconnecting with my coterie, I had forgotten all about Wu.

An Onca was changing the sheets, and I paused to ask, "Where did he go?"

Her head twisted left to right in a quick check that I meant her, that some other Onca nurse wasn't standing behind her. "He went on a walk last night, and he didn't come back."

"You just let him leave?" I hadn't meant to shout. I hadn't meant to advance on her either. But there I was, yelling and looming. Recognizing how close I skated the edge of my temper, I forced myself to take a step back before the cooling sensation in my core spread outward. "Was he okay? Delirious? What?"

Her eyes rounded, her pupils contracted, and her muzzle quivered. "I-I-I . . . d-d-don't know."

"Cole?" I turned my back on her and heard her relieved sigh to be out of the crosshairs. "We have to find Wu. He wandered off in the middle of the night, and no one thought to stop him. He's too valuable to lose."

"Your concern warms my heart," Wu drawled from behind me.

I spun and swept my gaze over him, a frown tipping my mouth. "You left to get fresh clothes?"

"The ones I wore yesterday were ruined." He studied me, and his voice hardened to a razor's edge. "As my invitation to frolic through the woods naked must have gotten lost in the mail, I thought I should procure more."

The blood rushed from my cheeks, anger or embarrassment, I couldn't tell. Maybe it was safer for him if I didn't peg the emotions roiling in my gut at his jab.

I knew then that he had followed us. He had *seen* us. What had drawn him out, I had no idea, but there was no mistaking the pinch of hurt at the corners of his eyes or the twist of disgust on his top-heavy mouth.

"You son of a bitch."

Aware I was forming a habit, I walked right up to him and slapped him hard across the face.

He didn't so much as blink, let alone demand an explanation. He was lucky I didn't use my fist.

"I have a lead on Bruster." He touched his fingers to his cheek. "I'm going to Nebo, North Carolina."

Blood still hot, I cut him a smile. "Then so am I." Turning to Cole, I cocked an eyebrow. "Give me a lift?"

"It would be my pleasure." He rolled that last *r* until it came out sounding like a purr.

Breaking his fifteen-year dry spell had definitely put him in a good mood.

"Meet you outside?" I wanted a moment alone with Miller before we departed, but Cole read me easily. He left and took Wu and the others with him.

Miller, propped up in bed, had been watching the show with

a half-smile that told me he could smell what we had been up to from where he rested.

"I heard you're a dirty faker." I plopped down in the seat Mags had faithfully occupied while he remained unconscious. "Has Maggie figured it out yet, or is she too polite to call you out?"

"I didn't mean to let it drag on." He fussed with the sheets around his hips. "It was nice ... having someone care."

"*I* care." I pinched his thigh and relished his yelp. "You mean it was nice having *Maggie* care."

"Yeah." Pink brushed his cheekbones. "That."

"I get it." I leaned back, crossed my arms over my chest. "I used to be so hungry for Cole's attention, I was starving to death no matter how many friends or how much family surrounded me."

"That's it exactly," he admitted softly. "Do you know if ... ?"

"I haven't asked her outright. I don't think she knows how she feels or wants to admit it if she does." I sighed. "You have to remember she was engaged. I don't mean to be the hammer hitting you over the head with that at every opportunity, but she had her whole life planned out before I dragged her into this world."

"Justin Sheridan."

"I'm going to pretend you remember that name because of our investigation into Maggie's disappearance and not because you're stalking her ex."

"I have an excellent memory."

"Mmm-hmm." I pushed to my feet. "Maggie would forgive a lot, but she would never forget you hurt Justin because of how you feel about her." I debated not saying the rest, but I might as well put it out there. "You would remind her of how War beat her to a pulp to punish me. You don't want her drawing that parallel. Trust me."

Tossing the cover off his legs, he swung them over the edge of the cot. "I do."

Snickering under my breath, I watched him stretch. "Don't give up the sickbed routine on my account."

"My back hurts," he admitted, sheepish. "This mattress is filled with gravel."

A sharp huff from across the room brought a quick apology to his lips for the healer he had offended.

"Let's get gone before they toss you out." I hooked my arm through his. "What are your plans for the day?"

"Santiago needs extra hands wiring the new security measures around the house and property."

"Ah." I hadn't realized that's what he had been doing to occupy himself, but I should have known it involved wires and some form of tech. "The real reason for your convalescence reveals itself."

He chuckled, well aware of our rivalry. "He doesn't give me the same trouble he does you."

Spotting the man himself, I grumbled, "He doesn't give anyone the trouble he gives me."

"That's how he shows his love," Portia sing-songed once we were in range. "He probably pulled girls' hair on the playground to show them he likes them."

"You know that's unacceptable, right?" The hair-pulling, not the love-showing.

Santiago wrapped her hair around his fist and yanked until they stood nose-to-nose. "What does this show you?"

"That you haven't brushed your teeth today. Your breath smells like the hot ass you don't have." She puckered up big. "I brushed mine twice — even flossed. I can kiss away the stink if you want me to try. It's hard work, but someone's got to be invested in your oral hygiene."

He recoiled so fast, she stumbled forward into the space he used to occupy.

"Works every time." She dusted her hands, but trouble sat in her eyes, an uneasiness that lingered in Santiago as well. "But seriously — do you want the gum or not?"

Attempting to shrug it off, he took the gum, chewed the flavor out of it, then stuck it in her hair.

I saw it coming from a mile away, and I should have stopped it. It was Maggie's hair too, but Santiago was at his most obnoxious when he cared. Having Portia go MIA had rattled him. So near what could be the end, when we were all focused on savoring our last moments with loved ones, I couldn't begrudge him his extreme reaction. Not where she was concerned. This was the game they played, and I wasn't about to step on their toes if they only related to one another on the level of two kids on a playground.

Once Portia realized what he'd done, she screeched and lunged for him. He darted aside, laughing maniacally, and ran. She gave chase, and everyone — and I do mean everyone — got out of their way.

"Mags was a kindergarten teacher," I said into the silence. "She's an old pro at getting gum out of hair."

Though she probably hadn't had to peanut butter or olive oil it out of her own since we were kids.

"We should go." Wu wasn't half as amused by watching Santiago soak up Portia's rage. "We don't have long before the office closes."

"What office?"

"An agent working undercover for the NSB called in the Bruster sighting. She's working at a car lot. We'll need to approach her as customers to maintain her cover."

Unable to believe my ears, I shook my head. "You act like any of that will matter if we don't stop your father."

"This world existed before you, or me, and it will continue on, in some form, after we're gone."

Framed that way, I had to mentally step back to view the entire picture.

Cadres had come before us, and unless we rewrote history, more would follow. The world at large would continue to turn, with humans blissfully unaware of the battle raging in their midst. The charun population would remain divided between the factions who wanted nothing to do with their pasts, or the cadres their ancestors heralded from, and loyalists who would bear arms in the cadres' name. Even among those, there would be division. Those who no longer had a horse in this particular race with War and Famine gone would sideline themselves and wait on the outcome, twiddling their thumbs until the next chance came around. Those who served Conquest or Death, however, would be scrambling to curry favor if they wanted a spot on the battlefield.

"If you die trying to wipe your father off the face of the Earth, do you really believe he will just let it go? That things will chug along as they have in the past? That he'll allow the NSB to maintain its charun taskforce when he's already detonated one secure holding facility at the cost of countless lives?"

"Luce — "

"And what about demis? His hatred for the enclave makes it clear he finds charun mixing with humans abominable. What about charun who mate outside their species? Will they, and their children, be targeted next? Will he really allow the system you implemented, that you maintained, to continue?"

Because if his father won, then Wu lost. We all lost.

Daddy Wu might forgive a lot of things in the name of family, but patricide was likely not one of them. And given that the enclave was Wu's blood kin, that meant he had to have loved a human, or at least slept with one, at some point. The offspring of that union, even generations later, was in danger of being exterminated by his father's prejudice.

"If I die trying to wipe Father off the map," he said after a long moment, "I'll never know how he handles any of this after I'm gone."

Cole was right. We needed to figure out Wu's game plan. Like now. Today. What had his father done to earn his son's hatred? Not just his stance against humans or his policies for controlling the charun populace, which were oppressive on both counts, but what he had done to Wu personally to deserve a knife in the back?

The knife Wu kept pressing into my hand after drawing on the bull's eye.

Nebo, North Carolina was a pinprick on the map. Picturesque, quaint, rural. I saw the appeal for a charun in hiding immediately. The car lot where Special Agent Deena Williamson worked held about a dozen clunkers in various stages of disrepair. The flashiest thing about them were the sale stickers in bold colors stuck to all the windows, some of them covering cracks in the glass.

Wu and I posed as a happy couple in need of transportation while Cole slipped off to scout the area for any nasty surprises.

"I'm shocked he let you out of his sight," Wu remarked. "He didn't even growl at me."

"Cole knows I love him." I kept my tone cool while the urge to slap Wu again prickled my palm. "He's got no competition." And neither did I. He loved me, not Conquest. And every day, he was proving it to me all over again. "There's no reason for him to be snarly because we're doing our jobs."

Slowing his pace before we reached the entrance, Wu forced me to hang back when all I wanted to do was shove inside and get this over with and behind me.

"I didn't follow you last night, and I didn't mean to follow you the night before. I didn't set out with that in mind. I was in Jackson when I . . . " His lips flattened, the top still fuller than the bottom.

"I'm sorry, Luce. I know how much you value your privacy. I left as soon as I grasped — or rather saw you grasp — the situation."

"The gasp was you." Heat prickling in my nape, I started piecing it together. "Cole was certain someone was out there, I had my suspicions too, but I played dumb so we got a few more hours where we could pretend all that mattered was us."

"That was reckless." His chastisement rang hollow, and we both heard it. "You can't trust your coterie to always have your back."

"Yes." I patted him on the chest. "I can."

As much trouble as Maggie and Portia had gone through to plan my romantic evening with Cole, I had zero concerns they wouldn't also have thought ahead to security measures for keeping our intimate bubble from bursting before dawn.

Done with Wu and his lip service, I marched to the dealership's door and shoved it open to the tinkling of bells. A man with white hair slicked to his scalp, who looked old enough to have been around when Wu was born, smiled at me from a receptionist's desk, showing off coffee-stained dentures. Behind him, I counted one office and a combination unisex restroom/breakroom. A fridge sat beside the toilet, and a microwave perched on top of that. Both appliances were close enough that the spare toilet paper had been stacked on top of them next to the paper plates.

I won't lie. I threw up in my mouth a little.

"How can I help you, young lady?" The man kept grinning his million-dollar smile. "Is this your husband?"

"No — " I started as Wu said, "We're engaged."

The urge to stomp on his foot surfaced, but I kept my shoes planted.

"No ring yet, I see." The man chuckled. "How'd you manage that?"

"It's getting resized," I growled before clearing my throat. "Family heirloom."

"That's nice. Real nice." Nodding, he pulled out a notepad. "Are you thinking sedan, SUV, or truck? Compact, mid-sized, full-sized?"

"We haven't decided yet." I swept my gaze over the prospects. "That green ... thing ... looks nice."

"Oh, that's a Ford Pinto. A classic." He pressed a button that caused a chime to ring out from the office three steps behind him. "Ms. Deena, we have two customers interested in the Pinto."

"I'll be right out, Sam."

She didn't bother with the intercom, and I liked her better for it. Then again, given the condition of the place, it might have been broken on her end.

Five minutes later, Deena graced us with her presence. She wore black stretch pants, a light pink short-sleeved sweater with a leopard print pattern in a darker shade, and shiny combat boots. Her hair was as wispy as cotton candy, her eyes the blue of Viagra, and her lips crimson and glossy like she had forgotten to wipe her mouth after eating a raw heart. Hopefully not from a person.

"Aren't you two cute?" She clasped her hands in front of her small chest. "I'm Deena Williamson. We'll start out with the Pinto and see where we end up. That sound good?"

"Yes," we said in unison and trailed her outside to inspect the slim pickings.

"Mistress, forgive me." Her voice softened, her tone reverent. "Sam is a good man, but he's human. I didn't want him to worry if I started acting peculiar."

Yep. It was official. I liked her. "You're fine. I'm not much into the whole reverence thing."

"I heard that about you. Figured it must be true since you're one of us suits." She gestured to her outfit. "I'm usually less ... colorful ... but tight clothes and big hair attract more flies to my honey or however that saying goes."

"You called me mistress. Does that mean you're a Conquest loyalist or just polite?"

"Momma was coterie back in the day. She met a remnant from a previous ascension, a previous Conquest in fact, settled down in Georgia, and here I am." She mulled it over. "I would say if I had to pick a side, it would be yours. Not because of your title, but because of who you are."

"I prefer to sway people on my own merits," was all I could say to that.

People who worshipped Conquest made me nervous, but people getting hung up on the idea of *Luce Boudreau: Savior* made me queasy beyond belief.

Deena picked up on my unease and switched topics. "Any particular reason you're looking for Bruster?"

"It's classified," Wu said before I could decide how much to tell her. "His services have been requested."

"He does a lot of freelance for the NSB," she said, fishing. "He's never been bagged or tagged."

"He's a valuable asset." Wu smiled, and it was glacial. "Is there a reason why you're protecting him?"

"I'm curious. That's all." She tugged on the hem of her sweater. "I don't see much action out here. I was starting to think I had pissed off someone higher up the ladder to end up in Nebo. Now the two of you are here, and it's just — exciting if I'm being honest."

"I get that." I got the same cheap thrills as a rookie. "You've done us a good turn by locating Bruster. We're not going to hurt him. We just want to consult him. After that, he'll be cut loose to disappear again."

"He likes the pie over at Martha's. It's a coffee shop about five minutes up the road, on the left. Stops by every night like clockwork around eight. That's how I've kept tabs on him. Drive straight. You can't miss it."

"We appreciate your time." I turned to go, but Wu stopped me. "What?"

"Your ride is gone," he pointed out, eyeing the Pinto with distrust. "We need a car to move around town. Unless you want to walk."

Just my luck, I hadn't purchased a return ticket on Air Cole.

Deena flashed a smile that probably had human men falling at her feet. "I'll make you a deal ... "

An hour later, Wu was the proud owner of a mint-green Ford Pinto. The interior was white leather, the small scrapes touched up with White-Out. All in all, it wasn't a bad deal for five hundred dollars. Plus, it made Wu's skin crawl to sit on the sagging upholstery, which I found hilarious. That and the way he drove with the tips of his fingers like he worried the steering wheel might give him cooties.

What a snob. I would have killed for this car or any other box with wheels when I was a teenager. Even my Bronco was bought used to spare me heart palpitations over showroom floor pricing. But Wu? I was betting he never got hand-me-downs. Only the best of everything for him from the moment of conception forward.

We arrived at Martha's before the dinner rush and claimed two seats at the diner-style bar. We ordered coffee and pie and settled in to wait. Three slices and two hours later, Bruster still hadn't showed, and I had to use the little girl's room.

After tossing back the last inch of coffee so black it absorbed creamer cup after creamer cup without changing color, I got Wu's attention from his phone. "Be right back."

I spun on my stool, smiling at the small thrill, then hopped off and headed for the bathroom. I had to pass the men's on my way, and a prickle started between my shoulder blades that radiated down my arms and through my fingertips. The urge to reach for the gun I wasn't wearing nearly overwhelmed me.

Pulling out my cell, I texted Wu.

> I got a bad feeling.

His head came up, a predator on alert, and his nostrils flared as he turned in my direction.

> I smell blood.

> What's our play?

> I'll pay the bill then check the
> men's room. Go to the ladies
> so you don't draw attention
> to yourself.

As much as I had to go, I wasn't thrilled by the idea of peeing while someone bled out the next room over. Sadly, one of the first things you learned as a cop was to take the breaks you were given. You never knew when you'd get another. So eat, drink, and tinkle when opportunities presented themselves.

Sliding my phone into my pocket, using the text as an excuse for why I had paused, I entered the ladies and handled my business while I waited on Wu to tell me what he found next door.

> We can go now.

Thumbs flying over the screen, I demanded,

> What do you mean?

> I found Deland Bruster.

Oh good.

                                     Not good. He's dead.

He can't be dead.
We need him.

I needed him. The night Kapoor had him read me, Bruster told me I was owned. I wanted to know by who. I had an inkling, but I wanted to be certain before I faced him.

                                  He's gone, Luce. I'm sorry.

Anger roiled in my gut, burning my hope to ashes.

How did he die? Who did
this? Why?

I might not be a cop anymore, but I used to be, and I had been raised by one. The instincts didn't quit just because I had.

                                      We need to go.

I want to see the body.

                            You'll draw too much
                  attention to us, and that will
                     bring down heat on Deena.
                       Bruster is dead. We can't
                         help him. We need to get
                     out before we can't help
                           ourselves, either.

I marched out of the ladies' room, out of the coffee bar, and out into the parking lot. That's where Wu caught up to me, but I had enough mad to spread around and texted Sariah with an almost grim satisfaction at thwarting her efforts to earn back her freedom. God knows I was locked into my fate. Why not spread the misery around?

Forget Bruster. He's dead.

Well shit.

My thoughts exactly.

This shouldn't count against me.

A man is dead. This isn't a game.
We aren't keeping score.

You honestly believe that, and it's why you'll never win. Ezra is still in play. We'll talk soon.

Fingers closing over the screen, I wanted to hurl the phone onto the asphalt and watch it skip like a rock on the water, but I reined in my temper before it got that far.

"I'm sorry." Wu guided me toward the Pinto. "I know you hoped he had answers for you."

"He had answers. He claimed someone owns me. It's not Cole. Our bond isn't like that. Even if it was, from what I understand, it would only affect him in a propriety way. This is something else, someone else, and I want to know what and who."

"Does it matter? Whoever it is hasn't exerted any control over you. We have no proof they have malicious intent."

"People don't bind themselves to other people, let alone kids they fish out of the swamp, with good intentions."

A defensive note crept into his voice. "You don't know that's when or how it happened."

"The only other option is that one of the doctors who worked on me . . . " I swayed on my feet recalling the procedures. The cutting, the bleeding, the screaming for help that never came. "One of those butchers would have had to have been charun. Do you think that was the real interest? They knew what I was, if not who, and they did something to me while I was on that table?"

One of those tables. There had been many. So very many.

The rose-gold metal under my skin was unlike anything the doctors had ever seen. They had no explanation for how it got there except for speculation on a tribal rite that didn't hold water given there were no records of such a thing being done, let alone to children, in Mississippi. And that was before they cut out a piece for testing . . . and it grew back.

The human body didn't produce metal, and it sure as heck didn't regrow it when it was harvested. If Dad hadn't used every ounce of his influence to steal me away before they had confirmation I was *other*, I might never have seen the light of day again.

"I wasn't there, so I can't say for sure. We kept an eye on you, but Edward Boudreau had already adopted you before the NSB put serious resources into learning more."

"Don't you get it?" I searched his face. "That possibility makes it worse, not better. My skin is crawling, imagining what some asshole might have left stitched up inside me." But no, unlike Santiago's trick with Wu, that's not how Bruster worked. He was a power, not a tech. "This is a soul-deep issue, right? It's not like I can just cut it out. Whoever did this, it's permanent."

"We need to go." He ushered me into the Pinto, and I let him. Behind the wheel, he sighed. "We should check in with Deena, let her know there's a mess to be cleaned up."

"A mess to be cleaned up," I repeated.

Charun, in general, didn't value human lives. I was used to that. Okay, so I would never accept it, but I expected the disdain from them. Bruster? He was charun. He had consulted with Kapoor and the NSB, if not Wu himself, yet Wu spared him less pity than he might show a squirrel who darted in front of a tire.

"You care too much," he said into the quiet.

"No." I angled my head toward him. "You don't care enough."

CHAPTER FOURTEEN

━━━◆◆◆◆◆━━━

Adam braced for the moment Luce entered the dealership to find Sam slumped over his desk, blood dripping down the sides from the slit across his throat. Her ragged gasp made his stomach clench in a way the fresh death hadn't bothered him.

After so long plotting his revenge, he was disconnected from the mechanics of achieving his goals. Through Luce, he experienced outrage, horror, and grief for the first time since ... a long, long time ago.

"Goddamn it." She rushed into the office, teeth bared. "Deena too."

Wu joined her in the doorway and took in the scene as it must appear through her impassioned eyes.

Deena hadn't gone easily. She clutched a dagger in her right hand, and her attacker's blood crusted the undersides of her fingernails. The cause of death was obvious. Her attacker had snapped off a chair leg and rammed the tapered end through her gut. The ratty carpet gleamed crimson beneath her.

"We have a leak. This is proof." Luce looked at him, her eyes cop-hard. "How else would they know to come after Bruster? Or Deena? They even killed a human to get to her."

"I reached out to trustworthy contacts to trace Bruster," Adam said slowly. "That's how Deena knew we wanted him. It's possible one of my other contacts turned on me. They might have fed the information to my father or one of his people."

A frown gathered on her brow that he wished he could smooth away with his thumb. "I need a list of your contacts. We'll have to eliminate each name to be certain we plug the right hole."

"We don't have time for this." Wu admired her tenacity, but Deland Bruster, and the fallout from locating him, was a loose end to be tied up. Not unraveled. "We have to focus on our preparations."

"You're big on telling me the world will keep spinning after I'm gone, just like it's rotating despite the dead bodies stacked around us. That's fine." She pointed a finger at him, as few would have dared. "But I want a record of this. If I'm a flash in the pan that's going to fizzle out, I want the NSB to investigate these murders after I'm gone."

"Write your report." Adam couldn't help the smile curling his lips. "I'll file it with Kapoor. He can get it to the right people when the time comes."

Assuming he survived. The odds weren't in his favor. He had done too much, helped too much, to walk away from this free and clear. And that was before Father decided to use him as a messenger. But that was the cost of revolution, a price they would all pay in the end.

CHAPTER FIFTEEN

———◆———

The farmhouse didn't feel much like home these days, but I was still grateful for the familiar when Cole landed in the driveway. Not even the dragon wrapping his tail around my ankle could yank me out of my sour mood.

No Bruster. No Ezra. And now Kapoor was officially MIA.

"Got him," Santiago yelled, trotting to us. "Took me long enough, but I found him."

Having my pity party interrupted derailed me for a second. "Kapoor?"

Utter disdain dripped from his words. "How many other hostages are we looking for?"

I narrowed my eyes on him, but it only made him smile. "How?"

"I have my ways." He scratched his cheek. "You might also be interested to know the top dog didn't inspect the blast site at the enclave bunker. He sent a fresh host of Malakhim to scout the area and report back."

"You had a head injury." I frowned at him. "When did you have time to mount cameras?"

They sure hadn't been there before since we hadn't known the place existed until Wu enlightened us.

"Rescue took forever." He rolled his eyes. "What was I supposed to do? Lie there and hope I didn't die?"

"Yes?" That's what a normal person would have done, but he wasn't normal, and I had doubts if I could classify him as a person. "You're telling me you've been monitoring the bunker site all this time?"

"That is what I just said, yes." He lifted the tablet. "My job is to cover the bases. I covered them." He threatened the power button with his thumb. "Now, do you want to know where they're holding Kapoor or not?"

"Hit me." I braced for the verbal smackdown.

Santiago lost his smirk and spun the tablet in his hand toward me. "Does this look familiar?"

"It's a hospital room." The list of recent visits to such institutions crowded my head. "Nicer than the one Jane Doe stayed in. Same for Jay Lambert. Not big or plush enough to be a maternity suite." He panned the room. "This is too nice for a public hospital." A sour taste coated the back of my throat when I spotted the view out the window. "This is the room where Wu recovered after Famine stabbed him with a poisoned blade."

Dad had been at this same charun-run facility, and that had me tasting bile.

"I don't see Kapoor." I studied the screen. "Where is he?"

Santiago angled the screen to give me a view of the ceiling. "There."

A shocked gasp stole my breath when it all clicked in my head, and I rubbed my eyes to see if the view changed. It didn't. I was seeing this. This was real. Kapoor was ... Malakhim. Half Malakhim. And I wondered if that's why his wings were the black of coal dust instead of the white of cumulus clouds.

Blood dripped onto the tiles from his hands where the nails pierced his palms. More pooled underneath the wounds in his feet where they crossed at his insteps. The worst might have been the stains from where his beautiful wings had been pinned behind him in a macabre display, a cruel mockery of flight, a nod to the avenging angel fallen.

"Wu needs to see this." Voice tight, I ripped my gaze from the screen. "Can you forward it to him?"

"Already done."

"Good." I knuckled my eyes, but Kapoor still hung there whenever they closed. "It's a trap, an obvious one."

"He chose an easily identifiable location for a reason," Miller agreed. "He might have thrown up some barriers to make finding him difficult, but he meant for you to recognize where Kapoor was being held. How else would he lure you there?"

"He chose Wu's room, not Dad's." Both, thank God, had been vacant. "Is this an attempt to corner his son? Or me? Or both of us?"

"He wanted a meeting with his son," Miller reasoned. "He asked Wu to bring you along. This tableau was tailormade to ensure neither of you had any trouble finding Kapoor, or him."

"There's no version of this that ends with me surviving without Wu in tow." I massaged the kinks out of my neck, wishing I could rub my own shoulders. "We wait for him, and then we strategize."

Santiago was already shaking his head. "You're risking your neck going anywhere with him as backup."

"She doesn't need him for backup," Rixton announced from behind me. "She's got me."

Snarl in my throat, I spun toward him. "Where the hell did you come from?"

"Is that a PC thing for a demon to ask? Just curious." He hooked a thumb over his shoulder. "And my ride is black and white. Hard to miss. Might look familiar to you? Oh, unless you're too busy stomping and raging in your driveway to hear me roll up and get out."

Lucky for him, the charun in residence would recognize a police car and its contents weren't edible.

"Who are all those people?" Rixton scanned the area. "There are dozens of them. Are they all . . . ?"

"Charun, yes. Coterie, no."

"Coterie," he repeated, and I could tell he was committing the phrase to memory.

"Forget about this, all of it. Go home." I slashed a hand through the air. "You can't be part of this."

"I need a signed permission slip from my wife before I do anything too reckless, but yeah. I can be. I am. I've been part of this since we met. I'm not backing out just when things are starting to get interesting."

I remembered then, his dream of joining the FBI, working major cases. The life of a small-town cop had been meant as a stepping stone for him. But then he met Sherry, and she asked him not to climb the rungs. Since he loved her more than the job, he did as she asked in order to keep her, to make her happy.

This was a second chance for him. One I was in no rush to give him. He had a bigger stake in the outcome than the rest of us, truthfully. He was one hundred percent human. This was his world, and he belonged here. His family, friends, and life were all here, all meant to be here. I was the aberration, and I didn't want to be the spark that breathed new life into old dreams.

"Sherry vetoed you joining the FBI. This is ten times worse than that on a good day." I gestured for Santiago to share the screen with him. "This is not a good day."

Rixton's eyes hardened to blue marble. "Who strung up your recruiter?"

"You'll die." The whos and hows and whys didn't matter when it came to protecting him. "These people . . . they don't care about humans. They'll kill you."

"Humans don't care about humans either," he pointed out before singling out the worst possible co-conspirator. "Santiago, right?"

"Yeah." Santiago flicked his gaze to me then back to Rixton. "What about it?"

"You like toys. You're always walking around with something in your hand. Maggie says you can do anything, build anything. That you're a big brain with a big mouth."

Brows slanting in consideration of the comment, Santiago conceded, "She's not wrong."

"Forge me armor," Rixton dared him. "If you're that smart, make me the next best thing to charun."

"We can't exactly press pause on the Kapoor situation while Santiago starts daydreaming a prototype. It would never be ready in time." As much as I admired his determination to join the cause, I was relieved to reiterate, "It's not happening."

"Well . . . " Santiago rubbed his jaw. "Here's the thing. Luce is right. I couldn't come up with a design on the fly, not in time to fabricate it and test it."

"Thank you, Polly, for repeating what I just said." I glared at him. "Would you like a cracker?"

"Portia is emocarre. She requires a host. Inhabiting a walking flesh suit with no defense mechanisms whatsoever is dangerous. She could die a hundred different ways — a thousand — and it would be a true death unless she managed to leapfrog into a new host."

"You've already been working on a design," I surmised. "You've been getting it ready for when she would need it most, to protect her."

"I needed a hobby," he said with a growl that dared me to make a big deal out of it. "It was a challenge worthy of my time. It's taken years to develop a prototype. Even then, it's never been tested by its target audience."

"You didn't tell Portia, or she refused to field test it?"

The hard glint in Santiago's eyes confirmed he had taken extreme measures, invested years of his energy into developing tech that might save her life, and he hadn't said a word out of fear she would think a gift of such magnitude meant he valued more than her friendly rivalry.

"Let me test it." Rixton played on Santiago's weakness like a pro. "I'm happy to play guinea pig."

"Luce is happy to separate my head from my neck too."

"He's right." I raised a hand. "I am."

"If it works," Rixton wheedled, "Portia will see its value and ask for one of her own. She doesn't have to know it was designed for her from the start."

"Are you listening to yourself?" I wanted to grab him by the shoulders and shake him. "You're volunteering to be a crash test dummy. That's how it feels when a Drosera plows into you, like you've been in a head-on collision, and these charun can fly."

"Think about this," Miller urged him. "Talk to your wife. Discuss the dangers."

"You mean get out of your hair while you make your move without me."

Frustrated as he made me, damn it was good having him back. Now if I could just keep him alive.

"With Thom recovering, we're a man down." Santiago eyeballed Rixton like a tailor sizing up a client. "Rixton has tactical experience. He knows the drill. Plus, you two worked together for years."

"You want to partner him with *me*?" I gritted my teeth. "Forget it. I have enough trouble keeping myself alive and watching out for you guys. I can't have my attention divided. It's too dangerous."

"She's right." Miller stepped in and saved the day. "He can pair up with me."

The betrayal stung, and I wondered, just for a second, if this wasn't payback for always letting Santiago partner up with Portia even though it meant Maggie went along for the ride, but that was crazy. Miller didn't have a vindictive bone in his body.

That meant he saw Rixton's determination, knew we couldn't beat it out of him, and that if we left him behind, he would find a way to follow. As evidenced by his unannounced appearance today. With a farmhouse chockful of winged charun, that wouldn't be hard to do. Miller was offering to watch Rixton's back so I didn't have to, and that was one of the reasons why he had been my first true friend in the coterie.

"Clear it with Sherry," I warned, still in a mood. "She ought to get a say in when she collects your life insurance."

"Ah, Bou-Bou." Rixton wiped beneath his dry eyes. "I missed that sunny disposition, that can-do attitude, that — "

"Shut it." I pivoted at the sound of Santiago's cackles. "That goes double for you."

Ignoring me as usual, Santiago devolved into belly laughs. "I like him."

"Of course you do," I growled. "He's a pain in my ass."

Tired of them both, I marched off in search of Cole. I found him huddled with four Oncas and three Cuprina, all of them running down their security measures and protocols, most of which Santiago had put in place. He might be a jerk, but he was a damn fine tech.

The expression on my face caused Cole to make his excuses and join me for a walk. "What happened?"

"Rixton wants to be my partner again." I kicked a rock skittering ahead of us. "He'll die, Cole, and he doesn't care."

"Have you asked him why it means so much to him?" Cole posed it as a question, and it came out sounding like one, but I got the feeling the answer was bundled in there too. "There's got to be a reason stronger than friendship propelling him to risk his life when he has so much to lose."

"He wants to protect his family." I kicked another rock. "He's paying me lip service about wanting to fight side by side with me, and I don't doubt that's true. You're right, though. It's not about me, and it's not about our partnership. It's about what happens to this town, to his family, if this situation isn't dealt with and fast."

"Talk to him," Cole urged. "Get him to put his drive into words. Force him to explain himself. It will give him perspective. Verbalizing his motives to you will clarify them for him."

"He's asking Sherry for permission to join the crusade." I sighed, accepting the heavy arm he wrapped around my waist. "She's going to say no."

Or so I kept praying.

Much to my dismay, Sherry signed off on Rixton testing the armor Santiago had devised. As tempted as I had been to snatch the phone out of his hand and plead my case, she hadn't asked to speak to me, and I figured that meant she wasn't ready to face my baggage yet. I couldn't blame her there. I didn't want to make eye contact with it, either. But, after Rixton got outfitted, I had to admit it was worth the price of admission to see him model the suit.

"Do you want me to take a picture?" I offered as I circled him. "Sherry would *love* to see this."

Baring his all too human teeth, he snarled, "Snap a picture and die, Boudreau."

Santiago being Santiago, and expecting to gift the suit to Portia, had made it both highly effective and highly offensive. The material was about the thickness of a dive suit with the same flexibility.

Its matte black finish meant it could be worn alone, but Rixton would want tactical gear over this.

Because the customizations didn't end there.

The material over the chest area puckered a bit where it was meant to cup breasts, and Santiago had added black sequin nipple covers in the center of each peak complete with tassels I was just waiting for him to tell me were motorized and whirled with the push of a button. The groin area had also been sequined over, giving Rixton a freshly vajazzled appearance, but that still wasn't the best part. No, the winner of this whole fiasco of design was the ruched fabric in the rear that gave a defined line between his butt cheeks, which appeared to be lifted and separated more than usual, not that I paid his rear that kind of attention. A shiny line wedged in his crack that drew the eye like a train wreck and made me wonder if the bottom had been meant to represent a thong. Maybe he ran out of sequins before he added decorative straps over the hips?

"I can't imagine why you thought Portia wouldn't love this," I said to Santiago, enjoying myself too much. "The subtle design is so classy, not at all what a porn star would wear on a set."

Confirmation he had successfully combined the offensive, the lewd, and the sexually explicit to the point of total and complete insult made his eyes glitter with what I suspected were tears of pride.

Never in a million years would I understand the facets of his relationship with Portia, and that was more than fine with me. It worked for them. Far be it from me to judge the line of *too far* when they both crossed it regularly enough it was smudged beyond recognition between them.

Regret and determination mingled on Rixton's face. "Tell me you have pants and a shirt I can borrow."

"You want to cover this masterpiece?" I chuckled while Santiago acted ready to snatch the suit off Rixton after having his design insulted. "Okay." I caught my breath and forced myself to be the adult here. "Hear me out."

The men shared a wary commiseration, both hoping the other got sank by what I was about to say.

"Santiago, if you're wanting to surprise Portia, this would do it. But you'll also never get her to wear it if she beholds its full glory on Rixton." That put a calculating gleam in his eyes, so I pressed on. "Rixton will test the suit. We'll make sure Portia sees he's now superhuman. And then, if she asks for her own suit, I'll even zip her into this so she can't escape the mental picture you've no doubt been holding in the forefront of your mind every day you've worked on this."

"Deal." Santiago disappeared then reappeared with a spare White Horse uniform. "Don't tip off Maggie, either. I don't want her tattling to Portia."

"My lips are zipped," I promised him, already making plans to keep Miller far, far away when this fashion show went down. Then again, maybe I ought to pass him one of Granny Boudreau's seam rippers on the sly, and he could de-sequin it before the show got started. Better him than me. "Let's get moving. Wu ought to be arriving any minute now."

I didn't make it far before Noel and Franklin found me, Mateo on their heels. "What's up?"

"Do you need extra bodies for you mission?" Mateo asked, his perpetual smile starting to curl.

"We can send six Oncas with you, if you like." Noel checked with Franklin. "Maybe even a dozen."

"We're good, but thanks. The coterie can handle this." Though it was nice seeing the various factions play nice. "The fewer bodies we bring with us on this mission, the greater its likelihood of succeeding."

"You're bringing the human." Mateo got to the heart of the issue. "He's the weakest among us. Taking him but refusing our help makes us look weak too." He wet his lips. "Our people are charged for a fight, and I don't want this to be what sparks one. They feel slighted, and it's raising tempers, making them question where your loyalties lie. With the humans, or with us."

Spearing Noel and Franklin with a glare, I asked, "Are you having the same problem?"

"No, Mistress." They bowed their heads low. "We are loyal to you."

Transform into a dragon, bite a few people, and you earned respect. No wonder Conquest had been so revered.

"Regardless, I'll give this speech to all of you." I pointed at the tent. "The human in there is John Rixton, a detective with the Canton Police Department. He was my training officer, my partner, and he taught me everything I know about procedure. I'm the godmother to his daughter, and that makes us family. I don't care that he's human. I don't care that charun are getting their feathers ruffled over it."

Three sets of predatory eyes narrowed on me, so I got to my point quickly. I didn't want to eat anyone today if I could help it.

"This is their world. They belong here, and they have as much right to defend it as we do." I held up my hand before Mateo lost points with me. "Many charun have made their home here as well. I have no issue with them. I *am* one of them. But when we're defending our new home, our new lives, our new world, just remember we're immigrants. We have to respect humans, and all other charun factions, if we expect this truce to hold."

A thoughtful expression crossed Mateo's features, and I wondered what side his judgement would land on.

"This is the reason why we follow you," he decided. "You pull us out of our old prejudices and force us to embrace your new philosophy of acceptance."

I waved them off and hunted down the others.

"You're more than he expected." Thom's voice carried, and I found him perched in a nearby tree. "Wu thought, perhaps he still thinks, he's forged a weapon in you." He leapt to the ground, landing in a graceful crouch. "But it's not the one he expected. You're nothing any of us expected. You've given us all hope this ascension will be the last."

Curious, I joined him off the beaten path, standing while he remained low. "Is that what you want?"

"What my people want is unrestricted access to knowledge of all kinds. We are scholars. We are curious about all things. But we don't want information paid for in the blood of thousands." He gazed out across the milling gathering. "The others didn't want me to accept Conquest's offer of a position in her coterie. They worried for my safety, and they fretted at the danger of me enlightening Conquest to a degree never before achieved. But I had this ... urge. A tug in my gut. I had to go. Instinct demanded I leave. And for a long time, a very long time, I regretted my choice. I came to accept my elders had been right to want me to find my own way." He leaned against my knees, and I scratched his scalp. "Then you came."

"Cole told me once you were leaving after the coterie achieved Earth."

"That was my plan, yes." He laughed, and he rolled his shoulders. "Part of me thinks I should have done just that, but it's cowardice talking."

Tightness in my throat made it hard to say, "You're not a coward for wanting to go home and avoid all this ugliness." For wishing he had left before he lost his ability to fly. "Every last one of us would choose that if it were an option. I would, if I had somewhere else to go."

"You have all the worlds that came before this one," he said softly, and I wondered at the plea in his tone. "You could leave, let the next Conquest fight this battle."

"And the one after her, and the one after her, and the one after her. All the while, innocents will die. I couldn't live with myself if I let that happen."

"That's what makes you Luce."

We remained together, in contented silence, and waited for Wu to arrive.

CHAPTER SIXTEEN

———◆———

Grief slashed Wu's face as he approached and demanded to view the live video feed. Anger followed. He began to vibrate, to softly glow, like the apocalypse I heralded was confined within his skin instead of mine.

Santiago obliged, but the scenery hadn't changed. Kapoor still hung pinned from the ceiling, his blood *drip-drip-dripping* on the tile floor beneath him.

"It's a trap," Wu said, shutting his eyes to block out the screen.

"Tell me something I don't know," I said to distract him.

"Lobster bladders are located under their eyes. Essentially, they pee out of their faces."

"Eww." Good thing I wasn't big on seafood. "I didn't ask for something I didn't *want* to know."

"Lobsters flirt by squirting urine on each other. The female's urine is chockful of pheromones designed to calm the male to prevent aggression and put him in the mood to mate."

"You made it worse." I shuddered. "How it could be worse, I don't know, but you managed."

"I have to save him." Wu opened eyes flushed with gold. "I can't leave him there."

"Leave no man behind." I puffed out my cheeks. "How do we do this?"

The gratitude shining in his burnished eyes made him more human than I had ever seen him, more vulnerable too, and I liked the glimpse of the man he must have been all those years ago.

"The Malakhim will be waiting." Wu ripped off his shirt, exposing his lean musculature, and his wings exploded from his back. "You'll need a two-pronged attack to make this work."

"I'm confused." I held up a hand like a kid in school. "You said *you'll* and not *we'll*."

"You wouldn't survive meeting with my father."

"And you will?"

"I have lifetimes of experience doing just that."

"Are you sure baiting him is wise?"

"Just the opposite, but I don't see another way for all of us to walk away to fight another day."

"Fine." I exhaled, trusting him to know his father best. "Two teams, one in the sky and one on the ground."

And one God knows where since Wu would be off cowboying during this op.

"Miller and Portia, you're ground. Cole and I will take to the skies." A voice cleared behind me, and I was forced to add, "Santiago, you're with us."

"No." Santiago folded his arms across his chest. "We stick with our partners."

"This is what you get for hanging out with Luce so much," Portia teased, attempting to defuse the situation. "You grow on people, Santiago."

"Like flesh-eating bacteria," I groused.

Unwilling to be placated, he pressed, "Are you really going to send her in solo?"

"Miller will be with her."

"Miller will be babysitting."

Portia slapped Santiago upside the head. "I don't need a babysitter."

"No," he said, getting in her face, "you need a partner."

"I get you're fried over what happened at Lake Bevin, but you couldn't have protected me then, and you can't protect me now." She placed her hand on his chest, where his heart might beat if he had one. "Miller won't let Maggie get hurt. He's already proven that. I'm as good as gold." She shoved him back. "Luce wouldn't have requested your delightful company if she didn't need you more than I do."

Brushing at his shirt like he might wipe off her concern, he joined us without another word.

"Rixton, Miller is your partner for this op." I clapped a hand on his shoulder. "Stick to his backside like toilet paper lint."

"You're grounding me?" His forehead pinched. "I don't get to ride the dragon?"

"Think of Air Cole as a crop duster. There's room for the pilot plus one. He's the pilot, I'm the plus one."

"Harsh." He crossed to Miller. "Looks like I'm with you guys."

Miller smiled, and it skirted the edge of patronizing. "We'll keep you safe."

"I haven't been safe since I graduated police academy." Rixton squared his shoulders. "Why should today be any different?"

I'm not sure I could have left Rixton with anyone other than Miller. Even Thom skirted the edge at times. Odd how the most dangerous among us was the most stalwart and reliable. Then again, maybe he had to be. Any lapse in control would cost him everything. Years of self-restraint may have evolved into a personality trait.

"Let's go." I turned my back on Rixton while I still could and marched off with Cole and Wu in tow. Santiago followed at a grudging pace. "What's the best way in?" I aimed the question at whoever felt they had an answer. Thanks to Dad's stint as an invalid, we had all spent plenty of time at the facility. The front and back entrances were obvious. I was betting Wu had a subtler way in. "Aerial attack is out of the question."

"You told the others — " Cole started. "You're protecting Rixton."

"Yep." I was as unrepentant as he was about donning that experimental suit. "We'll fly out to get a head start. By the time they arrive, it should be over." I acknowledged the grim set of Wu's jaw. "One way or another."

"Give me four hours." Wu rolled his shoulders, rustling his feathers. "I'll send Santiago the coordinates and instructions on how to operate the locking mechanism. I'll touch base with you before I go in, but I can't promise contact after that point. Father might not be fully acclimated, but he'll understand the significance of me texting or calling an undisclosed number after I show up empty-handed."

"You're going to use me to bluff him," I realized. "What happens when he realizes I'm a no-show?"

"I get the hell out of there using any means necessary."

"Any other charun aligned with your father we should be aware of?" Cole shifted his weight. "Are they all flight focused?"

"Father is a purist in all ways." The derision cut sharper than any knife. "He only employs charun from our home world. Those like me, the warriors, and the Malakhim, the foot soldiers."

"The Hole staff was diverse," I argued. Various charun species had worked there. "How did you manage that?"

"Wings." He made it sound obvious. "No creature born of the sky wants to live underground. I convinced Father it was in our best interest to cultivate certain species more apt to thrive in the deep and the dark."

"Makes sense." And it did. I could imagine the confinement wearing on skyborne charun over time, but I could also imagine his father telling them to suck it up and deal. "You've saved a lot of lives, haven't you?"

"Not enough." He ducked his head. "Not nearly enough."

Unwilling to let him leave on a down note, I mouthed off to get a reaction. "Well, go on then. Run along and get yourself smited."

A smile twitched at the corners of his mouth. "I'm hard to kill, remember?"

The polite thing would be to let it pass, but I couldn't resist. "Will there be trees where you're going?"

A chuckle escaped him before he shot off to do his damndest to provide us with a distraction.

And then there were three, and I would shave that down to two if I had my way.

"You don't have to do this, Cole." I danced out of his grasp when he reached for me. "You could go back to the bunkhouse, wake your daughter. Spend what time you have left with her."

A curl of frost escaped his mouth. "And risk never seeing you again."

"I want you to stay behind as much as I want you with me," I confessed. "I hate these options. I hate that every time we make the call to split up, it might be the last time we see each other. I hate all of this."

"I belong with you." He slid his coarse fingers through my hair. "I'm not letting you out of my sight until this ends if I can help it."

"What about Phoebe?"

"She's sleeping soundly, and she has been for a long time. Napping a while longer won't hurt her, and if she never wakes . . ." He shut his eyes, drew in air through his nose. "It might be a mercy."

"I love you." I cupped his face in my hands. "So much."

"Don't say your goodbyes." He brushed his lips over mine. "Not yet."

"Break it up." Santiago shoved us apart. "I thought regular sex would fix this, but it's just made it worse."

"You heard the man." I popped Cole on the butt. "It's go time."

Cole smiled before shifting, never a good sign, and the dragon returned the favor by snapping the tip of his tail against my rump.

"*Yowch.*" I rubbed away the sting. "How am I supposed to ride now?"

With his tail, the dragon encircled my waist, lifted me, and planted me on his back. He allowed Santiago a heartbeat to climb on before launching us into the sky to the sound of my startled scream.

As much as I loved the male, I just might have to kill the dragon.

Assuming Daddy Wu didn't do the job first.

We landed five miles east of the medical facility and covered the rest of the ground on foot.

With Malakhim sharing the skies with us, and no word from Wu, we couldn't be too careful.

"There are maintenance tunnels running beneath the building," Santiago said as his clever fingers accessed blueprints for us. "Looks like holding pens for various food sources, such as cattle and goats, are on the next level up. Then the labs and imaging center. After that, ground floor and the lobby. The rest of the layout we know."

The upper floors were patient suites, with the exception of the fourth floor, which was dedicated to physical therapy. There was a pool, a gym, a track, and various other amenities I noted during the tour they gave me prior to me leaving Dad in their care.

"Will they know to watch the tunnels?" Cole matched his stride to mine, even though I held him back with my shorter legs. "How much security are we talking about on the lower levels?"

"There's more and easier access from the roof and the higher floors of the building." Santiago glanced back at Cole. "Malakhim will be trained in aerial maneuvers, the same as all winged charun, and they'll be taught to never take the fight to the ground."

"They always look up for trouble." I nodded. "Gotcha."

Following Wu's coordinates, Santiago guided us to a stone wall so similar to the enclave's bunker entrance I didn't have to wonder how they had stumbled across the tech. Clearly Wu had been using his connections to protect his people in all ways. I could respect that. Admire it, even. As long as it didn't get us killed.

And there we huddled together until my phone vibrated. "It's Wu."

I'm about to go in.

Do you have visual
confirmation on your father?

I'm looking right at him.

I'm looking right at the
combination lock — or
should I say rock?

Be careful.

You too.

Santiago worked his magic, and the door opened with a hydraulic hiss. "I've got to get me one of these."

"You really need a secret lair with a stone doohickey on the door?"

Perfectly serious, he asked, "Doesn't everyone?"

Not waiting for an answer, he guided us through the labyrinthine twists of the maintenance tunnels.

Dim lights illuminated the space enough we didn't bump into each other, but the fit was tight. My shoulders brushed on either side, and so did Santiago's. Cole was sliding his back against the wall, the only way his broad shoulders would fit. Even then, it was touch and go. I worried he might get stuck, and that distracted me until I banged my head against a pipe. Hissing a curse, I kept going, shrugging off Cole's attempts to ascertain how badly I was injured when it was my pride that had taken the worst hit.

No wonder the Malakhim avoided this place. I didn't have wings. Well, I guess I did. *Weird.* But I hadn't used them to do more than stir a breeze. Anyway — I was claustrophobic by the time we reached a steel door with a heavy manual locking mechanism that Santiago manipulated without a hitch.

Lending him my weight, I eased the door open on silent hinges, and we crept into the gloom.

The smell hit me first. Livestock carried an earthy aroma all its own, and that was before you factored in the biological necessities. Cattle lowed in the left corner, and goats bleated to our right. Chickens clucked ahead, and I suspected their cries were answered by ducks or geese.

"Is there a butcher station tucked away in the kitchens?" I wondered out loud after grasping the scope of the operation. "There are enough animals here to feed — "

"These animals don't end up in the kitchen."

"Ah."

Santiago left me to imagine what that meant, and since I had witnessed a certain dragon downing cattle the way I popped Tic

Tacs, I didn't have to stretch my imagination. These must be meals for the more animalistic charun. The ones unable to blend with the human population. I hadn't realized this facility treated them, but I hadn't thought much past their credentials for treating a human, honestly. The fact they brought Wu here should have spoken volumes.

As the animals did after they caught wind of the predators in their midst.

The noise ratcheted higher and higher, and soon each stall we passed held frantic livestock flashing the whites of their eyes. Hooves kicked walls, inhuman screams pierced the air, and the commotion brought the handlers running.

"Nonpredatory species," Santiago murmured as we three ducked into an empty stall to wait.

I leaned in close. "How can you tell?"

Tapping the side of his nose, he said, "They make me hungry."

Putting a smidgen more distance between us, I inched closer to Cole.

Heavy footsteps thumped past us, and a male released a disgusted grunt at the uproar.

"Better not be another one of those damn cats. Last time Barns left the entrance open when he came in to take a piss, and a mountain lion got in. Scarred up the cattle before moving on to easier pickings. Ate every chicken. Every damn one."

"I brought the tranq gun," a female said. "If it's another cat, we've got it covered."

A tiny voice in my head wondered if Wu had anything to do with that cat finding its way in, with planting the seed that there were other explanations for livestock panic aside from facility infiltration, but maybe that was paranoia talking. We were up in the mountains, after all.

Santiago gestured toward the door the pair had entered

through, and I glanced back at Cole to make certain he saw. He was busy tracking the immediate threat, so I caught his hand and tugged to get his attention.

The problem with touching Cole was, once I had him, I didn't want to let go.

Tick-tick-tick.

That's what I kept hearing. My ears rang with it. Any moment could be our last. Any misstep could be the one that gave us away, the tipping point that cost us all our lives.

Never one to utter empty placations, Cole leaned forward, resting his forehead against mine. We stayed like that a moment, our breaths mingling, our gazes locked, and I mouthed, *"I love you."*

Lately I was tempted to start and end all my conversations with that phrase. I couldn't say it enough. It was like a physical pressure building behind my chest, ready to explode from my lips at a moment's notice.

The only way to go forward was to pull on the cold place enough to ice my racing heart, my sweaty palms. Cole watched the transformation, unable to hide the tightening around his eyes, but he cupped my cheek and mouthed, *"I love you, Luce."*

Turning away so he didn't see how far down I had tunneled, past the point of his gesture warming me, I locked gazes with Santiago. He slid the bolt on the stall door free, scanned the aisle both ways, then gestured for me to follow. I did the same, clearing the way for Cole.

We reached the door leading into the facility without incident, and Santiago locked it behind us.

"This will slow them down," he murmured.

"They won't be suspicious?" We kept going, opting for the stairwell over the single elevator. "Doors like those don't close themselves."

"Standard protocol when working a security detail is to shut any doors behind you, but they left this one open in case they needed to make a quick exit." He picked up the pace. "Memory is a funny thing. They'll each wonder if the other shut it out of habit and be pissed to find their escape route blocked. This will too." He pressed a few more buttons, and the green lights holding steady above the door flashed red. "Buh-bye security feed. We're cloaked, now let's move."

Putting our head start to its best advantage, we quit jawing and got jogging up to the main floor.

The door marking the lobby had a glass panel inset into its front, and I peered through it, curious if Daddy Wu had cleared the facility to set the stage. The bustle of staff and trickle of visitors shouldn't have surprised me. According to Wu, his father was loyal to his own terrene, and that was it. He wouldn't care about a few extra fatalities if this went sideways.

"How do we get to the fourth floor?" I ducked out of sight as an orderly passed by our hiding place. "There must be another stairwell, right?"

"There is," Santiago confirmed. "It's opposite this one."

"That's great, but how do we get to it without being spotted?"

"We're going to have to walk out of here, play it like we're visiting a patient." Cole laid it out for us. "The staff is familiar with us. Most won't give us a second glance."

The peaceful folks staffing this place understandably didn't want to get on the wrong side of Conquest.

"It's not a great plan, but it's the only one we've got." I puffed out my cheeks. "Who wants to go first?"

"That would be me." Santiago spun a tablet across his palm. "I'll scout and report back."

"You and I always visited your father together," Cole agreed. "They won't blink at seeing us together."

"You're Conquest," Santiago broke it down further, "and it's the time of ascension. Anyone who hasn't met you, or who is loyal to Conquest, will gawk. You'll cause a scene, and that's the last thing we need."

"Don't be a hero." I jabbed him in the chest. "Do *not* engage until we arrive."

"Aww." Santiago hitched his lips to one side. "You do care."

"Whatever," I said, speaking his language with a fluidity that should have alarmed me.

Santiago cracked open the door then set a casual pace toward the stairwell across the inviting lobby.

Alone with Cole, I leaned against him, watching my phone. "I should have gone to see my dad when I had the chance."

He and I had talked, and I had made empty promises, but I hadn't set eyes on him in what felt like forever.

"You did what you had to do to keep him safe." Cole pressed a warm kiss to my temple. "You did what he would want you to do, what he would do in your position."

A text chimed, Santiago giving the all-clear.

"Thank you." Because he wouldn't have said it if he didn't mean it. He would rather tell the truth than soothe a hurt with a lie. Pulling away from him, I tugged on the cuffs of my shirt, pulling them into the palm of my hand in a tight ball, an old habit I was slow to break. "We're up."

The one good thing about our exit was we got to make it together. Cole threaded his fingers through mine, and I clutched that precious lifeline he had tossed me. We kept our pace easy, casual, and we almost got away with the incognito bit. But, as Santiago had speculated, we drew attention from two young men who goggled at me like I was a legend come to life. To them, I suppose I was. I almost tripped over them when they darted in my path and hit the floor on their faces, arms stretching for my feet.

Lip curled, I threw on the brakes. "Get up."

Cole squeezed my hand in a gentle warning. We didn't want to draw more attention. These two clowns were already causing a scene.

"Please," I gritted from between clenched teeth. "I'm happy to let you lick my boots later, but I need to go to the little girl's room."

Their heads shot up, eyes wide, and they pointed at the bathroom blessedly close to the stairwell entrance.

"Thanks." I waved as I pivoted on my heel and hauled Cole — no easy feat — behind me.

"Lick your boots?" Amusement threaded his deep voice, and it rumbled through my bones. "Will you make good on your promise?"

"I didn't say the actual word," I reasoned, "so it's not really a promise. That makes it a statement."

"Is that cop logic?"

Thinking of Rixton shot fresh worry through me, but I managed a smile. "I learned from the best."

We reached the restrooms, and using Cole as a shield, I slid into the stairwell with Santiago. I counted the seconds while I waited on Cole to join us, and when he did, he wore a crooked smile.

"They're still prostrate," he said, "awaiting your return."

"Their extremities will go numb eventually, and they'll figure out I'm not coming back."

A girl could hope anyway.

CHAPTER SEVENTEEN

————◆————

No one had been posted in the stairwell. Not a single Malakhim.

We walked right up and exited onto the floor where Kapoor was being held without incident.

No one guarded the door to his room. Not even a feather drifted through the hall.

"I've got a bad feeling about this." I reached for my service weapon on instinct, but there was nothing to draw, and bullets didn't do more than piss off charun. "I should have brought a sword."

"Hard to hide those on your person," Santiago said, stepping up beside me. "Plus, they tend to incite panic when wielded by Conquest with an *I'm on a mission* look in her eye."

A trap within a trap, and there was no way to discover its mechanism until it sprung.

"I hope Wu knows what he's doing," I muttered and shoved open the door.

"Fucked up ... coming here," Kapoor whispered through split lips. "Should've ... let me die."

"Hello to you too." I walked a slow circle beneath Kapoor, checking for wires or triggers we might bump when we pulled him down. "I'm not leaving you behind. That's not how this works."

"Get . . . yourself," he rasped, " . . . killed."

"Not today." I glanced around the room Cole and Santiago were busy clearing. "Wu is distracting his father. Where is everyone else?"

"Strung me up." Kapoor panted, running out of energy fast. "Left in a hurry."

A cold wash of dread swept through me. "Did they say anything?"

"No." He clenched his fists, and fresh blood dripped. "Didn't give 'im a thing."

The blood loss was wreaking havoc on Kapoor, and confusion was setting in.

"No," I murmured. "You wouldn't have told them anything."

Even if it cost him his life, and it nearly had — it still might — he would keep his silence.

Idiot.

Wu wasn't worth this.

The enclave? Yeah. They deserved our protection, but this? This was preventable. Wu should have kept tabs on Kapoor. He should have brought him in when his situation ran too hot. But Wu had tunnel vision, and it paid to remember that the next person found strung up could be me, or a member of the coterie.

"I'm going to pull the bed over and stand on that." I kept a dialogue going more to cover Kapoor's ragged breathing than anything else. "I need to pry out the nails first."

"Take your . . . " Kapoor's head went limp on his neck.

Time.

Cole moved the bed into position in the time it would have taken me to figure out how the locks worked on the wheels. I stepped up, stood on the mattress, and set to work beneath Kapoor but a noise brought me up short.

"Do you hear that?" I rubbed my hands over my ears. "That buzzing?"

Bees. Trapped in my skull. Driving their stingers into my brain.

"I don't hear anything," Cole said warily. "Santiago?"

"On it." He pulled out a second tablet and set it on the counter. "Scanning for ultrasonic emissions."

Over the noise, I yelled, "What?"

"Four speakers. One in each corner where the wall meets the ceiling. Probably hidden behind the tiles." Santiago might as well have been whispering. "We don't know what the hell they're doing to her, but it can't be good. Smash them, Cole."

The droning sound filled my head, stuffed itself in me until my brain felt swollen, ready to burst.

And then ... I did.

CHAPTER EIGHTEEN

———◦◉◦———

Adam sat in the lobby of a posh hotel, one of many his father owned thanks to his financial oversight, for over three hours. Decorative glass panels etched with wavy designs separated him from the conference room, giving him a prime view of his father.

Golden head bent, he read from a leather-bound tome brittle with age. He appeared quite at his leisure, a businessman enjoying the solitude prior to his scheduled meeting, immersing himself in a place other than here, a time other than now.

And every second that ticked past set Adam's jaw grinding.

There was a trick here, a trap, but he couldn't figure out which of them had been sprung.

Was Adam keeping his father occupied, or was the reverse true?

A quick check of his watch told him more than enough time had passed for Luce and her coterie to complete their mission. Done wasting his time, he shoved to his feet, ready to make his escape.

"Are you familiar with how a dog whistle works?" Ezra asked from the doorway of the conference room.

Brought up short by the question, he answered without considering why his father might have asked. "It emits an ultrasonic frequency in a range that humans can't hear but some animals, and some charun, can detect."

"Some animals," he agreed, "and some charun."

As his father made it clear he saw little division between beasts native to this world and any other, he didn't waste breath renewing an old argument.

"What is your point, Father?"

"That just as a dog can be taught to obey unspoken commands, so too can cadre."

Adam shifted his weight, caught himself, forced his posture to relax. "You can control them?"

"Quite the opposite." His smile was benevolent, indulgent. "As it happens, the right frequency causes an Otillian to completely lose control of their faculties." He chuckled. "The phenomenon was initially dismissed due to Famine's mental instability, but it has since been proven effective on a secondary subject."

"Luce."

"Conquest," he corrected, "but yes."

"That's why you kept me waiting."

"No, that was to remind you of who I am, who you are, and where your loyalties lie."

"What have you done?" he rasped, heart thudding against his ribs. "Damn you, what have you done?"

"The next time I request a meeting, perhaps you'll be punctual, and we can be civilized to each other, avoid all this unnecessary ugliness."

"Father . . ."

"I will help you see her as she truly is, and then we will put her down together, as you should have already done. If you refuse, if you deny me, if you act in any way other than grateful, you will force my hand."

"You would kill your only son?"

"I am eternal. I can make more children. That I have been content with you thus far is a glaring mistake I face with each rising. Do not tempt me to sully myself in the name of procreation when you are as fine an heir as any I might sire."

Without dignifying him with a response, Adam turned on his heel and marched out the door, terrified by what awaited him, and uncertain if he was grateful his father released him to discover it.

CHAPTER NINETEEN

———◆◆◆———

Metal bit into my wrists and ankles. I swallowed to clear the sour tang in the back of my throat, and chains rattled. Opening my eyes required too much effort. Breathing hurt. Everything hurt. There must be crushed soda cans in better shape than I was right now.

"She's waking," Thom said, tone clinical. "I have the tranquilizer ready."

"Give her a chance," Maggie pleaded. "Please. I know what happened last time but — "

Strong hands bracketed my shoulders, the fingers sinking into bruised tracks that ached. "I'll restrain her." Miller applied pressure, and I whimpered. "Open your eyes."

For a second, I didn't get that he was talking to me. And then I wished I hadn't grasped the magnitude of his order.

"Can't." I winced as my split lip cracked. "Hurts."

"They're swollen shut," Thom confirmed. "We'll have to apply a compress to reduce the swelling if she's lucid."

"Lucid isn't the issue," Santiago remarked. "Luce is."

"We should get Cole." Portia added her two cents. "He can always tell."

"Get him." Miller kept his grip firm. "We need confirmation."

"Her scent changed." Warm breath tickled my face, and Thom said, "She smells right again."

Fresh blood filled my mouth when I asked, "What happened?"

"Conquest happened."

That was Wu. Him being here had to be a good sign, right? That meant we escaped. We were all alive. "Kapoor?"

"Recovering." A gentle hand rested on my forearm, and warmth radiated down to my bones. Definitely Wu. "I thought we lost you."

"I don't remember." I swallowed again, working to clear my throat. "Did she … ?"

"Conquest seized control of you." Wu stroked his fingers over the delicate bones in my wrists, sliding the tips beneath the cuffs slicing into my skin. "She brought the building down around us."

I didn't want to ask, didn't want to know, but I had to find out. "Casualties?"

"You aren't responsible for what she did." Miller hadn't loosened his grip, but he wasn't hurting me. "You don't have to shoulder that burden."

"Tell me."

"Eighteen patients," Santiago replied when Miller kept quiet. "Twenty-five staff members."

A sob hitched in my chest, but I hurt too much to release it.

"There were sixteen injuries, but none serious." He kept going, driving the knife deeper. "The livestock escaped unscathed except for one chicken that I suspect the janitor ate while no one was looking."

As much as I wanted Cole, I wasn't sure I could face him. I wouldn't ask for him. I wouldn't. I would stay strong, let him make the choice. He could come to me or not, and I would abide by his decision. We had both known this day was coming, when I fractured enough she slipped through the cracks, but I hadn't expected it this soon. I thought I was handling it, handling her. But I hadn't factored in Wu's father.

A door opened and shut to my left, and heavy footsteps I knew by heart thumped closer.

I wanted to curl into a ball, but I couldn't move. I had been restrained, and now I knew why.

"Don't." I was helpless to stop the hot tears from seeping through the cracks of my lids and rolling down my cheeks. "Please."

Cole didn't listen. It shouldn't have surprised me. He only heard what he wanted to, but I figured he would have gotten this message loud and clear.

"Please." I struggled against Miller, against the chains. "Please."

No matter how wide I opened my mouth, that was the only word that came out.

Miller eased up the pressure on my shoulders and then withdrew. Heavier hands replaced his, thicker fingers dug into my skin, but Cole didn't restrain me to the table. He lifted me upright and settled me against his chest.

"Luce," he breathed against my throat. "You came back to me."

The tension in the room eased as the others accepted his assessment as proof I was me and not her.

"How can you stand to touch me?" Sobs hiccupped out of me. "How can you — ?"

"I love you." He kissed my swollen lids. "Only you."

Weak, I was so weak, but I couldn't let him go. "What are we going to do?"

"It's already done." He rested his cheek against mine. "I hope in time you'll forgive me for it."

"Ease her back," Thom ordered. "She's too bruised to sit upright comfortably yet."

"I want Cole." I sounded like a child begging for her teddy bear, and I didn't care. This was my coterie. They were my friends, family, and they understood I was out of strength and needed to borrow his. "I can deal with the pain."

"Hold still." Thom fussed at me, his nimble fingers massaging ointment over my eyelids. "That will help with the swelling. You should be able to open in a moment."

Charun medicine was definitely the good stuff. Thom could be my medic any day. As long as you didn't stop to wonder what part of his body his wonder drugs came from, it was all good. "Thanks."

"I'm releasing her." Miller started with the wrists tucked against my chest, and I folded myself as tight against Cole as I could wiggle. "She's not a danger to herself or us when she's Luce."

The others murmured assent, and their relief was a balm to my soul.

I was back.

I was me.

I had won.

This time.

Next time ... I might not be so lucky.

After he moved to my ankles, I noticed a cool weight still encircling my wrists. Testing my eyes, I cracked my lids and sucked in a gasp at the rose gold bangles weighting my arms. "No."

I recognized their design. These were the bangles Lorelei had made for Cole from the rosendium she harvested from his wrists. The last time I saw them, Sariah had been wearing them, ensuring our control over her and the remaining Drosera.

"Forgive me," Cole whispered against my temple. "I had no choice."

"Sariah is free?" Shoving against his chest, I gained enough space to squint at him. "You freed her?"

"I had no choice," Cole repeated, tormented. "When she heard about your ... condition ... she came to us. We had no choice but to take her up on her offer."

An icy prickle down my spine caused me to stiffen. "What offer?"

"Her freedom in exchange for the one thing that might control Conquest."

Even with Bruster dead and Ezra a freaking ghost, she had managed to strike a deal that got her what she wanted without her lifting a finger.

No wonder she had survived War and Thanases. She was cut from the same brutal cloth with the same ruthless shears.

Sick to my core over who and what they had unleashed to save me, I surprised myself by finding room in my heart for fresh panic. "Who's holding my leash?"

"I am," Cole said, and I heard what it cost him to admit he had done to me what Conquest had done to him all those centuries ago.

"Okay." I rested my hand over his heart. "This is fine. Great even. She can't get out?"

"I gave you a direct order to suppress her. She didn't go easily, but it appears to be holding."

"That's why I feel like hot shit?" I pressed a hand to my ribs. "She fought being contained."

"Like her life depended on it," he confirmed. "It took all of us and Wu to restrain you. He was in critical condition afterward, but Thom revived him."

"You said Kapoor got out?" Pain dragged at my senses, the edges of my focus unraveling. "He's okay?"

"He'll survive," Thom confirmed. "I was able to save his wings."

The way he lumped them together, as if they carried the same importance, was a sucker punch to the gut. I might have failed Thom, but at least Kapoor was intact.

"Where are we?" I couldn't see well, mostly shadowy figures, but even the scents in the air struck me as wrong. "It smells damp."

"It's a bunker." Wu caressed my side, and warmth spread through my tender ribs. "One the enclave uses for . . . Suffice it to say, the cells and chains were already here. It made the most sense to make use of them. We couldn't hold Conquest long. We couldn't get her down here until after Cole got the bangles on her. Even then, it took several days of you rising to consciousness, and Cole refining his commands, to get you back."

"We'll take you to our new HQ." Santiago wavered into view, and his belief I was blind as a bat was the only reason he let me see the worry pinching his expression, I was sure. "We've pulled out of the farmhouse. It's an enclave-only outpost now."

Better for them all to be as far away from me as possible. The coterie, at least, had survived Conquest. They weren't in immediate danger from her. "What about the Oncas and the Cuprina?"

"They'll remain with the enclave," Cole told me. "We recruited a few to help us track Conquest and corner her, but they've returned to their clans."

Cole held on tight, like Wu might pluck me from his arms, but I had news for him. I wasn't going anywhere. This was right where I wanted to be. Well, not in this cell, but with him.

"Putting a bullet between my eyes would have been simpler," I joked, well aware it took more than that to stop a charun, let alone a cadre member. A harpoon gun maybe?

"I'm not giving up on you." Cole framed my face with his wide hands. "That means you can't either."

Cold stung my hip, and the room smudged a bit more. "Hey . . ."

"It's a sedative to help you rest." Thom stroked my hair. "I'll heal you while you sleep."

The fact they shot me up as I was coming around wasn't lost on me. Whatever it had taken to restrain Conquest, they didn't want me to see the evidence of it. Morbid curiosity kept me blinking, trying to take in the damage to my arms and torso, but I couldn't focus. I was too tired. Too damn tired to do more than curl against Cole, twine my fingers in his shirt, and let the darkness claim me.

CHAPTER TWENTY

Warmth surrounded me, and I drifted in a cozy bubble of contentment until my bladder refused to be ignored any longer. Opening my eyes didn't hurt, and I could see the source of the comfort snuggled around me on the bed. Cole to my right, Maggie and Portia to my left. Thom, in his boxy tomcat form, slept on my feet. Miller had fallen asleep at the foot of the bed with his arm resting across my shins. Santiago sat beside him, and though he didn't touch me, he had fallen asleep angled toward me, a guardian too exhausted to maintain his watch.

For a long time, I soaked in the moment. Surrounded by my coterie, I felt safe, loved, protected.

But our enemy was still out there, and it was only a matter of time before he figured out Conquest had stopped rampaging and set another trap for us.

"Morning," I whispered to Cole as I climbed over him. That had been the plan, anyway. Once I got my leg swung over his hips, he gripped mine and held me straddling him. He was hard and eager between my thighs, and I shivered from wanting him. "Knock it off."

"I haven't moved," he said, sleep making his eyes soft.

"Crap." That meant I was the one grinding on him. "I have to pee."

Before my hormones got away from me again, I slid onto the floor and scrambled to the bathroom.

The harsh overhead light stung my eyes, and I gritted my teeth as my temples throbbed. As much as I hated mirrors, I sought out this one.

The woman staring back at me had lost weight in recent weeks and gained muscle. Her complexion was more golden, thanks to all those daytime trips on the back of a dragon. Her eyes were . . . haunted. But the swelling was gone, so were the dark circles. I traced the outline of my lips, but the splits and cracks had healed.

I could almost pretend it never happened. I was good at locking away what I didn't want to deal with.

Eighteen dead patients.

Twenty-five deceased staff.

Sixteen injuries.

One dead chicken.

Exhaling slowly, I backed away from the reflection before I saw too much. I used the facilities, washed my hands, and entered the bedroom to find the coterie stirring.

Thom shifted midstride and crossed to me. "How do you feel?"

"Good." I pressed my fingers against my ribs to test for an ache but found none. "I'm not in any pain."

"Glad to hear it." Mags tackled me, slamming me into the wall at my back. "You were gone, Luce. *Gone.* We couldn't bring you back. I was terrified."

I wrapped my arms around her, breathed in the comforting scent of Maggie and coterie, and a fraction of the weight on my soul lifted. Conquest might be resting, but the coterie bond still hummed beneath my skin. "Thanks for fighting for me." I glanced past her to the others. "That goes for all of you."

A door opened and shut to my right, and a familiar voice called, "Threesome!"

Rixton slammed into us, dragging Maggie and me against his chest, and held on tight. "You two have to stop dying on me. I'm only human. My heart's only got so many beats, and you're making mine go triple time fretting over you. I don't want to run out before I get back home."

"I didn't die," I huffed, shoving him away before he noticed my discomfort and took it personally. Yep. Even with Conquest down for the count, I was still hooked into the coterie's feedback loop, which begged the question if Cole had made that an order too. A way to ground me. Then again, much like the rosendium beneath our skins, it might be too intrenched to remove. "I just ... went away for a while."

"I died." Maggie shrugged, keeping an arm around his shoulders. "In more ways than one."

Guilt hit me quick and hard, but I did my best to shield her from it. I had made the choice to save her. I had no right to also make her feel bad about how torn I remained. I would do it again in a heartbeat, and that meant I wasn't as sorry as I wanted to be, as I maybe ought to be. Until that changed, or she pressed the issue, we had nothing left to discuss on the topic.

"I'm glad you made it back," Rixton said, and the sentiment encompassed us both.

Maggie gave him a look that melted into Portia's huskier tones. "How did you take those hits?" She raked her gaze over him. "That punch to your ribs should have broken several, but you're still standing."

"Santiago designed a flexible armor suit for me." Rixton kept right on script. "Doesn't do much to keep my head on my shoulders, but it protected everything from the neck down like a pro." He skirted the edge of my gaze when he added, "Those things would have killed me otherwise. Humans aren't built to withstand that type of punishment."

"Hmm." Portia measured Rixton then prowled toward Santiago with purpose in her stride.

"You fed her to the lions without batting an eye." I snorted. "Impressive."

"Hey, I pay my debts." He sobered. "I owe Santiago. Big." He offered me a weak smile. "I wasn't lying. Those winged bastards would have killed me if not for that suit."

"You fought?" The blood drained from my cheeks in an icy rush. "I thought — "

" — if you held me back far enough I wouldn't see action?" He laughed. "Your plan would have worked if your cork hadn't got popped. After you went nuclear, it was all hands on deck."

"I'm sorry you had to see that." I shuddered, thinking of the face in the mirror, the haunted eyes I never met if I could help it. "I'm sorry you had to be part of this at all."

"Luce, I have a little girl, and I have a wife. They're everything to me." His mouth tightened. "I don't want to be here, risking my life, throwing away what time I have left with them, but it's my privilege to protect my girls." He punched my shoulder. "You included."

Cole's words rang in my ears. Rixton had answered the question without me having to ask. It was no less than I had assumed, but the words carried more weight when he spoke them.

"I'm going to get you home in one piece."

Stop making promises you can't keep, Boudreau.

"You'll try." He rolled his shoulders. "That's all any of us can do. Try."

"This isn't your fight." I had to say it, at least once more. "You could go home now. Leave this behind."

"Doesn't it strike you as odd that Earth is at stake, but no humans are fighting to save it? No humans even know it's at risk. We aren't equal to the task. I know that. But it seems like we ought to be given the option to protect our homes, our families, instead of being kept in the dark while the decisions are being made without us by beings from other worlds."

"We're not little green men." Really, I was just glad he hadn't called us *creatures* or *things*. *Beings* implied sentience at least.

"Your boyfriend is a dragon. *You* are a dragon. Don't talk to me about little green men." He cut his eyes to where Portia prowled after Santiago. "That's the weirdest thing yet. Maggie's body. I mean, I see it. It's her. But it's not her. The expressions, the inflection. It's someone else. *In her body*. Maybe Sherry was onto something with her alien obsession. Body snatchers are clearly a thing."

Unreal to be having this conversation with him when I thought I would never see him again, let alone talk to him or cut up with him. A miracle. That's how it felt. And it left me jonesing for another reunion. One long overdue.

I wanted to see Dad. I was ready to face him. There were no guarantees how long the bangles would contain Conquest. They hadn't been fashioned with that in mind. She was a power, and using rosendium harvested from her — *our* — body against her was a losing proposition.

Dad deserved to see his daughter one last time while I was still me. And damn it, I deserved to tell my dad I loved him, to hug him, before I left him behind to deal with the fallout.

"Luce." Thom urged me over to the coterie side of the room. "Sit down. I want to examine you."

Rixton pointed at the door and slipped out of the room, giving me time alone with my coterie.

"Fiiiiine." I didn't wait for his permission to latch onto him. "Thanks for putting me back together."

"You're welcome." A purr was in his voice when he rubbed his cheek against mine. "I won't let you go without a fight. None of us will."

A thought occurred to me, and I reared back. "Hey, the enclave is in seclusion. Why are you still here?"

"I'm done licking my wounds." A tight smile played on his lips. "I'm not at full strength, but the coterie can't afford to continue on without its medic."

Not with Conquest playing whack-a-mole with them when they came after her.

"I'm glad." I did my best to be a grateful patient and not a grumpy one. "It's selfish, I know, but I'm glad you're back. I missed you."

"We talked every day." Amusement glinted in his eyes as he sat me on the edge of the bed. "Video chatted every other day at least."

"It's not the same." I let him work through his battery of tests. "I feel better putting my eyes on you."

"What happened wasn't your fault." He nodded to himself, appearing content with his results. "You must stop blaming yourself."

I didn't remind him he was my responsibility. He knew that. I didn't promise he would never be harmed on my watch again. He knew that too. Anyone who wanted at Thom would get to him over my dead body. The same went for any member of my coterie. I had lost enough, more than enough. Protecting those who remained wouldn't bring back Aunt Nancy or Uncle Harold, but it was a step toward the only form of atonement within my grasp.

"You're fully healed," he announced to the room, and I noticed Cole push out an exhale at the news.

"The real question is — " I stood, anger rising with me. "What are we doing about Wu's father?"

"You must recover." Miller crossed to me, rested a hand on my shoulder. "What you've been through is enough to rattle anyone. We don't have to strike back right this minute."

"Luce." Cole didn't manage more than that, but the look we shared conveyed the rest.

He wanted me to heal. He wanted me to wait. He wanted to protect me.

But I couldn't be coddled, and we couldn't afford to wait.

"Where is Wu?" I searched the room in case I missed him. "Kapoor?"

"They're in the suite adjoining this one." Santiago pointed at a door. "I bought this hotel years ago as an investment. Penthouse is too obvious, so we're staying in king suites. There's no paper trail tying this building to any of us, or to White Horse. We should be safe here for a while."

Hotels with penthouse suites in Canton didn't happen. "Where are we?"

"Jackson." Santiago walked to the window and yanked back the curtain, revealing a view of the Mississippi River. "There are two clans loyal to Conquest in the area. I've put in calls to them. They're handling security for us to cut down on time we spend on the streets, out in the open." Before I could argue, he raised a hand. "I vetted them personally. They're loyal to the bone. Think Veronica. They don't require you to eat, maim, or otherwise digest any of their members to swear fealty to you."

Placing a hand over my stomach, I grimaced. "That's good to know."

Hoping Kapoor fared as well as I had under Thom's care, I knocked on the door to the suite next door.

Wu answered wearing loose pajama bottoms, with his bare chest and wings on full display. "Luce."

"Wu." I arched an eyebrow at him. "Well? Can I come in?"

"You?" He surveyed the gathering behind me. "Or all of you?"

"Whatever gets me through the door." I shrugged. "I'll tell them everything. It's up to you if they hear it first or secondhand."

"I'll leave the door open, but I would prefer the others not to enter. Farhan is ... having difficulties. A crowd might kickstart his fight or flight reflexes, and he wouldn't get far in the shape he's in."

"Thom said he saved Kapoor's wings." I peered into the suite but saw no sign of him. "How's the rest of him?"

"Physically? He's recovering." He stepped back and gave me room to enter. "Mentally? I'm not so sure."

Braced for the worst, I was surprised to find Kapoor sitting on the couch reading a report. He looked the same as always, except he wore the same loose style pants as Wu, baring a lightly muscled chest. A pair of black wings draped over the back cushions and swept across the floor.

"Hey." I started to tuck my hands into my pants pockets, but the pajamas I wore had none. "How are you doing?"

Slowly, Kapoor faced me. His eyes were full black, and the traceries of his veins mapped his face, the blood gone dark as pitch. Ridges fanned his cheeks, and tough plates covered his forehead.

Thanks to interacting with my coterie, I had gotten better about shielding my knee-jerk response to the natural charun form. That pesky inner voice cranked up its wailing a few notches, but I muffled it to a bearable level.

I had been wrong about Kapoor. Whatever he was, he wasn't Malakhim. Mixing in a little human wouldn't have resulted in these stark changes.

"I'm alive." He didn't so much as blink. "There's that."

"You and Wu are a match made in fatalist heaven." I moved to take the seat opposite him, and six black horns burst from his forehead, in the center of those hardened plates. Chest heaving, he clenched his fists. The muscles in his arms and chest tightened, his core fluttering as his abs flexed. *Fight or flight.* "I'm not going to hurt you."

"Give him his *me* space," Thom coached from the doorway. "He'll calm down once he ceases to feel threatened."

Easing back, I gave Kapoor plenty of room to find his calm. All the while, my mind raced, pieces clicking into place.

This was the face of the NSB's janitor. This was what all those charun marked for death had seen before their lives were snuffed out of existence.

For some reason, probably the fact I clung to my humanity so hard, I figured he had hunted them down in his suit and tie then popped a few rounds in them. Except I knew from personal experience unless he had a weapon calibrated to take down charun, he wasn't going to get far with bullets. Plus, it was in their nature, the urge to hunt. To kill. To feel blood slicking their hands, wetting their throats.

I swallowed hard to force my own urges to take a backseat to reason. "We good?"

Still heaving breaths, Kapoor nodded. "Good."

"Luce?" Wu straightened his shirt. "Can I speak to you in the kitchen? I have a few questions."

From there, we could pretend to get coffee while keeping an eye on Kapoor.

Settled in with my mug, wishing for flavored creamer, I got to the point. "What do you want to know?"

"All of it."

And that's what I told him.

Afterward, he returned the favor, filling in the blanks about the meeting with his father, explaining what had triggered me, and conveying his ultimatum.

Now that I had been captured and tamed, his father would be looking for his son to choose a side. For good.

That didn't give us much time, but it didn't change my mind. "I want to see my dad."

"That can be arranged." His attention zoomed back to me. "If you're sure you want to risk it."

"I do." I worried the bangle on my left wrist. "I want him to know how much I love him."

"He does." Wu's expression softened. "He's never doubted it for a moment."

"I want to say it, I want him to hear it." And, I had to be truthful. "I want to hear it too."

"I'll make the arrangements." Wu rested his hand on my shoulder, but no warmth accompanied the touch. "The bangles are more effective than I expected." His eyes flashed gold. "There's no resonance between us. For all intents and purposes, you're . . . human."

Hmm. That trick had Cole's fingerprints all over it.

What a mess. What a flaming hot mess. Astronauts could probably view it from space.

"Most of my life I had no idea there was another person smothered by my conscious mind. You'll have to forgive me if I'm not convinced she's restrained and not resting. From what I hear, she went on quite a tear before she was captured." All those lives lost, all my fault for not being stronger. "I feel like me, more like myself than I have in a long time, and it's great. But it won't last. It never does. It can't." The smile I offered him was brittle. "I'll be feeling the leash tug before you know it."

The shock of learning where Wu had transferred my father almost bowled me over. This was no NSB facility. It wasn't a facility at all. It was a personal residence. *His.* A mansion built into the side of a mountain I couldn't name, that I doubt Wu would confide if I asked him.

He instructed us to wait on the ledge where we landed and went in to clear the visit with his personal security, giving me a moment to compose myself.

Cole placed his hands on my shoulders, anchoring me, and I was reminded of Wu's dilemma. "Can you feel our mate bond?"

"No." He didn't sound bothered by the lack. More proof he had tinkered with me. "It went silent before you woke the last time. It gave me hope the bangles had done their job."

Twisting around, I studied his face. "You're good with that?"

"I don't need a mate bond to tell me how I feel." He stroked his thumb across my jawline. "Or to tell me you feel the same."

Since I had been throwing myself at him from the moment we met, I wasn't the one in doubt. I had been drawn to him on a soul-deep level from the moment I first spied him through my security feed at the farmhouse the morning after Jane Doe — War — had been rescued from the swamp.

"It's a relief." One of us had to say it. "Wu told me I read as human, that Conquest is dormant. That means I'm just Luce. No shadows. Only me."

Now he was the one studying me. "Did you think it would change things between us?"

If I was being honest, I had to admit, "Yeah."

Sliding his hand to the back of my neck, Cole pulled me to him. He lowered his head, eyes fierce, and claimed my lips in a scalding kiss that caused spots to dance behind my eyelids. "I love you, Luce Boudreau."

For the first time, I felt he could mean it. Really mean it. And it shattered my heart in a good way, not that you could tell by the tears streaming down my cheeks. "You're really mine."

"I'm really yours." He brushed his mouth over mine again, softer this time. "I shouldn't have given you so much reason to doubt me."

The secrets and lies I couldn't pin on him. He was protecting me from Conquest, and the coterie as well. Not to mention those he knew I cared for. Keeping me in the dark allowed me time to cope, room to expand my perceptions, and a chance to develop bonds with him and the coterie that were unique to me. The fact he had been torn over pursuing me as Luce when he shared so much history with Conquest wasn't a blip on my radar. I was too grateful he saw me for myself, that he wanted me, that he loved me.

Me.

What that said about soulmates, fate, destiny, or whatever you wanted to call it, I had no idea. I might never be sure if I felt drawn to him because of what lurked beneath my skin or his own appeal. He would have to guess on his end as well. We were too tangled to unknot. But I could say with absolute certainty that I loved him just as much, wanted him just as much, needed him just as much, with her muted.

For me, for Luce, there would never be anyone but Cole. That's all that really mattered in the end.

"You're cleared." Wu stood in the doorway flanked by two guards who wore the same uniforms I remembered from The Hole, and I prayed they hadn't been reassigned here, that they didn't have to carry the guilt of knowing one slot on the schedule had spared them and damned their comrades. "Your father is waiting for you in his suite."

Nerves made my hands clammy, but I held on tight to Cole as we followed Wu into the lush hallway dotted with ornate doors that could have led anywhere. He stopped at one, seemingly at random, and knocked twice.

"Come in," Dad called, sounding at ease.

"I'll wait for you out here." Cole pressed a kiss to my forehead. "Call if you need me."

"Sure." I wet my lips, eyes sliding to Wu. "You going to wait out here too?"

"No." He shared a look with Cole. "I'll be in my office down the hall, to the left, when you're ready to go."

Out of time to procrastinate, I turned the knob and entered a room straight out of a magazine spread. Hardwood floors. Silk wallpaper. Plush rugs. A bed big enough for Cole to splay without our outstretched hands touching.

"There's my baby girl." Dad crossed to me and brought me in for a hug that smelled like home. "I wondered when you'd get around to visiting your old man."

"I wanted to come sooner." I held on tight. "Work got in the way."

"Saving the world does that." He chuckled as he pulled away. "I made a few friends. Other residents of this . . . House isn't the right word. Manor?" He gestured toward the pair of chairs angled toward an unlit fireplace. "Turns out I'm the only human in residence."

"The only . . . " I curled my fingers into the armrests of my seat. "Human?"

"Luce, I've known you're special for a long time." He leaned back, gazing into the darkened hearth. "I understand just how special now." His stare would have fit had there been flames, but their lack made his concentration eerie. "I had no idea other worlds, other beings, existed. But it doesn't surprise me." He flicked me a brief smile. "Not after you."

Mouth full of cotton, I couldn't get my tongue to work. "Dad, I wanted to tell you but — "

"You wanted to protect me. I get that. I respect that. Understand it even." He reached for my hand, and I gave it to him. "I'm not mad." He chuckled. "I was pissed at first. Not at you, but at the confinement. I'm not allowed to leave, to make phone calls, or have contact with the outside world except for you. I was not the best house guest. I suppose that's why the others took pity on me.

They must have figured I'd settle down if they explained what was going on and why."

Unsure where to start since my whole mental speech had been derailed, I just sat there like an idiot.

"I know about Harry," he said, softer. "I heard about Nancy too."

"I'm sorry." I almost choked on the inadequacy of the words. "I tried to save him, but I couldn't. I didn't even know she was sick. If I had, then maybe I could have — "

"Luce." Dad's voice remained gentle but firm. "What happened to them was not your fault. Nancy would have died, and Harry . . . " He shut his eyes a moment. "He made his choice, and I can't blame him for it. I would have done the same for you."

"War and Famine wouldn't have targeted them if not for me."

Finally, he looked at me. Until that point, I hadn't realized he would rather stare at ashes in the hearth than my face. "What do you want me to say?"

A distant part of me realized I had been spoiling for this fight, and having it whimper instead of bang was a disappointment. I wanted him mad. Fuming. Pissed-the-hell-off. I wanted him to point a finger and damn me for what I brought into his life, into the lives of his friends. Forgiveness was too easy.

"You brought me home with you, and all these deaths followed. How does that make you feel?"

"Like I made a mistake the day I saved you? Like I should have turned a deaf ear when your screams echoed through the hospital? Like I should have my head examined for adopting you?"

"Yes." The weirdest sense of relief swept through me. "All of that."

"I hate to disappoint you, kiddo." His eyes went cop flat. "Cops don't last long if they don't listen to their gut, and my gut told me you were mine. Blood doesn't mean a damn thing to me. What you are matters even less. You're my little girl. End of story."

There was more bubbling under the surface, and I couldn't stop myself from peeking.

"What aren't you telling me?" I cocked my head, really looked at him. "What did you know that made this leap of logic so easy for you?"

"Easy?" Coarse laughter erupted from him. "I wouldn't call any of this easy."

"You ought to be more upset than you are." I searched the room but saw no pill bottles. "Are they giving you sedatives to calm you?"

"Michelle Fortenberry."

The name struck no chords with me. "Who?"

"That was your name." He scratched his jaw. "Your description flagged a missing person's report."

"Missing?"

"Michelle was kidnapped and held captive for three weeks. Her abductor tortured and killed her. Her body was found five days before you were spotted in the swamp. Before more than a preliminary examination of the corpse could be performed, her remains disappeared from the morgue."

Resting my elbows on my knees, I stared at the floor between my feet, afraid I might get sick.

"The child was pronounced DOA. The estimated TOD was six hours earlier." He raked his fingers through his thinning hair. "I had a choice to make. Call Michelle's parents and tell them I found their child running naked through Cypress Swamp, the child they had already held a memorial for, or bury the connection. It didn't sit right with me, but neither did turning over an amnesiac kid suffering from obvious trauma. One that shouldn't be alive, let alone thirty miles from the morgue on record."

The choice must have eaten him alive. "Did Uncle Harold know?"

"He did all the digging." Dad shrugged. "I took a leave of absence. Had to. I was missing shifts to stay at the hospital."

Eyes prickling, I rubbed them with the backs of my hands. "That couldn't have been an easy decision for you."

"Hardest one of my life," he admitted. "I didn't realize I wanted kids — *a* kid — until you fell in my lap. I thought the urge driving me was a sense of responsibility, but Harry was the one who cut through the BS and made me see it for what it was." He shrugged again. "Love." His shoulders hitched for a third time before he caught the nervous gesture and stilled. "He asked me point blank if I thought anyone else could love you, provide for you, teach you, as well as I could, and I told him no without hesitation. That's when I knew what I had to do. I filed paperwork the next day. I considered you my daughter when I brought you home from the hospital, but we made it legal a few months later."

"You made all the difference. I hope you know that." I clutched his hands in mine. "Everything I am is because of you. You made me a decent person, a good friend, a hard worker. That's all you."

"Oh sure." Eyes glassy, he coughed into his fist. "Blame it on your parent."

"I call 'em like I see 'em." I smiled, and that ugly tangle in my gut unfurled. "And what I see isn't what I expected. We need to talk about next steps."

"I've been reassured I'm safe here. Remote location, armed guards, weresomethings down the hall."

A laugh snuck up on me. "Weresomethings?"

"One turns into a duck/wolf/spider combo I still see in my nightmares. Another looks like a kitten half eaten by a snake. The third one — " A flush warmed his cheeks. "She's the next best thing to a mermaid. I, ah, found that out by stumbling across her in the saltwater pool."

"Mmm-hmm." I chuckled at his embarrassment. "I'm guessing she forgot to wear her seashells?"

"Well . . . I . . . " His blush darkened, giving lobsters a run for their money. "I didn't check."

Except he must have caught a glimpse of something to be this mortified. Worried about his stress levels, and not at all interested in learning my dad had not-dad thoughts, I got us back on track. "You want to stay here?"

"I do." He tapped his fingers on his knee. "As much as I hate the idea of sending you out there alone, I'm too old to fight. I don't want to be another burden on your conscience. Staying put means you know I'm safe, and you don't have to worry about me. It might be boring as hell, but there are perks."

Perks that involved tails, scales, and the lack of seashell bras.

"You're being very rational about all this," I pointed out, still amazed by how well he was coping.

A soft knock on the door drew my attention, and I called out, "Come in."

Too late I realized the knock had come from a different door than the one I entered through, and the petite female with silvery hair edging toward lavender who stuck her head in the room was not looking for me.

"You must be Luce," she said, her voice soft as the robe she wore. "I'm Miranda."

"You're the mermaid Dad mentioned." I stood to shake her hand. "It's nice to meet you."

"Mermaid?" Her cheeks pinkened. "Oh, you." She crossed to Dad and kissed his cheek. "Flatterer."

Before I discovered whether she was wearing anything beneath the robe trying hard to slip off her shoulder, I made my excuses. "I should go."

"You don't have to rush away." Miranda glanced between us.

"Please, don't let me run you off. He's been so worried. I didn't realize he had company, or I wouldn't have bothered him."

"It's no bother," Dad grumbled. "Luce, are you sure you can't stay?"

"The longer I'm here, the more dangerous it is for you all." I managed to keep a straight face and not tease him when he stood and came in for a hug. "I'll see you soon, okay?" I kissed his cheek. "I love you, Daddy."

"I love you too, baby girl." He squeezed me one last time and held on tight. "Be safe out there."

"I'll do my best," I promised. "Miranda, it was nice meeting you. Keep an eye on this guy for me, will you?"

"It would be my pleasure." She beamed at me. "Edward is such good company."

Edward.

I blinked.

Over the years, I had heard Dad called a lot of things, not all of them complimentary, but Edward was not one of them. Most folks called him Eddie or Boudreau. Hearing his entire first name used as a form of address struck me as weirder than the fact he was cozying up to a woman, let alone a charun, at all.

Waving goodbye, I exited the room to find Cole wearing a grin. "You heard all that?"

"I did." His wide shoulders jostled with laughter. "Your father has made interesting friends."

"Seashells," I grumbled. "She's nothing to worry about, right?"

"Her kind are harmless. They aren't mermaids, but their lower bodies are fishlike."

"As long as she won't eat him, or mate him." I frowned. "Or mate him then eat him. We're good."

"Charun can't mate humans," he reminded me. "As to the other, given your father's love of fishing, I would say she's in greater danger from him than the reverse."

"You're a funny guy." I elbowed him in the side then winced. "You're also made out of poured concrete or something. Seriously. *Ouch.*"

Wry humor glinted in his eyes. "You don't like my body?"

There was nothing wrong with his body, and we both knew it. But now he had me thinking about our sprint through the woods, the splash of our bodies hitting the water then crashing together on the bank. And all the times that came after that first one.

Chewing my bottom lip saved me from answering long enough for Wu to come fetch us.

"I thought I heard voices." Wu flared his nostrils. "Am I interrupting?"

"Sadly, no." I heaved a sigh. "Five more minutes, and maybe."

"I could leave and then come back."

I caught him by the arm before he could make good on his offer. "Why didn't you tell me Dad had been briefed?"

"I wasn't aware until we arrived. Miranda informed me the group made the decision to bring him into their inner circle to help him adapt to his situation."

"Miranda has the hots for my dad." I narrowed my eyes at him. "She's way too young for him."

Wu's smile was slow to spread, but it stretched from ear to ear. "She's two hundred and three."

"Oh." I hadn't factored charun biology into the equation. "I guess that's okay then."

Cole was working hard to keep the amusement off his face, but I wasn't buying into the innocent act.

"He's my dad. I'm entitled to vet the people he dates." I huffed out a laugh. "God knows he's done the same to me." I jabbed Cole with a finger. "He did the same to you."

"I wouldn't call what they're doing *dating.*" Cole captured my hand. "They're too isolated for that."

"Ugh." I stuck my fingers in my ears. "Why would you imply that? Dads don't have sex. They just don't."

Whatever he said next made Wu laugh, but I couldn't hear either of them, and I liked it that way.

The look on Wu's face had me lowering my arms. "What?"

"Can I have a moment of your time before we go?"

Figuring he wanted to discuss Dad or security details further, I shrugged. "Sure."

"Let's use my office."

How he could tell one room from another was beyond me. The doors were all identical, as was their spacing. "How many rooms does this joint have?"

"Thirty bedrooms," he said without missing a beat. "Fifty rooms total."

Stunned, I pinned him with a stare. "Who needs thirty bedrooms?"

"This place was built on hope." He touched his fingers to his chest. "For the day I could bring the enclave here to live with me, as a family."

A dream made reality. I almost tasted the bittersweetness of his longing. "Who are the others?"

"Staff." He lowered his hand to his side. "There are more of them, but your father hasn't met them yet."

"He thinks they're all guests." And that didn't sit right with me. "They want to tell him the truth, fine. Tell him the whole truth. I don't want him getting hurt later when he finds out his new friends are on your payroll."

Learning Miranda was paid to do a job, even if that job wasn't playing maybe-girlfriend, should be disclosed before he got any un-dadlike ideas about her.

"I'll leave word that total transparency is a requirement when dealing with your father."

Nodding my thanks, I pressed my luck. "How would you feel about more house guests?"

"I'm willing to accommodate a select few others. The more we bring in, the more these are at risk. Currently your father is the only human, the only civilian, in residence. I assume you're wanting to add to that number."

Thinking of Sherry and Nettie, and Phoebe, I admitted, "Yes."

"Make your arrangements," he said after a time, "and I'll see to the rest."

"Wu?" I wasn't sure how to frame the question without insulting him. "Why didn't you bring the enclave here if this is the home you built for them?"

"We made an even trade. My people are at your home, and your father is in one of mine."

"That's not an answer," I pointed out, but he was right. We had balanced the scales without me knowing it.

"I want this to be their sanctuary. I want them to be free to come and go as they please, do as they wish, and live their lives in the open."

"You don't want to tarnish this place." Death always left a mark, and no battles were fought without casualties. "This is your Eden."

Biblical references ruffled his feathers, but having a godlike father who named him Adam was just asking for it. This was his ideal, his wish for his descendants. It was, perhaps, more for him than he realized. It was a gift he wanted to give them, a symbol of the future he envisioned for them, and he didn't want to pass off the latter until the former had been realized.

At the door to his office, he asked Cole to wait outside.

He agreed, without a fuss, since we had just established he could hear through the door just fine.

"Ezra is ready to meet with you."

"Are you serious?" Tingles swept across my skin. "You located him?"

"I've always known where he was," Wu admitted, moving to stand behind his desk, like a hunk of oak would stop me from throttling him. "I never intended for you two to meet. I'm still not convinced it's the right thing to do, but I have to tell you before you find out some other way, and it gets you killed."

Fury rolled through me, hot and fast, that he would keep this from me. "Where is he?"

Wu rolled an elegant shoulder. "He's right here."

As quick as my temper had ignited, it snuffed even faster, replaced by an icy shock that paralyzed.

"W-w-what?" I would have hit the ground if I hadn't backed into the door. "You? *You?* You can't be him."

"I'm not, really."

Shoving off the wood, I demanded, "What the hell does that mean?"

"All those years ago, you begged me for a name. I gave you one, but it wasn't mine. It was my father's."

A tremble started in my calves, the muscles turning to water. The higher it rose, the more I wobbled, until my knees gave, and I hit the floor. "No."

"Yes." Wu rounded the desk, but he kept a safe distance from me.

"Why tell me now?"

"Sooner or later, you're going to encounter my father. Sooner, at the rate he's going. Father is going to introduce himself as Ezra. Do you really want that to happen when you're feeling indebted to him? Do you want to keep wasting your hope on answers he can't give?" Wu tucked his hands into his pockets. "I don't." He shifted his weight. "I don't want you anywhere near him."

"All this time ... " I couldn't make the pieces fit in my head, could barely look at Wu. "You lied to me from the start."

"I did." He didn't sound sorry about it, either. "I wanted to gain your trust on my own merits. I didn't want you to look at me the way you are now, and I didn't want you viewing me through the idyllic lens of your childhood relationship with me either."

Doing what I do best, I packed away the sharpest hurts and locked them in the back of my mind, allowing the cold place to numb the sting and clear my head. Once the haze thinned, my cop brain kicked in, and I sat upright, ready to grill him. "How did you stop the pain?"

"All you needed was to hear my voice. Trial and error made it hard on you during the first few years, but I conditioned you to only need feedback from me once a year in order to function."

A steady vibration rumbled through my chest as I processed what Wu meant.

"Why you?" I made fists at my sides. "Would any charun have sufficed, or did it have to be you in particular? Would contact with the coterie have cured me?"

The NSB had been watching me since the first headlines splashed front pages. They had tracked my life, my development, my loyalties. I figured that meant Wu had paid closer attention to me than he let on, but I didn't peg him for this. I never could have imagined subterfuge on this level.

"No." Wu paid the buttons on his shirt particular attention. "It had to be me."

"You're the one Bruster meant," I realized. "You're the one he said owned Conquest."

I had been right all along. Ezra did own me. I just hadn't realized he and Wu were one and the same.

"You are owned. Conquest is owned."

That's what Bruster told us while in his meditative fugue.

"I know a lot of things, Wu." Bruster rasped out a chuckle. "More every day. Soon your daddy's going to know them too."

A wink and a nod to Wu. I hadn't picked up on either.

"I am, but it's not what you think." He glanced up then. "It's worse."

"Explain," I barked, patience wearing thin. "What have you done to me?"

"I established a mate bond with you." Quick to cut off my horror, he pressed on. "It was nothing physical. I wouldn't have abused a child."

No matter how many times I played it back in my head, it didn't get any better. *"You mated me?"*

As the wheels in my head spun, a vicious snarl eclipsed their whirring, and the door behind me thumped hard, and then again, and then again.

"When you breached, I was there. Waiting. As I had been so many times before, with so many other Conquests. I had experimented on them all to one degree or another, but I never got it right. They never changed enough. They all retained their Otillian sensibilities."

The spit dried from my mouth, and I couldn't even think of another question to hurl at him.

The fact talons had pierced the door and begun prying it from its hinges didn't help matters. It might have been forged with charun in mind, but it wouldn't hold against a pissed-off dragon for long.

"But this last time," he pressed on through my shock, "I made more headway than ever before, and I brought the previous Conquest to The Hole for monitoring."

The frequency trick that had cost me my humanity ... That had been his doing. Maybe not personally, but he had employed the scientists responsible and provided them with test subjects. Then again, so had I. I was the reason Famine was in The Hole in the first place, and she was the reason Daddy Wu — no, *Ezra* — had blown it to kingdom come.

Metal screeched, bent. Wood groaned, splintered. And the dragon . . . roared as it flung the door skittering down the hall.

The serpentine curve of his head and neck shoved into the room first, darting straight for Wu, teeth snapping an inch from the tip of his nose.

"Luce is every bit as much my mate as she is yours." A ghost of a smile flickered on Wu's lips. "Maybe more since I claimed her first as this person, in this body."

"Are you trying to get him to kill you?" I rushed over, braced my hands on the dragon's chest to keep him from advancing. "He'll do it, and he won't feel bad about it. I bet you taste just like chicken."

Tongue darting between his teeth, the dragon growled his agreement.

"Talk fast, Wu. I can't hold him long when he's like this."

And honestly, I didn't want to. Learning I was a thing Wu had hand-crafted made me sick. Watching Cole eat him wouldn't help, but it would be satisfying in its own way.

"There's a moment when Otillians breach where their essence is . . . flexible." He rubbed his fingers together. "Tangible."

How many previous cadres had been sacrificed to learn that much? I didn't ask. I didn't want to know.

"When Conquest breached, I was waiting in Cypress Swamp for her with the body of a ten-year-old girl who had died six hours earlier."

"Conquest isn't viscarre," I protested. "Even if she was, they require living hosts to feed on."

"There was no soul in the body," Wu continued like I hadn't interrupted him. "When Conquest began her transformation, when she was essence waiting to be given form, I coated my hands in healing power, balled up as much of her as I could hold, and shoved her into that little girl." Wu wet his lips. "And then I performed CPR until she revived." He looked at me then, the wonder of the moment cutting through all the rest. "You went mad when you woke. You screamed and scratched and bit me to escape, and then you ran into the swamp. I thought I had failed. I left you there, thinking you would die or that the swamp would kill you."

Truth. Brutal truth. Nothing else would hurt like this.

"But fishermen spotted the Wild Child and called it in," I finished for him. "That's how the cops ended up out there searching for a girl without a name or a family. That's how Dad found me."

Telling him this, if I ever worked up the courage, would lay any lingering guilt to rest. He had been right to keep me for his own. I had been dead to them, and it was right that I stay that way.

"I thought about killing you before he discovered your true nature. It would have been easy." His voice took on an almost philosophical tone. "Any one of the visits to the hospital could have been your last."

"Why let me live then?" I demanded. "Why risk exposure?"

"I was there the night Officer Boudreau marched into the OR and decked the head surgeon. He brought a nurse with him. The same female a member of War's coterie later claimed as a host."

Ida Bell. I remembered her. All too well. And it hurt knowing she had been the one to risk her job, to rush in with Dad, probably at Uncle Harold's request, and unhook me from all those machines so he could take me home.

"He was so fiercely protective of you," he said, "it made me curious what might come of letting him raise this thing I had created."

This thing I had created. Yep. Daddy Wu's god complex was genetic.

The hit landed with the force of a fist to the gut, knocked the breath out of me, and made it clear he viewed me, my life, my struggles — not with his own eyes, but through the lens of a microscope.

"I was an experiment start to finish for you." I unlocked my jaw, forced myself to stop grinding my teeth. "I get that. What I don't understand is how or why you think you're my mate."

"Conquest was dying. As Cole said, she isn't viscarre or emocarre. She's not made for what I did to her. After I shoved her essence into that dead vessel, Conquest began dying too." His eyes lifted, locked with Cole's. "There is no greater connection than a mate bond." His gaze slid back to me. "Your mate wasn't there. You had no anchor in this world, so I became one."

"You mated a ten-year-old dead girl?" I blinked at him. "How the hell is that even possible?"

"We can't mate humans." His bitter laughter scraped my ears. "They don't have enough soul, enough life, to bind what scraps they have to the vastness of our existence."

Thinking on the enclave, I laughed bitterly. "Speaking from personal experience?"

"Yes, damn you." The muscles in his jaw flexed. "I am."

"You once talked to me about resonance. You were hitting on me."

"You're my mate, even if it's only a technicality." He lifted his arm, like he might touch me, but he let it fall without making contact. Probably worried I might twist it off and beat him to death with it. "Any male would be tempted."

"That's what you meant that night." The night we raided the Drosera nests. The night I failed Thom. "I thought you were being cocky, acting like you had the right to award me to Cole like a prize, but you were conceding your rights as my mate."

"I never intended to ... " He shook his head. "You were a child when this started. The temptation didn't come until later, until I dared believe in you. Even then, I'm not sure I could ... " He cut the thought short. "You've given me hope these last few years, and that's been in short supply, but thinking of you in that light feels like betrayal." His gaze lifted to mine. "That doesn't mean I can stop."

Not gonna touch that comment with a ten-foot pole. I didn't want to catch whatever madness had infected him if he thought for one hot second I would choose him over Cole.

"That doesn't explain how you did it." This scheme was more in Death's wheelhouse than his. Maybe she would have better answers for me. "Why did it work?"

"I didn't mate the girl." Wu sounded tired. "I mated Conquest. That link between us rooted her in that body. Otillians are the most adaptable of any charun species. I gambled that she would make it work, and she did. She survived. Or so I thought."

"Oh, she survived."

Eighteen dead patients.

Twenty-five deceased staff.

Sixteen injuries.

One dead chicken.

"What I mean is, I wasn't sure for a long time that you weren't her. She's a gifted actress, they all are. They're skilled at adaptation, at blending in, at letting others see what they want to see. But after a while, when your coterie made no attempt to contact you — or you them — I began to wonder. And I watched until I was almost certain you were the genuine article."

"How do the phone calls fit in?" With me under surveillance, he wouldn't have needed to make personal contact. "The pain — did you cause that? Or did you cure it?"

"The pain was caused by Conquest rattling the bars of her cage," he explained. "She was aware, more in the early years, and she wanted out. She wanted to claim her own body, her own identity, and not be trapped in a shell she had little control over."

"The girl was dead." I rubbed my forehead. "Why wasn't Conquest in total control of the body?"

"I believe a combination of my healing power and the infusion of soul woke part of the girl's mind. I believe Conquest fused with her on every level, making you some combination of the two, and wiping you blank." He raised his eyes. "I also believe the longer your amnesia smothered her beneath this new identity, the weaker she became until you — Luce — became the dominant personality."

"I needed you every year like clockwork. If I have her leashed, why is that?"

"She's diminished, but she's not vanquished. You're able to pull on her power, but you can't access her knowledge. That's why I'm convinced part of the girl's brain survived. Had Conquest simply filled a vessel, she would have woken trapped in a human body, but that's all. She would have still been herself, not this. Not you." He shook his head. "The phone calls were easiest. They kept our paths from crossing. They kept you in the dark, where I wanted you to stay for as long as possible."

The dragon had stopped fighting me to get closer to Wu, so I began petting him to comfort us both.

"Conquest never stops trying to regain the upper hand, to crush that kernel of humanity lodged in her brain. She's always pushing. You're a splinter she wants removed at all costs. You can feel it, can't you? I can. Through our mate bond, I sense her." His eyes dimmed. "I'm the only thing keeping her contained, Luce. Remember that before you or your dragon attempt to digest me. You have to have regular contact with me, or she will punch through that final barrier given time, and your human mind will be crushed as she floods it with her presence. You'll revert, and Conquest will be unleashed."

That shocked the man right out of the dragon, and Cole paled until his complexion almost matched his silvery-white scales.

The silent horror contorting his expression gave me all the proof I needed without asking if Cole had known Wu was my mate, if that was why they had called a truce when remembering

Phoebe had almost broken me. Their reasons must have been more practical, more tactical.

Clearly, that truce had just gone bye-bye.

"You waited until War breached." I leaned against Cole, both for comfort and so I could restrain him again if necessary. "That's when you decided to set yourself in my path, using Kapoor as a conduit."

"Yes." He ducked his head. "At that point, I couldn't afford to let you interact with your siblings without supervision. I had to be sure they didn't have means of drawing Conquest to the surface. After nurturing you for so long, I feel ... proprietary ... toward you. Part of that is what I did, and part of that is the natural course of the mate bond."

"How can I be bonded to two charun?" Accepting I had one mate still gave me heart palpitations.

"Otillian biology," Cole answered for him. "They're adaptable to any terrene, and that includes ones where females keep multiple mates."

"Conquest was pure potential when I molded her into the shape I required. That included allowing her to be responsive to a dual bond. She didn't accept it, of course, but that doesn't change the fact that I am her mate, even if she refused to acknowledge me as hers." He exhaled. "My kind isn't so different from yours in one respect. We can mate without reciprocation. It grants us a hold on the other person, with or without their consent."

"That's a handy fail-safe you built for yourself," I said at last. "I can't kill you, and I can't let you die." Bile soured the back of my throat. "What about Cole? War told me he must remain in close proximity to me, or he'll die. She claimed the same was true for the others. Does that mean it's not the mate bond but the coterie bond that binds them to me?"

"Luce," Cole rumbled in warning, but I had to know.

"What was true for Conquest might not be true for you. What War thought she knew about the bond you shared with your coterie, with your mate, might not be accurate either. You're one of a kind. The truth is, we have no idea if Cole or the others will survive you. Previous coteries have outlived their masters by being set free or through a weak bond. Yours is ironclad, your people are loyal to you."

"You set us up like dominoes." I exhaled through my teeth. "One falls, we all fall."

"Unless the pattern is disrupted," he said quietly, "yes."

Pattern. Yes. The weft and warp of life was a pattern, and how dare he pluck the strings with such careless fingers? "You'd try this again, with the next cadre, wouldn't you?"

"I can't." Wu's eyes darkened. "I can only mate once, and I have, with you. You're my last chance to get this right, to end it once and for all." He spread his hands. "You die, I die, remember?"

All Cole's warnings rang in my ears when I looked at Wu. He had gambled it all, both our lives, to see this through. We might not have a clear picture of his endgame yet, but he was busy painting it.

"How do we know you're the better bet? Why should we support this coup of yours? You're quick to tell us that life goes on between ascensions. You've trained the NSB to wipe out the cadre as it surfaces, and all the while you're quietly adding hand-selected coterie members to the population. How are you any different than your father?"

"I cherish mortals." Wings burst from either side of his spine when he lost control of his temper. "I cherished one above all others. I was married. I had a wife. A mortal wife. A human wife. She was my entire world, she was all worlds to me. Father learned of her shortly before our third child was born. He walked into our home, spotted her in the birthing bed, killed the midwife, and snapped her neck. She died by his hand, our unborn child died by his hand, and so did the midwife's young daughters. He thought they were mine, you see, and I didn't tell him otherwise."

"There was no point." Cole tightened his hands on my arms. "Keeping your silence let their deaths mean something."

Aware the absolution came one father to another, I covered his hand with mine. "He's right."

"I raised my girls alone, and they went on to found the enclave to give their families a safe place to live." He softened his voice. "I gave them money, supplies, protection. When that wasn't enough, when technology advanced beyond what I understood, I joined the NSB and learned all I could about how they tracked charun, how they located them, what they did to undocumented charun. Eventually, I rerouted satellite surveillance, I tampered with official documents, I made them disappear." He exhaled. "But the attack on the bunker proved Father knew all along. He might not have discovered them for generations, but he did in the end, and he hit Knox hardest. He's my direct descendant. He's … important to me. So is Kimora. So is Lira. They all are."

"He knew where to strike to hurt you the most." As much as I hated asking, someone had to push the issue. "What are the odds you have a mole in the enclave? That our leak sprung from there?"

"They're my family." Wu stiffened his spine. "My blood."

"Family can commit atrocities just as easily as anyone else. Maybe more so." Look at mine. War. Famine. Death. My sisters were bloodthirsty nightmares come to life, and so was I. "They know us well enough to anticipate how to twist the blade to make it hurt the most."

Aunt Nancy and Uncle Harold had been selected for just that reason. Because I loved them. Because they were important to me. Because the cadre thought they could shatter my foundation by smashing my support pillars one by one.

"Eliminate the enclave," I tried again, "and the only people with access to that information would be Kapoor, or someone else within the NSB who got curious enough to do some digging, right?"

"Kapoor would never betray me." Wu sounded grieved about that, about what his loyalty had cost him. "No one else within the NSB, to my knowledge, is aware of my family ties."

"Your father has NSB resources at his fingertips. He had you watched. I guarantee it. You've been careful, and so has the enclave, but all it takes is one misstep for all their supposition to fall into place."

"Your father might be vain," Cole agreed, "but he would understand he had made an enemy of you that night."

The possibility intel was being passed from the inside voided all the enclave's carefully stocked resources.

"Knox knows his people best." Wu looked rumpled in his expensive suit. "He won't want to do it, but he can interview them, see if anyone's story doesn't check out."

"Get the ball rolling," I said, and it felt good to have that much control in this situation, even if it was an illusion.

Wu watched me for a moment, some mixture of envy and misery clashing on his face. The face I had dreamed of seeing for so many years. Ezra. He might not be *the* Ezra, but he was *my* Ezra. I ought to be pissed. I *was* pissed. But I ought to be more . . . I don't know. I wasn't sure how I should feel given what I had learned.

The girl Edward Boudreau fished out of the swamp wasn't a skin suit. She was a real girl, or she had been. Upon reflection, there was comfort in that. I might be an echo of Conquest, but I was rooted in this world, in this life, deeper than I imagined possible.

I really was a Real Girl.

"I had no right to use you the way I did," Wu all but whispered. "But if I hadn't, then Luce wouldn't be here. She wouldn't exist. You would be Conquest, and only Conquest. Just another monster unleashed on an unsuspecting world, the same as my father." He shrugged. "The same as any of us."

"Oh yeah, your idea of shoving charun into human corpses is much better."

"You're the answer to the question I've been asking myself for centuries — What if Conquest had a human conscience?"

Sliding a finger around the collar of my shirt, I couldn't find relief. "I need air."

Not waiting to see if they followed, I exited the office and the mansion until I stood on the cliff's edge.

"We should go," Wu said from behind me. "We put Haven at risk every moment we linger."

Haven. The name fit, and it was already living up to it by sheltering my dad.

Wu shook out his wings and leapt over the edge.

"Phoebe would be safe here." I touched Cole's shoulder. "Something to consider."

"He gave us the perfect leverage," he said bitterly, "didn't he?"

Our lives were tied together. All of us. And while Wu might have been the only thing keeping me alive, I was an Achilles heel of his own making. Cole was on point when he said that gave us leverage. Perhaps more than Wu realized.

Placing my hand over his heart, I felt its steady beat. "Think it over."

Cole shifted without another word, and I climbed on.

It's not like dragons are big on talking, but he didn't dip, dive, or roll. Not once. He flew in a straight line, his thoughts kept to himself.

Aware his breaths were being counted, Wu also kept his own counsel. He followed at a safe distance, well out of range of Cole's whiplike tail.

CHAPTER TWENTY-ONE

———◆———

Rixton and Maggie were playing chess when we got back to the hotel. Wu made his excuses then slipped off to check on Kapoor. The coterie, scattered around the room, looked to me for an update as Cole walked in.

"I visited Dad." Hardly earth-shattering news for them. "He's doing well, and he's in a secure location."

"I'm glad to hear it," Miller said with genuine warmth.

"He will recover fully," Thom promised me. "It's best he rest until the lingering effects of the toxins pass."

Santiago offered no comment. He was lost, as usual, in a tablet's screen.

"He's really okay?" Rixton searched my face. "Are you?"

"Yeah and yeah." I dropped on the couch next to Mags. "The staff briefed him on my situation, so I'm just ... processing. I expected a showdown, I guess. I didn't get one, so I can't shake this feeling of having unfinished business on that front."

"Your dad loves you." Maggie leaned back, the game forgotten.

"He was always going to accept who you are." She shared a smile with Rixton. "You're the only one surprised here."

"Your dad has a sharp mind, Bou-Bou. An analytical mind. I was working my way toward a revelation when I saw Thom. He expanded my horizons ahead of schedule, that's all."

"You're saying you always, on some level, thought I was different." And didn't that sting? "So learning I was just clicked right in place for you."

"It didn't change the fact we were friends. We *are* friends. What you are doesn't matter to me, but it does help me understand you better. You can't blame me for wanting answers. Not when the stakes are this high."

"I guess not," I groused. "As your friend, I have a proposition to make."

"I'm a married man." He held up his hands, palms out. "The threesome comment earlier was out of line. The only three-ways I'm into involve hugs. Unless you and Sherry have something planned, in which case, I'll just remind you my birthday is coming up in three months."

Maggie kicked him in the shin. "Pig."

"I'm a man."

"Pig."

"Man."

"Pig."

"You two are worse than Portia and Santiago." That earned me a glare from eyes that were no longer fully Maggie's. "Sorry, that was out of line." When Portia slipped under, I mumbled under my breath, "But true."

The way Maggie kept staring at me told me I hadn't gotten away with a thing. Damn charun hearing.

Knowing my luck, I had just kicked off a competition between Portia and Santiago to prove which duo was more annoying.

One day I would learn to keep my mouth shut.

"Rixton," I began before the bickering resumed. "Wu has offered your family a spot at Haven. Talk it over with Sherry, figure out if that's what's best for your family."

"She won't like it." His amusement vanished. "She won't want to leave home."

"I understand, but I had to make the offer. The enclave was meant to host our safehouse. But that's where the Malakhim struck. They zeroed in on the bunker, and that tells me there's a leak. Wu has his reasons for not inviting his people to Haven, but that's mine. I don't want to put Dad at risk. And that goes double if Sherry and Nettie decide to ride this out there."

"I'll make the call." He stood. "I'll be in my room. Knock if anything interesting happens."

"I'll do that." I waited until he left to look over Maggie. "How does it feel to return from the dead?"

"Ask me in a few days, after I've had time to process." She put on a smile. "It's good to see Rixton. I missed the jerk."

"But you wish you could reach out to others." Her fiancé, her parents, her job. "I get it."

"No." She hesitated before continuing. "I just made peace with having a clean slate. I liked the idea of starting over from scratch. A new me. This makes that impossible."

"Ditching your old life wasn't your choice, but I'm not sure if it's healthy to be glad about it. It's not like you. You're rooted in family, in your community, in . . . " What she hadn't said dawned on me a beat too late, and I got it. "I'm sorry I cost you all those things."

"You and I are past that." She waved a hand. "All I meant was I'm starting to get a foothold on who I am with Portia, and Rixton showing up makes me look back instead of forward."

Miller wandered over, but Maggie slipped into the room after Rixton before Miller reached us.

"I didn't mean to run her off." He frowned at her quick exit then studied me. "You look upset."

Since she didn't say either way, I figured it probably had more to do with all the looking back she had just mentioned, which included her ex-fiancé, than wanting to give us privacy. But I wasn't about to tell Miller that. Not when he already looked slighted by her avoidance.

"I could use an ice-cold Coca-Cola." I indicated the door. "Walk to the vending machine with me?"

Nice place like this, I doubted there was one. More like a mini mart secreted behind the front desk.

After the day I'd had so far, I wanted cold and caffeinated, and I wasn't picky about where I got it.

I used the walk to explain Wu's confession, minus the complication of having a second mate, and it made so much sense in hindsight I felt like an idiot.

Thom had verified Wu's scent around my window weeks ago, called it layered and old. Learning that didn't surprise me. I was under constant surveillance from the coterie, the NSB, and the locals. What was one more thing? But even the phone Wu gave me, the way he left the cell tucked under the base of that stupid rotary phone, should have tipped me off. And that was before I noticed the ringtone he had chosen for me.

It's like he was trying, in his subtle way, to push me toward connecting the dots on my own. But he hadn't sounded happy to come clean, so maybe it was his subconscious at work. Maybe he wanted me to know, and on some level, he couldn't stop dropping hints. Maybe he wanted the fight, wanted the anger, that came from discovery versus the stunned silence that came after confession.

"Do you want me to kill him?" Miller asked when I finished. "I wouldn't mind."

"Thanks." I leaned my head on his shoulder as we walked. "You're a real friend."

"How do you feel knowing you're more human than you thought you were yesterday?"

"Good. Weird. Sad." I shook my head. "I'm a walking corpse."

"You're not Death." He chuckled. "The child might have been dead when Conquest possessed her — for lack of a better word — but that little girl was brought back to life. Otherwise, Conquest would have found herself trapped in the body of a ten-year-old." At my look, he shrugged. "Dead things don't grow, don't change. Most don't maintain. They begin to deteriorate. You're not dead. You're very much alive."

A hard breath punched out of me and left me lightheaded. "It's not that I object to being charun." I straightened, combing my fingers through my hair. "I love you guys. I feel like myself when I'm with you, like I belong."

"But you were raised human by a human father, and it feels good to have an anchor within yourself to that upbringing and those people." He touched my arm. "I understand. The coterie won't hold it against you."

"Santiago will," I grumped.

"Santiago holds the rising of the sun against the moon." Miller smiled. "Ignore him. Attention only whets his appetite for more. He'll act out until he gets what he wants or gets bored trying."

"How is he not toddling around in diapers? Honestly?" Miller's bark of laughter felt good, and I grinned at him. "On the topic of men acting out — what's up with you and Rixton?"

"No one outside the coterie has touched Maggie or Portia since their transition. Have you noticed that? I didn't realize it until Rixton had his arms around her the first time. The instinct to claim her almost got the better of me."

Setting aside the claiming remark, I smiled. "I'm glad it didn't. Rixton is human, and they break easily."

Admitting that was beyond weird. So far beyond, I couldn't see the shape of the words on my horizon.

"She's not mine. That's what stopped me. Not kindness, rationality, or consideration."

Nerves fluttering in my belly, I had to ask, "Do you want her to be?"

He hesitated. "I'm not sure. I've never wanted anyone the way I want her."

"Miller ... stop me if this is too personal, but have you ever?" I rolled my hand. "You know?"

"Had sex?" His lips twitched. "Yes, but it requires a lack of control I'm no longer allowed to experience."

Or he would wipe out life on this planet as we knew it, strangle it in his ever-expanding coils. He was an ouroboros, a self-devouring serpent, and he would keep eating until he devoured everything.

"Well, lucky for you there are other benefits to being in a relationship that don't require ... that."

A delicate flush pinked his cheeks, and he cleared his throat. "Are we hitting the campaign trail again after you've recovered?"

"Ugh." That was the last thing I wanted to talk about, let alone do, but I respected his redirection. "We have no choice. Armies don't raise themselves, apparently."

"Luce."

My head shot up, and my heart rate was quick to match it. "Santiago?"

"The Malakhim," he panted. "They're converging on Canton."

"Shit." I advanced on him. "Where?"

Genuine regret filled his eyes when he said, "The police station."

Gut churning faster than my feet, I sprinted upstairs and shoved inside the suite.

"Fuck. Shit. Damn it." I shoved open the door to find everyone had gone to their own rooms. "*Cole.*"

"I don't know how I feel about my name being the last in that string of obscenities." He read my expression, and his hardened. "What's happened?"

"The Malakhim are in Canton." I gripped his arm, tugging him toward the window that shouldn't open but Miller had modified for our winged coterie members. "They're heading for the police station. We have to move."

"All right." He cast a look over his shoulder at the rest of the coterie. "Grab Wu. Meet us there."

"Tell Rixton," I called to Maggie. "Make sure he suits up before he leaves this building."

Maggie caved to Portia, and she gave me a tight nod. "I'll get him prepped and ready. He can ride with me."

Out of time for instructions, pleas, or prayers, I watched Cole fall out the window, twist midair as his body expanded to suit his dragon. And then I took a leap of faith.

There was nothing left of the Canton Police Department by the time we arrived. Santiago's warning had come too late. The building was a smoking husk garishly illuminated by the flashing lights mounted on firetrucks dousing the sated inferno.

Cole set down a few blocks away, and I hit the pavement, running full speed before he shifted and caught me.

Heart clogging my throat, I burst through the police line being held by two officers and fisted one's shirt. "What the hell happened here?"

"Gas leak. One of the old timers lit up in the breakroom, and the whole place went up." The rookie didn't fight me, and shock was to thank for that. It's not like I had a badge to whip out these days. "We don't have numbers yet." He swallowed hard. "There were no survivors."

The fight drained out of me, and I released him to do his job, tempted to help, to fall into old patterns, stand shoulder to shoulder with the uniforms. But it wasn't my place, not when it was my fault. These people have been targeted because of me. I had no right to stand beside the survivors and grieve.

Rixton arrived fifteen minutes later and flipped the switch from friend to cop between the long strides that ate up the distance to the first responders. He talked to each officer present, shook hands with the firemen, nodded at the grim words murmured by the paramedics. When he had done all he could do, all anyone could do, he joined me where I sat in a puddle of muddy ash.

"Sherry is going to Haven," he said softly.

Numb, I forced myself to focus. "She agreed?"

"No, she fought like a wildcat." He surveyed the damage. "I don't give a damn. I don't care if I have to toss her over my shoulder like a bag of the world's sexiest potatoes and carry her there on foot. She's going, and so is the baby." The hand he wiped down his face left black streaks. "Who do we make pay for this?" He cut me a look. "And don't give me the bullshit answer this was your fault. You didn't do this."

"Ezra."

The mental war I fought to separate the man I thought I had known all those years and the real Ezra caused my emotions and temper to fray. My Ezra didn't exist. He never had. He was a figment of my imagination, dreamed up by Wu. Considering his relationship with his father, I couldn't begin to fathom why he had chosen that name to give me when I asked for his. Maybe the name was a bullet, and Wu had loaded his weapon with it in the hopes its aim would be true.

"Then we find him," Rixton said, "and we put him down."

There was no arguing with that tone, and it soured my stomach. As grateful as I was to have him with me, I wished he had never forgiven me. "Are you ready to walk away from your family knowing you might never see them again?"

Head down, he stared at the swirl of charred particles mixing with hose water. "As long as Ezra is out there, every time I leave my house I'm risking never seeing my family again."

"You could go to Haven too." I had to put it out there, had to make a final push. "You would all be safe."

"For how long?" He flicked the water with his fingertips. "I'm not stupid, Luce. I can see you're on an end run. I'm not thrilled about it, but I get it. I've never been one of those cops who dreams of going out in the line of duty. I want to fall asleep after a night of making love to my wife, probably with the aid of pharmaceuticals at that age, and never wake up. That's my fantasy death." He smirked. "Not many of us get to live out our fantasies."

"Okay." I wiped my hands but only stained them worse. "I'll stop fighting you on this. You want in, you're in." That didn't mean I wouldn't ask Miller to stick to him like white on rice. "You need to go home, get your family packed. Wu will meet you there and take you to Haven and get them settled. He'll bring you wherever the coterie is when you're done."

"Are you sure this reasonable act isn't a trick? You're not still trying to ditch me?"

"I'm tempted." I wouldn't lie about that. "But you'd just get yourself killed if I don't keep an eye on you."

"How does it feel?" He stood then offered me a hand up. "The role reversal?"

"I'm not training you." I thought about it, frowned. "Guess I am sort of training you. I don't like it much. I prefer the days when I came to you with my questions. Your answers didn't always make sense, and there was that one time you came to work dressed as a banana, but you did your best."

"That's the first rule of leadership," he commiserated. "Trying to foist responsibility onto another person. See, kid? You've got this in the bag."

From the corner of my eye, I spotted Wu standing apart from the crowd, the wash of red lights painting his face crimson. I pointed him out to Rixton and set that ball rolling.

"We'll make him pay for this." Miller looped an arm around my shoulders, and I leaned against him, soaking up the coterie bond. "I swear it."

Because he was Miller, and I could ask him without shame, I did. "Where's Cole?"

"He's going to offer to fly the Rixtons to Haven. If the missus is resistant to that idea, then he's going to provide cover for them while Wu drives her minivan." He squeezed my shoulder. "We'll get them there safely."

"Too bad Haven isn't big enough for everyone." Sorrow burned through my chest, a slow ache that poisoned. "I would put them all in a bubble if I could."

The town, the human race, the world. I wasn't sure what I meant, but I trusted Miller to understand.

"No bubble is large enough to contain them all." Thom stepped up to my side. "We'll just have to make the world safe enough no bubbles are needed." A frown marred his forehead. "Except for those catnip bubbles you sometimes blow for me. Those will always be appreciated."

Making a mental note to buy another bottle of them, I pulled away from Miller to kiss Thom on the cheek. There was a simple happiness in being around him that made me understand why Conquest was a crazy cat lady. He was the most feline of the coterie, and his purrs soothed better than a cup of chamomile tea.

"Santiago?" I didn't see him in the crowd. "Portia?"

"He's in a vehicle heading this way. Portia is driving while he monitors the Malakhim situation." Miller waved to an unfamiliar face and guided me in that direction. "They'll be here soon."

We trudged through the muck to greet a thin male with a receding hairline who managed to look happy in spite of our circumstances. It was awe, I knew, from beholding Conquest. But that made me dislike him on principle. I couldn't stomach his smile against the backdrop of wailing voices, police radios, and sirens.

"Mistress, it's a pleasure to meet you at last." His bony knees quivered, threatening to buckle. "I heard you were rallying your supporters, and I wish to add my clan's might to your numbers."

"Thank you." I forced out a polite tone. "You can start by tracking the Malakhim who did this."

"We have eyes on them." He bobbed his head. "We didn't realize their intent here until it was too late."

Hearing he tried bumped him up in my estimation. "I doubt anyone could have anticipated this."

As the words left my mouth, Thom looked at me, nodded. He wanted me to take them to heart, to accept and believe I was blameless. Clever kitty. I couldn't very well dispute my advice while the guy I was attempting to soothe stood an arm's length away.

"Misha." A short female in a powder-blue jumpsuit burst through the wall of milling people, aiming straight for us. "They're on the move." Her panted breaths worked on the zipper covering her ample breasts, each inhale forcing it down a few clicks until I saw she was naked beneath the thin jacket. That, or she went bra-less, a dangerous proposition for a female of her cup size. "They're heading toward the outskirts of town."

Ice slicked my spine. "Which way?"

"Northeast." She cocked her head, listening to something beyond my hearing. "There are a few older homes in the area, all with large tracts of land." Her eyes widened. "There's a commune of some kind."

"The farmhouse." I rubbed my eyes, smearing soot like war paint over my face. "The Malakhim are going after the enclave." I looked to Miller and Thom. "Ezra punished me, and now it's Wu's turn."

"We have a clan of thirty in the area," the female said. "They're tracking the Malakhim with orders to engage if they assume battle formation. Human lives will be protected at all costs."

Now I was the one smiling wide, standing out. This was music to my ears. A clan of charun who valued human life, who wanted to join me because our views aligned.

"Cole and Wu have their hands full." I paced between my coterie and the others. "Santiago and Portia won't arrive for a bit. There's only the three of us. We're it." I slid a glance toward our new allies. "And you, of course."

"We understand coterie is family to you." Wonder shone through the male's voice, and it hit me. The root of his awe wasn't in meeting Conquest. It was in meeting *me*. The abnormality masquerading as cadre. "It's only right that you would prefer to have them at your back. We're unknowns, and we must prove our loyalty to you. Let us begin that process now. Come. We will lead you to the Malakhim."

"I know the way."

It was time to go home.

I had no concept of how the title of host applied to the Malakhim until I beheld their formation from the ground. Looking up, the sky was clotted with winged humanoid figures, most dressed in white, with varying shades of golden blond hair and luminous blue eyes. Weapons strapped to backs, swords clutched in hands, quivers rattling with arsenals of arrows.

I felt small, insignificant, overshadowed by the aerial army come to return my first real home and Wu's family to dust.

But more than that, I felt pissed. And a pissed-off female defending her home was mightier than the sword, or so I had to believe.

"How far to the farmhouse?" Miller crept through the underbrush beside me. "We're almost to the head of the host."

"Ten minutes." I calculated the distance by the bend of a familiar pine. "We're not going to beat them."

"No." He kept pushing himself, harder, faster. "We won't."

Thom, used to playing scout, shifted into his cat form. After I threatened to collar and leash him to keep him close, he elected to jump onto my shoulders and curl around my neck, securing himself with his claws. The message was clear: *You want me to stick close, you've got to carry me.*

Thanks to the extra weight — Thom and I seriously needed to chat about how many mice he was eating — I was panting hard and tasting blood in the back of my throat when we hit the edge of the rolling lawn leading to the farmhouse.

Heartbeat pounding in my ears, I soaked in the picturesque setting. The old clapboard house we really should have painted a few years back, the gleam from the new bay window, the lighter boards alternating weathered ones where the porch had been rebuilt.

I absorbed every detail, committed it to memory, a snapshot in my head, and before I could tell my childhood goodbye, they were upon us.

"Get to the house," I snapped. "The enclave's safety comes first."

There were kids in there. *Pregnant* women. Elders too.

The enclave males stood on the lawn behind Knox, faces grim and eyes tight, ready for battle.

The women able to fight flanked Kimora, their teeth bared and fists clenched, eager to draw first blood.

But that had already happened, a few miles away, as far as I was concerned.

"Thom, you're with me." I ripped the cat off my shoulder and tossed him. The cat twisted midair, landing in a crouch as a man. "We'll evacuate the farmhouse. Miller, provide cover."

A whistling noise preceded the first arrow strike. An Onca yards away jolted, impaled by the wooden shaft, and went down on her knees.

"Damn it," I snarled. "Goddamn it."

We passed through the lines, and I met Knox's gaze for a frozen second. He didn't have to speak for me to hear his plea to take care of his people.

The front door of the farmhouse swung open, allowing us to enter at a run and slam it shut behind us, for all the good the thin wood would do.

"We have to go." I counted children, my stomach sinking as the number grew higher. "Leave everything. The Malakhim are outside. We have to run."

Mothers gathered their infants. Expectant mothers gritted their teeth. Toddlers were slung across shoulders or encouraged to hang off backs. I spotted Lira and her mother. She had quite the brood. As the oldest, Lira would be on her own, and her short legs would never keep pace.

"I don't have any chocolate on me." I knelt beside her when her eyes brightened in recognition. Wu had gotten the kid hooked on sweets her parents frowned on, but desperate times called for grand promises. "I'll give you a whole bar if you can hold onto me long enough to get somewhere safe."

"I can do that." She made grabby hands at me. "I'm a big girl. Just ask my mommy."

"Mommy, do you mind?" I hadn't met her mother, but it was obvious who she belonged to when the female almost fainted at having her child singled out by me. "My life for hers, I swear it."

"I'll hold you to your vow," the female promised, hope and terror clashing in her eyes.

"Come on." I hauled Lira onto a chair at the kitchen table. "Hop on piggyback style."

The first time we met, she told me her father called her Monkey. I could see why. She climbed me like a vine, swinging from my shoulders to peer at my face, her eyes wild with excitement.

Her mother caught me staring at the closed door and read my inner conflict over fleeing the battle. "You're too important to lose."

Until she pointed it out, I hadn't realized I was running scenarios in my head. Leaving the Oncas and Cuprina to fight my battles for me didn't sit right, and I didn't even have a name for our newest allies, but they were here of their own free will. This was their choice, their fight. Figureheads had power. Without me, the resistance would crumble, and the world would spin until the next ascension, doomed to repeat the cycle for all time.

"Move out." It was all I had left to say. "We'll head to Cypress Swamp. There's a bunkhouse there. It's full, but we have airboats. We'll use them to transport the children somewhere safe."

As soon as Wu told me where that might be. Aside from Haven, a leak meant nowhere known to them would be secure.

Searching the room to see where Thom had gone, I found him carrying three laughing children who were scratching the furry black ears he had sprouted to amuse them. He crossed to me, took in Lira, and smiled. "Don't feel bad. I lived among them for a time, and the children favored me."

"Until you mentioned it, I didn't realize this was a popularity contest." On reflex, I reached out to tickle the nearest child, much to his delight. "Hold on tight to Thom. We're going on an adventure."

The children were young enough to be fooled into believing the shouts and grunts from outside were part of the game, the ones being carried at least. There were older kids, teens, and their eyes held adult knowledge.

The last mother grabbed the final child, and I led them out the backdoor and into the cover of the trees. It burned to know they were all winged, that flight was so much easier and safer, so much faster. But the Malakhim had wings too, and they trained on how best to use them to inflict maximum damage.

Behind us, Miller took up the rear guard. I was forced to let him set the pace to match the slowest of our group, a female who looked seconds away from giving birth. With that fear lodged in my gut, I chose the gentlest paths, the ones Dad and I troubled to keep clear of debris to make for easy walking for me and easy hunting for him.

We passed the spot where I encountered my first Drosera, and where I first met the dragon.

The trip to Cypress Swamp would be long and ugly, and we only had so much time before the women tired, the babies started crying, and the kids began complaining. I wanted to put as much distance between us and the farmhouse as possible before that happened.

With Lira a warm weight on my back, her touch prickling down my spine, I cut a path toward Death.

Miller had the hindsight to text Portia and Santiago our new location, and we hoped to meet them at the bunkhouse. Wu and Cole were still MIA, I assumed delivering the Rixtons to Haven, meaning Rixton wasn't here to lighten the mood with jokes inappropriate for young ears. Then again, that might be for the best.

"Sister." Death stepped from behind a cypress tree into our path. "I wasn't expecting you." She examined the ragtag band of refugees staggering behind me. "Your mate was here not so long ago. He reclaimed the pod for safekeeping."

There was no time for relief, not with so many other children still at risk, but it was good to know Phoebe was out of the crosshairs for the moment.

"We need a place to stay for a few hours. Portia and Santiago ought to be here in thirty minutes or less. I'm not sure when to expect Cole and Wu." Rixton I didn't mention since his name would mean nothing to her, and I didn't want to pick a fight about the value of human life when all of ours were on the line. "We should be out of your hair before dark if we're lucky."

"This is your home," Death said with a welcoming smile. "Do with it as you will."

"Thank you." I jerked my head, ushering the females toward the pier. The most heavily pregnant ones took the patio chairs. The rest sat with their sore feet dangling in the murky water. Janardan, upon spotting guests, rallied his children, who rushed to offer the females bottled water and the kids snack-size bags of chips. "Have you heard the news from Canton?"

"Janardan saw a news report on the tablet." She frowned as she spoke, unsure she had it right. "He said the police station was reduced to ash." The lines on her forehead deepened. "You worked there, as a law enforcer, correct?"

"A cop, yes." I didn't ask if fatalities had been tallied yet. I would hear the news soon enough. It would be broadcast on a loop until avoiding it became impossible. "You have more experience playing this game than I do. How would you strike back? How would you hurt the one responsible?"

"You're thinking of the wrong sister." She chuckled softly. "War would have been the one to ask. She thrived on revenge, and look where it got her."

The jab sliced deep, as it was meant to, but I was already bleeding from a hundred tiny cuts.

Placing her hands on my shoulders, contact which made me break a sweat after recalling how War met her end, Death advised, "The best revenge is a life well-lived. Given who we are, our expected lifespans once we reach Earth, we have so very little time, don't you think?"

"I can't kick back and enjoy what's left. There's too little of it." I cupped a hand to my ear. "Don't you hear the clock ticking? I do."

"Survive." Fierce, she held my gaze. "Thrive." She lowered her arms. "That's the worst punishment you could dole out to any enemy."

"Thanks." I managed to keep from rolling my eyes. "That's ... great advice."

Beaming at me, she set out for the pier. "Our philosophies aren't so different, yours and mine."

On that, I couldn't agree. I wanted blood. I had a taste for it now. I couldn't let Ezra get away with what he had done.

"I need to make contact with my team." I took out my phone. "I'll join you in a minute."

Santiago answered on the second ring. "What?"

"You have the best manners. They never cease to amaze."

"Busy here. What do you want?"

"That's better." I swept my gaze over the exhausted masses. "The enclave is secure, for now. We're at the bunkhouse."

"What?"

"You keep saying that." I frowned. "What is your problem? I just told you mine."

"We're ten minutes from the farmhouse. No one told us the party switched locations."

"The Malakhim attacked," I said slowly. "Miller, Thom, and I evacuated the vulnerables to the bunkhouse. It was the closest, safest place I could think of to stash them, but we need alternatives yesterday. This is the first place they'll look."

Thom deposited his charges then returned to me. "What's wrong?"

"Hold on," I told Santiago then addressed Thom. "Santiago didn't get Miller's message. They're en route to the farmhouse, not here." Meaning help was farther away than I would like. Being on the water only increased the impression we were sitting ducks. "Check with Miller. See if the text shows as clearing. Find out if there was a response."

A niggling sense of doubt was worming its way into my brain, a worry I couldn't pinpoint. I was missing something. Something big. There was a connection here, on the edge of my memory, but I couldn't pull it into focus.

Thom went in search of Miller while I gazed off into the swamp, in the direction of the seal between terrenes.

"The message shows as read," Miller said, coming up behind me. "There's no response, but I wouldn't have expected one."

"I don't like this." A fist of dread squeezed my heart. "We're vulnerable here, and we're isolated from the rest of the coterie."

"Death is here." The fine lines bracketing his mouth hinted my paranoia was creeping up on him. "Her mate and coterie are here. We've got backup if — "

Death was here. So was Janardan. So was I. Only Cole missing prevented a clean sweep, a total coup.

"I've done a stupid, stupid thing." I whirled toward Miller, panic fluttering along my nerve endings. "I've put myself in the same place as Death. One strike here could wipe out the entire cadre."

"We can load up the enclave, get them on the airboats." He half turned, searching for Thom, the only other pilot we had on hand. "There are other places they can hide, farther away from the epicenter."

"Where?" I hadn't meant to snap at him, but I couldn't shake the horrible feeling that old debts were coming due. "We're running out of hidey-holes." Opening Haven's doors ahead of schedule would jeopardize Dad, Sherry, and Nettie. Ezra was hunting these people. He was bent on eradicating them. He wouldn't stop until he punished Wu in the worst way left to him — erasing all traces of his mortal wife by wiping out their bloodline. "We need to move, and Death does too. Her coterie won't be safe here."

A sudden wind blew my hair away from my face, and chills dappled my arms in response.

The old-growth trees creaked, their branches rustling. Water rippled, debris skating farther out into the swamp. And overhead . . . the sky turned black.

Hundreds of Malakhim swarmed above us, blotting out the sun.

They had followed us. I expected some would. The scouts must have turned back to rejoin the host, point them in our direction. Maybe they had already been heading here. Maybe Ezra had pieced together enough about me to know where I would go to ground and who I would take with me. He captured Kapoor, tortured him. He could have told Ezra anything, everything. The NSB had files on me for days.

"What do we do?" I looked to Miller. "What the hell do we do?"

The end was upon us, and backup was nowhere in sight.

"We do the best we can, for as long as we can, and hope for the best."

Dread soured my stomach, and I screamed to the enclave, "Get inside. Get inside now."

Arrows rained down on the pier, peppering the bunkhouse, and turning the slowest of our group, the female primed to give birth at any moment, into a pincushion.

Thom sprinted for her before I could scream at him to take cover and hauled her into the relative safety of the bunkhouse.

I promised him, and myself, he would never get hurt again on my watch.

I promised, and I kept my promises.

Rage that the Malakhim would jeopardize that vow blanketed my vision, turning it a vibrant crimson.

Blinking, I couldn't shake the haze, and that meant one thing — I was about to go dragon on their asses. That meant Wu was right. The dragon was a biological function. Even with Conquest locked away, I had access to that part of me. Too bad the chances of me retaining control were fifty-fifty. I really, really hoped I didn't eat anyone important.

Without the cold place buffeting the change, I kept a clear head, even as that head rose a dozen feet above the ground. Higher. I was in control. Total control. For the first time, the dragon felt like an extension of me rather than an intruder. This must be how Cole felt all the time — invincible.

The smile Miller wore was one I had never seen on his face, and I was surprised how well it fit him.

An instant later, he swelled into his charun form, and a massive snake lashed its tail through the trees.

Quick as lightning, he sped toward the bunkhouse, to defend the enclave.

Since taking to the air was a no-go, I climbed the tallest tree capable of supporting my weight and used my whiplike tail to knock Malakhim out of the sky. Their arrows bounced off my scales, and I didn't let them get close enough to find out if the same was true for their swords. Cole had been injured with bullets the night I first met his dragon, so I wasn't invulnerable in this form, even if it turned out females were more heavily armored, as sometimes happened in nature. While it might not kill me, it wouldn't feel great, and it would slow me down enough for the Malakhim to finish the job.

Too bad there were no dragon-size mirrors. For once, I would have loved to take a look at myself, compare my form to Cole's.

And that was the panic talking. Vanity would have to wait. I had to focus. Push out the inane thoughts meant to soothe or distract. I needed my head on right if I wanted to keep it on my shoulders.

Through the leaves, I spotted Miller striking, capturing Malakhim in his jaws and gulping them whole. I tried not to watch the struggle as they lodged in his throat. He didn't seem concerned, so I couldn't let myself be either.

No sign of Thom, but that was a good thing. It meant he was inside, working on the wounded, and safe.

Free to refocus on the swarm buzzing around me, I lashed out with my tail, knocking three soldiers into each other and tumbling them into the trees along with a fourth.

My endurance in this body was phenomenal, but I couldn't hold the line against so many for long. A few were skirting me now, diving for Miller. Once enough of them got on the roof, they would infiltrate the building, and we would lose.

"We must take the fight to them," Death called from below me. "It's the only way."

The rumbling groan issuing from my throat sounded close enough to *what the actual hell* to work for me.

"You can fly, Luce." Her eyes burned, dark voids with red embers in their centers. "It's muscle memory for that body. Trust me." She reached out her hand. "We must defend our people, or they will perish."

Using my tail, I coiled it around her offered wrist and hauled her up to me. She settled on my back in the spot where I rode Cole, making me think she — or we — had done this before. I flinched as a fresh volley of arrows whistled through the sky, but they disintegrated, rotted clean away, before touching her.

I gulped hard and tried not to think too much about what she could do to me with the same ease.

"You're high enough." She peered around me. "Spread your wings and leap. The wind will catch you. You'll glide, even if you can't achieve lift."

I might have argued with her, as much as I was able, if I hadn't spotted movement behind Miller, near the rear of the bunkhouse.

Lira.

She had taken a sword from a body or a cache in the house, and she stood with the weapon in her hands, ready to defend the others with her life.

A deafening roar exploded from my throat, and I lunged for her, wings spread as far as I could stretch them. I glided, as Death said I would, but at this rate, I wouldn't save Lira. I would squish her flat and maybe topple the bunkhouse too.

Muscles screaming from the strain, I managed to backbeat enough to scoop Lira up with my tail and deposit her in Death's lap. The roof scratched my stomach, but I made it over the top. I wouldn't last in the air. This body might be made for flight, and it might remember the mechanics, but it hadn't flown in too long. I was too weak to maintain without Conquest's power boosting me.

"Get me to them, and I will kill them." Death yanked on my mane. "You can do this. Just a moment longer. Hold your position."

I hadn't meant to slow enough for the Malakhim to catch us. I was that tired, that winded, that I couldn't have escaped them if our lives depended on it. Which, of course, they did.

"A little closer," Death murmured, and I remembered what a patient hunter she could be. "There."

From the corner of my eye, I watched her reach up like she would clasp forearms with the soldier above her. He startled at her bare hand, and it cost him. She rested her palm on top of the fingers clutching the dagger he hadn't thought to use, and the light went out of his eyes. He dropped like a stone, his corpse splashing into the water.

Mild panic tingled down my spine, raising nubby spikes, but Death stroked them smooth again.

"I won't hurt the child." She sounded amused when she added, "Or you, sister."

Chest heaving, muscles trembling, I reached for the sky. The Malakhim sensed weakness and crowded in, not close enough for me to bite or claw, but enough I had to veer to avoid them or risk falling. They were herding me toward the swamp, clocking my decline until it was obvious I would smash into a copse of ancient cypress trees then plummet into the water. We would all be sitting ducks then.

"Hold tight, little one." Death pressed her lips to the dagger in Lira's hand, and blood trickled down her chin. "Nick anyone who gets too close. My kiss is death, and you carry it with you."

"Okay." Lira's voice didn't tremble. "I'll be careful of the sharp end."

Clearly, Death had no experience dealing with living children. Her offspring were dead, reanimated somehow. Giving small kids poisoned blades and trusting them not to kill you, or themselves, with it by accident was overreaching. But I couldn't find the oxygen to grumble a disagreement.

"Hold steady." Death stood on my spine, her toes digging into my scales, and raised her arms. "I am Death, and you are mine. I claim you, as is my right." Springing onto the back of a Malakhim who had flown too close, she leapt from soldier to soldier, dropping them like flies with a touch. "You cannot defeat Death. I am inevitable."

But she wasn't indestructible. Obviously. Or this terrene would be lousy with the remnants from her namesake's previous cadres.

Lira held on tight, one fist twined in my mane, the other gripping a weapon no child ought to wield.

A sharp cry pierced my ears, and I twisted to find a spear jutting from Death's shoulder. She fought to dislodge it even as the soldier beneath her plummeted in empty-eyed silence.

Maybe it was a dormant sibling bond roaring to life, or maybe it was the simple fact Death had helped when she could have elected to sit on the sidelines. She was aquatic, and so were her coterie. They could have fled underwater faster than the Malakhim could trace them from above. But she had stayed. She had called me sister and meant it. And I couldn't let her die, no matter how inevitable Death might be.

With no better options, I used my tail to encircle Lira, swung her around to my chest, then caught her in my clawed hand. She was safer there, where I could protect her and my tender belly, than on my back. The child laughed and brandished her dagger while I tried valiantly not to get cut or stabbed with its sharp tip.

Groaning from the effort, I pumped my wings harder, not bothering to go higher. Just closer. Death rode the fallen soldier like a surfboard, no longer struggling to remove the spear but bracing for grisly impact. I flew as hard, as fast, as my flagging body allowed, but Death's fingers slid over the tip of my wing without purchase. Gritting my teeth, I whipped my tail after her, snagging her wrist in a wrap tight enough to do Cole proud.

Bone snapped, and Death cried out in pain, but her eyes were grateful when they met mine.

I glided over the bunkhouse and dropped Death on the pier. She turned the fall into a practiced roll and came up cradling her wrist. A half turn kept me from flattening Lira as I released her in the space Miller had cleared around the front door. But I was done. I couldn't lift my wings again. They weighed too much. A headache pounded in my temples, and my tongue went dry. For some reason my stomach hurt. Not hunger. Not overindulgence. Just pain. Searing, burning, almost like . . .

The last thing I saw before slamming into the water were the fat tears streaking Lira's windburned face as she stared in horror at the knife in her hand, and then in misery at me.

CHAPTER TWENTY-TWO

———◆———

I woke on a battlefield littered with corpses. Feathers drifted on the air, and the reek of death stuffed my nose. Sour blood caked me, and I wish I could say it turned my stomach rather than made me hungry.

"She's coming around." Thom's gentle hands touched my face. "How do you feel?"

"Did we win?" I groped with a very human hand until a wide palm clasped mine. "Cole." I hadn't realized I was searching for him. It had been instinct. "Hey."

"We won," Miller said from my left. "It cost us."

The enclave weren't my people, but the news still hit hard. "How many?"

"Three." He worked his jaw like he wanted to say more but had decided against it. "Death lost two members of her coterie. She's in mourning. We're on our own for the next seven days, long enough for her to observe Otillian funeral rites."

"She saved us." I clutched Cole tighter. "We would have been wiped out if she hadn't pitched in."

"For that, I'm grateful." He kissed my knuckles. "I should have been here."

"You got the Rixtons to safety." I attempted to shove upright then wished I hadn't as the world sloshed. "Phoebe too. Death told me you came for her."

"I took your advice." He attempted a smile. "Your father will protect her."

"My ... " I squinted harder, like that might boost my hearing. "What?"

"As far as he's concerned, Phoebe is his granddaughter."

That was guaranteed to have him polishing his shotgun in preparation for future boyfriends. "You told him Phoebe is our daughter?"

"She *is* our daughter." Cole helped me sit upright while I regained my equilibrium. "Your relationship with her is complicated. His will be too. I didn't think it was wise to tell my mate's father she wasn't the mother of our child."

"That ... sounds worse than it is." I had lost all perspective. "I will agree Dad wouldn't have taken you stepping out on me lightly, even if you technically aren't. Haven't?" I leaned my forehead on his shoulder. "My head hurts."

"I should have consulted you first." He raked his fingers through my hair. "I didn't anticipate him meeting us." He kissed my temple. "When he showed up expecting you, I didn't know what to tell him."

"I suggested the truth." Wu walked up from behind me. "But you're the one who wanted transparency."

Biting the inside of my cheek to keep from growling, I had to admit he was right. "He would find out about her eventually. This isn't how I planned on having the talk with him, but maybe it's all for the best. After all, you did it for me, and I didn't have to be there to witness it."

Once I was sure my stomach wouldn't invert when I stood, I got to my feet and surveyed the carnage. So much senseless violence. Life spilled in red rivulets at my feet. Such a waste. The Malakhim had been raised to hate, nurtured on vengeance, and that upbringing had killed them every bit as much as teeth or claws.

Checking on my coterie heartened me.

Miller wasn't looking so hot. I couldn't begin to imagine how many Malakhim he had swallowed to prevent them from entering the bunkhouse, but he was standing. The indigestion would pass.

Despite being coated in blood from his head to his shoes, Thom didn't have a scratch on him. I had done that much right at least.

Rixton was standing at the edge of the pier, a distant expression on his face, a stiff set to his shoulders, but soothing him would have to wait.

Guilt throat-punched me a second later, and I couldn't believe I had forgotten to ask. "How is Lira?" I touched my shoulder. "Death? She had a . . . spear? Lance? Giant arrow thing? Sticking out of her."

"I treated Death," Thom reassured me. "She'll recover in a day or two."

The fact no one rushed to reassure me about Lira left me cold. I searched each of their faces, waiting.

Santiago, who I hadn't noticed lurking in the water, was the one who let me have it.

"Lira's parents are dead. Her mother was struck by an arrow while she was helping with the wounded. Her father was shot through the heart during the farmhouse skirmish."

"That explains why she took up the dagger." I scrubbed my hands over my face. "No wonder the kid was primed for a fight. Her parents were murdered." I sought out Wu, found him pale-faced and grim. "I'm sorry for your loss."

Wu managed a nod, but his expression didn't change.

"She's got family to take her in, right?" I rubbed my arms, and dirt flaked off in handfuls. "She isn't alone?"

"The enclave believes it requires a community to raise a child," Thom answered to spare Wu. "She is with her aunt, uncle, and cousins. They'll take her in, love her like their own."

"We need to establish a new safehouse." As the dizziness cleared, I got my brain back on track. "The survivors need shelter."

"I'm sending them overseas." Wu watched a single white feather, speckled with crimson, dance in a whirl of leaves. "I own a small castle in Scotland. It was a gift from *heri*, General Valero. We were careful. It will take a while for Father to ferret out the deed." He lifted his foot when it danced closer ... and crushed it flat. "He won't look away from the Deep South. Canton is the epicenter." He scraped the crud off his shoe. "The seal is here. Your home is here. It will end here."

Santiago's hiss of breath drew my attention back to the water. "We've got movement near the breach site." His fervent tapping on the planks led me to believe he had left a tablet within easy reach. "Pulling up camera four now. Camera five. Camera — " He bared his teeth. "There you are."

Exhaustion weighted my limbs, but I started toward him. "Who?"

"An unidentified Drosera." He zoned out for a few seconds. "Winding back the video. Back, back, back." He smiled from ear to ear. "Clever, aren't you? Hiding out of range of the doppler sensors."

"Are you done talking to yourself or ... ?"

"The Drosera has been dormant in the swamp, watching for hours. It didn't trip any of my sensors, so the cameras didn't activate."

"What are the odds of a random Drosera not bumping into the minefield you rigged out there?"

"None to none." He stared at the tablet, his face lit by the screen. "Whoever this is knew we had sensors in the water and had an idea of how to trigger surveillance that would let us know they were there when they were ready."

"Let's greet our guest." I waited for Cole to join me. "Fly in or airboat?"

"Let's take the boat." He rolled a shoulder, grimaced when it made a popping noise. "We've all exceeded our limits today. We need all the help we can get."

While Cole and Miller readied the airboat, I stood on the pier with Rixton. The silence between us pressed in on me, his inattention almost a blessing. Until I couldn't take it anymore.

"The first time I saw Maggie ... after ... she was sitting right here." I scuffed a boot over the planks. "I don't know why I told you that. I wasn't going anywhere with it. Just a random thought."

He made a humming sound that was drowned out by the buzzing motor of an approaching airboat.

Black, streamlined, shining. It was the new boat, the stealthy one. Cole was at the helm, and he bumped its edge gently against the pier. Thom leapt on without help. Miller, ever the gentleman, took my arm to hand me across.

Glancing over my shoulder, I noticed Rixton hadn't moved. "You coming?"

"I'll stay here." He shook his head, eyed the bunkhouse. "Help the remaining survivors onto the second boat. You were unconscious during the first load. They ought to be here any minute to pick up the rest."

"All right." I got the feeling he needed to help them, to be among the living, after so much death.

"Wait for me," Portia yelled as she took a running jump and landed on the deck in a Thom-worthy crouch. "Phew. Just made it."

Looking her over to make sure she and Maggie were okay, I asked, "Find anything?"

"The Malakhim have withdrawn from the area. I estimate

two-thirds of their force was depleted. We don't have firm numbers on the exact size of the host, so it's difficult to gauge how hard this loss will hit Ezra."

"Not half as hard as it hit us." Each member of the enclave would be mourned. I doubted the same could be said for Ezra's legion. "Santiago? You coming?"

"I texted Miller the coordinates." He eased back into the water. "I'll follow."

Once his head was good and underwater, I muttered, "He knows that just makes me wonder what he is that much more."

Portia chuckled, her eyes dancing with amusement. It should have been obscene, the contrast between her easy laughter and the bodies stacked behind us, but I had been a cop long enough to know people cope with horror in myriad ways. Laughter, snark, anger, sorrow. All were valid choices. Whatever eased the burden. Whatever made the senseless make sense. Whatever dulled the images that danced behind your eyes when they closed at night. As long as it hurt no one, there was no wrong answer.

The airboat glided over the water like butter across a hot skillet, and soon we spotted the spine of an animal too large to pass for an American alligator. Miller leapt into the water, and the head of a giant snake reared over us, fangs glistening. Between him, the boat, and Santiago, we cornered the Drosera.

Since it hadn't shown aggression, we returned the favor. Odds were good Sariah had positioned a scout in the area to keep tabs on Death. I wasn't a fan of being spied on. The fact she might know about the pod, what was in the pod, chilled me. Phoebe might be out of reach for the moment, but Sariah was cut from the same cloth as her mother. If she needed leverage, a child gave her plenty.

The unformed thought from earlier returned with a vengeance. The text Santiago hadn't received would have turned the tide of the battle against me and my coterie if Death hadn't joined the fight. Coincidence? Electronic malfunction? Somehow, I doubted it.

"Shift," I called to it. "Let's talk this out like civilized folks."

A safe distance away, the Drosera shifted into Sariah, her wrists uncomfortably bare.

Shock at seeing her doing her own dirty work numbed to a cold certainty that whatever brought her here was nothing good.

"How are you so hard to kill?" She looped her arm companionably around the knee of a bald cypress tree to keep herself afloat. "Conquest usually dies first. First in, first out. Did anyone tell you that? By surviving for this long, you're beating the odds in more ways than one."

Slow halting steps guided me to the end of the boat. "How are you enjoying your freedom?"

"How are you enjoying your captivity?" Her lip curled at the sight of me wearing the bangles. "Though, I suppose, Cole might have developed all sorts of dominance fetishes over the centuries. Have you slept together wearing them? How did that work? When he said to come for him, did you do it because he'd worked you up to it or because he'd given the order?"

"I'm not comfortable discussing my sex life with my niece. Let's keep this conversation PG."

"Prude." She clucked her tongue. "Conquest mated Cole in the middle of cadre meetings. Trust me, there's not much about your male I don't know." She raked her gaze over him. "Or haven't seen."

Rage kindled in my center, cold and burning, and all mine. "Why are you here?"

"I came to watch the show." Her cheeky smile chilled me. "You really need to work on your technique. You almost crashed a half dozen times. You resembled a drunk chicken more than a dragon."

"Chickens can't fly."

"Exactly."

"I don't see any popcorn." Or any backup, Drosera or otherwise. "How did you know where and when to be?"

"Lucky guess?"

"Your luck ran out when Luce gave you a second chance." Cole stared her down. "Who's your source?"

"*The* source." The amusement on her face shifted to icy calculation. "Ezra."

"He hates charun." I snorted in disbelief. "He wouldn't align with one."

"I came to you with an offer of alliance," she reminded me. "I told you then I had seen what lay beyond this terrene. I wanted no part of it then, and I want no part of it now. How do you think I found out? Who do you think told me? I went sniffing after the source of power on this terrene, as I have done for Mother on all other worlds, and rumors of Ezra are what I found."

She flicked duckweed off her arm, giving me a second to absorb the fact she had known damn well who I was talking about when I set her task but lied to my face about it. She had wanted to have her cake and eat it too.

"I don't believe in gods," she said. "I've seen no evidence of them in any civilization we've visited. Unless their divine plan was to universally let us wreck and ruin their flock. Faith is a lie, but most lies are rooted in truth. I just had to dig deeper to find it, that's all."

"You found Ezra." Doubt coated my tone. "And he — what? Took a meeting with you?"

The figment I had searched for my entire remembered life, and she just stumbled across him? Granted, she had been hunting the apex predator in this terrene. Without knowing it, I had been tracking his son. That was the whole problem. All I had was a name, and it had gotten me nowhere. I had been exhausting human leads, through human means of investigation. She had a leg up on me there. She had known he was charun, and that's how she researched him. Considering I hadn't had a clue about my heritage, I had done the best I could given my resources, but she had lifetimes of practice doing her mother's dirty work.

"Can you picture me in a pencil skirt?" She glanced down her stolen body. "Actually, there was this one host. Legs for days. I wouldn't have tossed her body if I hadn't needed this brain, but human technology is rather advanced for a bunch of monkeys. I had to adapt and quickly."

Santiago got there ahead of me. "Your host was a programmer."

"The best." She tapped her temple. "Too bad knowledge degrades over time. I had to act fact, memorize as much as possible, before that little voice screaming in my head went silent."

"You intercepted the text from Miller." The bigger picture loomed, and I felt like an idiot for not seeing it sooner. "You hacked the feeds the night Death killed War."

"Turns out you don't have to tell the truth while wearing the bangles unless you're explicitly ordered to be honest." She shrugged. "It's not my fault you missed an opportunity."

"You're big on casting blame as long as it doesn't land on you, huh?"

"You don't have the stomach to do what it takes," she shot back. "This is how the game is played, Luce."

"This isn't a game," I snarled. "It's my life."

"And it's pathetic." She slapped the water in front of her. "You're ambitionless. You've lost sight of our mission."

Our mission.

Cops had to trust their gut or be willing to pay the price for ignoring it, and it looked like my tab was coming due.

"You led your mother into a trap." How I mustered surprise, I couldn't begin to guess. "You killed her."

"No, Death killed her. Sibling bonds don't mean much to either of us, but the Drosera are a dim lot. Generations of inbreeding will do that. They wouldn't have followed me if I killed Mother. Neither would War's allies on this terrene. I needed her blood on someone else's hands before I could take the reins."

"Ezra hates charun," I said again, firmer. "I don't believe for a hot minute that he met with you."

Someone with enough talent not to leave fingerprints for Santiago to track could stick her fingers into all sorts of pies without alerting us. Including our databases. There were files on Ezra, and on Wu. On their familial connection.

Wu, who downright loved humans and had roleplayed Ezra before.

Wu, whose involvement would explain the enclave leak in the worst possible way.

Damn it.

There was no way he would stoop so low. No way. No possible way he would align with her.

Was there?

He was a liar, a good one. A professional one, in fact. But who had he lied to this time? Her? Or me?

I was a sucker for a hard luck story. The human wife, the demi offspring, would appeal to my protective instincts where humans were concerned. Had he invented a wife? His kids? The enclave's origin story?

No. Well, yes. He would lie if it suited him. But that depth of grief, of guilt couldn't be faked. I might be taken in, but Cole would have scented Wu's emotions. It all but made charun lie detectors. He would have suspected Wu was being less than honest instead of offering him solace. That meant — big surprise — Sariah was fibbing to us about her source.

"Not my problem." She released her grip on the cypress knee

and trod water. "I have to go, Auntie. It was nice catching up. I would say it's good to see you survived, but we both know I wouldn't mean it."

"You aren't cadre." I balled my fists. "This isn't your fight."

In giving her a second chance, I had enabled her to realize her dream of usurping her mother.

Sariah wanted to become the next War, and she was well on her way to declaring it between us.

"You denounced Conquest, and that means you're not cadre either." Ripples skated across the murky surface as she sliced her arms. "This ascension is different. *We're* different. One way or another, it ends with us."

As much as I wanted to believe her, I had doubts. Whatever future she imagined wasn't the one I envisioned. I wanted Ezra's head on a pike. I wanted a way to seal the breach sites for good. The charun who lived here could be governed and maintained by the NSB, but this constant upheaval? This battle for ownership of an entire ecosystem and its inhabitants? Charun weren't gods, despite what Ezra might believe, and they shouldn't play at it. It was time for the fate of this terrene to rest in human hands.

"Give me your source." I caught Miller's eye, and he sank lower in the water. "Tell me that, and we'll let you leave in peace."

"As tempting as that offer sounds . . . " She tilted her head. "I'm going to have to pass."

Desperate to buy us more time and answers, I threw out a wild card. "What about Bruster?"

"That one wasn't mine." She frowned. "I didn't hear about it until after."

Meaning there was one more rogue out there killing people only a select few knew I was after. Great.

"Sariah — "

"I brought you a present. Unwrap it. Maybe the answers you

want are inside." A wiggle of her fingers, and she dove beneath the murky surface.

"Go after her." I gestured to Miller. "Don't let her slip away until we nail down who's feeding her intel."

"We've got movement in quadrant four, on camera one." Santiago had bellied up to the boat and toyed with one of his billion tablets on the deck. Seriously. The things were like rabbits. They bred when you weren't looking. "Sariah didn't come alone."

"Drosera never do." I twisted the bangles on my wrists, reassuring myself the coterie had chosen the lesser of two evils when they restrained Conquest over Sariah. "You're fast in the water. Help Miller round up Sariah. We'll go after her backup."

Santiago vanished, leaving only a ripple across the surface to betray his direction.

"Portia, can you read that thing?" I pointed to the tablet. "We need coordinates. Quadrant names and camera numbers don't mean crap to me."

"On it." She scooped up the device then settled in with it balanced on her lap. "Got it."

"Cole." I touched his shoulder. "Let's see how much trouble we can get into before the others return."

A smiled touched his lips, and he kissed me. Hard. "Plenty, I'm sure."

I sank onto the bench across from Thom, who crouched on the deck, eyes sharp in the growing darkness.

He drew in great lungfuls of air, parsing the scents, and his spine went rigid. Our tracker at work.

"What is it?" I ruffled his hair. "You look ready to hiss and spit."

"I recognize this scent." His reflective green irises flashed when the light caught them. "I know it well."

"You can ID our target?" That ought to be cause for celebration, not sorrow. Meaning one thing. "Who betrayed us?"

Gut tight, I half expected him to name Wu. As certain as I had been a moment ago that his backstory was legit, that his grief and drive for vengeance was honest, I braced for yet another loss. The hits just kept coming.

"I didn't betray anyone," a soft voice challenged overhead. "I'm doing this for the enclave."

"Kimora." A stone sank in my gut that kept me rooted to my seat. "Does Knox know what you've been up to?"

"No." A stubborn twist of her lips betrayed her age. "Dad doesn't understand that we can't hide forever. He thinks we'll be safe if we keep to ourselves, but he's wrong. We've lost our home, access to our resources, and now we've lost lives. This will prove to Dad we can't hide behind Adam forever. He can't protect us, not from Ezra. We have to take matters into our own hands."

"You fed Sariah the intel on Ezra."

The relief that Wu hadn't turned on us never arrived. Learning one of his descendants had stabbed him in the back gutted me. He had given so much for them, all in memory of his wife and their daughters. But those figures were historical to the enclave. No one alive had met them, known them, loved them. Only he carried their faces burning in his mind's eye. Blinded by the past, he might be, but he was also their best chance of survival in the long run. His love might have painted a target on their backs, but it had kept them fed, sheltered, and as safe as he could make them for as long as possible.

"I spotted her on our property during a patrol." Kimora kept to the skies, sealing her advantage. "She offered me a trade. I briefed her on this terrene's hierarchy, and she gave me the inside track on the cadre."

"But your collaboration didn't stop there."

"The cadre is different this time. We've all heard the whispers. The elders believe this ascension will be the last. Why shouldn't I do everything in my power to help make it true? Without Otillians battering their way through the seal, the charun population on Earth will stabilize. Ezra won't have any reason to strike us down."

"Except his hatred of humans, demis, and basically any charun not of his terrene. Without the cadre distracting him, dividing his forces, he'll have nothing to do with his endless days except plot how best to exterminate the inferior beings making his paradise imperfect."

A spark of fury kindled in her eyes, rage vibrating through every wingbeat. "You don't know what you're talking about."

Half the time it felt that way, this new world too surreal to be real. "What about Bruster?"

Chin up, defiance clear in the set of her jaw. "What about him?"

"Did you kill him?" I thought it over, frowned. "Sariah knew I was searching for him. She could have let it slip to you. You had to know if we offered him protection in exchange for his cooperation, he might come into contact with you at the enclave, and he would have read the betrayal in your soul. The gig would be up. Your father would cast you out, and all your scheming would have been for nothing."

"He would never cast me out," she snarled. "I'm his daughter."

As far as confessions went, it was hardly a noose by which to hang her, but the rest was damning enough.

Cole brushed his fingers along mine, and I gave a nod. We had found our leak. Now we had to plug it through any means necessary.

"Think of her father," I said under my breath, barely an exhale. "Take her down easy."

With as much effort as I expended sneezing, Cole transformed into his dragon and lunged for the spot where Kimora had gotten comfortable. The boat rocked, water sloshing over the sides, and I held on to the rail until it stilled. By the time I looked up, it was over. Cole had lashed out with his tail, wrapped her up tight, binding her arms to her sides and her wings to her back. She hung limp in his hold, unable to do more than kick her legs.

"Take her to the bunkhouse." I reclaimed my seat. "I'll wait on Santiago and Miller. We'll meet you there."

After he left, and Portia and I were alone, she ceded the body to Maggie.

Mags looped an arm around me, resting her chin on my shoulder. "I'm sorry it was someone you knew."

"Her dad isn't going to take this well. Her father is fiercely protective of her. He's going to fight us." I exhaled. "There will be an internal trial, I'm sure. The enclave is an insular society."

"Can we trust it to be a fair trial when Knox is the leader of the enclave?"

"I don't know, and I hope I'm never in his position and have to find out."

We sat there, listening to frog song, waiting for the others to report back. I had no doubt Sariah had escaped. The guys were good, but she had been planning this. She wouldn't have tripped one of the sensors if she hadn't been anticipating a confrontation and had her route plotted in advance.

A present.

Kimora had been a present. What did you call a peace offering exchanged before going to war?

"I have to give Wu a heads up." I found my phone in my pocket, the screen cracked but the device functional. I punched in his number and waited for him to answer. "Adam."

"You called me Adam." Suspicion clouded his voice. "What's wrong?"

"We found the enclave leak, but you're not going to like it."

"Who?" He bit off the word. "Did you handle them?"

"Uh, no. Cole has her secured at the bunkhouse, which we have to evacuate ASAP." I wet my lips. "It's Kimora. She confessed it all. Sariah must have invited her here for a private meeting then sent us to greet her instead. They've been sharing intel about both sides of the conflict. Any safehouses or plans she knows, we have to assume she told Sariah."

The line went silent, and I rushed to fill it to avoid hearing his grief.

"Sariah hacked the cameras the night Death took out War. She planned and executed a coup to gain control of her mother's coterie and allies. She intercepted a text we sent Santiago and Portia to direct them away from the farmhouse. That means she left fingerprints on our equipment and programs while she was our guest. There's no telling how deep she dug, or what she's done with the information."

"She got what she wanted, or she wouldn't have outed herself."

As much as I hated to throw my family in his face in light of our circumstances, I had to ask, "Is Haven secure? Does Kimora — or Knox — have any reason to suspect it exists? Would it show up in a title search? Tax records? Any official paperwork?"

"Haven was always meant as a gift," he said softly, brokenly. "I kept the details private. No one except my staff, who has no ties to the enclave, are aware it exists. The architect and builders have long since died. Its secret is safe with us."

Sweet relief swept through me, and I sagged against Maggie. "What about the castle?"

"*Heri* meant it as a sanctuary, for me." His voice roughened over the endearment. "No one knows it's mine. I've never seen it. Never taken the vacation she wished for me. There was no time." He went quiet. "I had all the time in the world, and it wasn't enough. Vengeance takes precedent. You're always one step away, one move away from realizing your goal, and you can't relent, or you lose traction. You lose … everything. All over again."

Because he was my partner, and he was in this up to his neck, I confessed. "I worried you might be the leak. You're a double agent. I wasn't sure how many times you would double back."

"I wish I were to blame." His exhale blasted the speaker. "I'll pick up Knox and meet you at the bunkhouse."

"Adam." Using his name twice in one conversation gave it weight. "Are you going to be okay?"

"I haven't been okay in a long time, Luce." His voice warmed a few precarious degrees. "But I'll manage. I always do."

He ended the call before I could think of what else to say.

"He's walking a thin line," Maggie said, stating the obvious. "His balance must be spectacular."

"I worry about him," I confessed. "He was cocky and sure when we first met. Full of himself. The Hole hit him hard. Losing the general wounded him. I don't think he realized he could still hurt that much. All his careful plans are unraveling, and he can't get a grip on any of the strings."

"He does seem to have set himself on a collision course of some kind." She frowned. "I worry more that he's dragging you along for the ride."

"Kimora wants to seal the Otillian breach site. How is what we're doing any different?"

"You want to seize control of this terrene then hand it back to humans, not some deranged all-powerful icon so caught up in his own myth he can't tell fact from fiction. That's a noble thing, Luce. This world is a battleground, and we never had a clue. All the wars and famine and plague — We have a chance to end the worst of them by wiping out their cause."

"Ezra is only the first step." I spotted movement and rose. "We still have to figure out how to seal this terrene off from the others, assuming it's possible."

Santiago broke the surface first and slung his head like a dog to shake off water, splattering us. At Maggie's squeal, he looked chagrined. "Sorry," he grumbled. "I thought you were Portia."

"No problem." She wiped her face dry. "Where's Miller?"

"Definitely Maggie," he muttered under his breath. Louder, he said, "Right behind me."

Wishing he was in range for me to thump him on the head, I pressed, "Any luck?"

"She got away." He hoisted himself onto the deck. "She set traps. Simple ones, but too many to diffuse and still catch her. She was prepared for this. She had it all planned out ahead of time."

Moments later, Miller came into view, his arms slicing through the water. He reached the boat, and I offered him a hand. Content to drip dry, he raked his gaze over Maggie first then turned his attention to me. "We lost her. She was smart keeping her host body. It got her in places her Drosera form — and I — couldn't go. She's spent a lot of time out here to know the place so well."

"Her primary job for War was to gather information," I reminded him. "I'm not surprised she mapped out a place as critical as the breach site."

"True," he allowed. "Usually, she's more thorough on points regarding a new terrene's native population, societal hierarchy, and information gathering."

What he meant was, "She had a particular interest in this breach site."

"It looks that way."

"How about you?" Santiago glanced around. "Have any luck?"

"Sariah served up her source on a silver platter." I couldn't get Knox's craggy face out of my mind, and I was grateful not to be there when Wu broke the news. "Kimora was the leak."

"How did Wu take the news?" Miller twisted to face me. "Is Cole with her?"

"Wu is close to Knox, Kimora too. This will hit them both hard." The entire enclave would be rocked. "And yeah. Cole apprehended her. They're at the bunkhouse." I sat back. "Actually, we should head there now that you two are back."

Once the guys settled in, Thom cranked the boat and pointed it toward what used to be home for them.

Talking over the motor was wasted breath, and none of us had much to say in any case.

Wu and Knox stood on the pier, awaiting our arrival. Cole and Kimora were nowhere in sight. Rixton was MIA as well.

Thom guided the boat close then killed the engine. Gliding in, it bumped off the nearest post, and we stepped onto the pier. Knox was on me a second later, his metal teeth bared, his mechanical hand crushing my airway when it closed around my throat.

"We invited you into our home, provided for and protected one of yours, and this is how you repay us?" A vein bulged in his forehead. "You implicated my daughter — my *daughter*. You're forcing me to bring this infraction to the attention of the enclave. Her reputation will be ruined. She'll be banned from scouting missions and stripped of her security clearance."

"She confessed," I panted. "She wasn't coerced. She was here, in the swamp, waiting to meet Sariah."

His gaze shot to my hands where they clawed at him, to the bangles clanking on my wrists. "No."

"She'll get a fair trial." Wu appeared behind Knox and rested a hand on his shoulder. "It will be up to her peers, not the cadre or their coteries, to decide what punishment she's earned."

"You're hurting. I understand that." Thom prowled over to us, his fingers tipped by claws. "But you're taking your anger out on Luce, and I won't abide that. It's not her fault your daughter made the choices she did, and you will not punish her for them."

A flicker of betrayal brightened Knox's eyes, but then he

nodded, almost to himself, as if remembering Thom was coterie first. He was no longer living among the enclave, and no longer subordinate to Knox.

One by one, Knox loosened his fingers then pried them from my throat like the effort cost him.

"I want to see Kimora." He took a step back, metal hand flexing down by his side. He wasn't done with me yet, but he was lucid enough to recognize he was outgunned. Payback, when it happened, wouldn't come in front of witnesses. "Where is my daughter?"

A door creaked open, and heavy footsteps hit the planks. Cole rounded the corner with Kimora in tow. He had zip tied her hands behind her back, but she otherwise looked fine. In contrast, he noted the tender skin on my throat that would bruise, and then he turned a glacial stare on Knox.

"Luce ordered leniency for your daughter on your behalf." Cole stopped an arm's length away from Knox. "Touch my mate again, and I won't show mercy."

Knox paled under the threat, but he barked, "Release my daughter."

"This isn't your daughter." Cole drew a pocket knife, flicked it open, then stabbed her in the gut. "Show him."

Knox roared his fury, but Wu caught him around the middle before he could attack Cole.

"Daddy." Kimora writhed in Cole's grasp, pain washing the color from her cheeks. "Help me." Blood spilled down the front of her shirt, saturating the waistband of her pants. "Please, Daddy. I'm sorry. Don't let him hurt me again."

Mouth tight, Cole ripped the knife free then plunged it in again. He repeated the process three more times while Knox fought Wu for every inch he gained, but Cole stood firm. The fifth wound broke her, and her skin bubbled, stretched, ripped. At the last second, Cole turned her loose, and a Drosera exploded from her body, almost landing on top of Knox.

"No." He hit the pier on his knees and stared into the gaping mouth of the beast who had murdered his daughter for her body. "*No.*"

Shock glued Wu's feet to the planks, and he made no move to scoop Knox out of harm's way.

"Shit on a shingle." I dove for the Drosera, landing on its back. "Get out of the way." I locked my thighs around its heaving sides and pummeled the base of its skull with my fists until the skin split. "*Move.*"

Cole lunged for Knox, shoving him back into Wu, and they all three hit the water seconds after the Drosera's meaty jaws snapped closed over the air where Knox had been kneeling.

"Little help here?" I slid down the gator's spine as it whipped its body back and forth. "My eight seconds are up."

Light of foot, Thom leapt onto the Drosera's back. Thanks to its attempts to death roll me off its back, he sat in front of me. Claws out, he sank those sharp anchors into that tough hide and held on. He opened his mouth, and his canines elongated into needlelike points he drove into the Drosera with each savage bite he delivered to the heavily plated neck.

The narcotic effect of Thom's saliva wasn't working fast enough. We were all too tired, too beat, for yet another fight. Eager to end things, Miller piled on in front of Thom with a dagger he sank into the Drosera's side. With a sawing motion, he started cutting down its body until blood and organs spilled across the planks. Thank God Knox was too shocked to equate what was being done to the Drosera with his daughter from where he watched from the water.

Kimora was gone. Just as Uncle Harold had been gone. Until this moment, I hadn't realized a viscarre charun could take another charun as a host. But she had been a demi, at least half human with plenty more in her family tree. That must have given the Drosera enough of a toehold to slip into her skin. What it bargained for, how it tricked her, we would never know. Though I could guess their deal involved protecting her father and the enclave.

After the fight went out of the gator, we hopped off and watched until it quit twitching. Once we were certain it was dead, we rolled it off the pier into the water where it landed with a splash and floated belly-up, bobbing slightly.

The chaos meant I hadn't noticed when Cole climbed onto the pier. I wasn't sure if he bodily hoisted Knox onto the planks or if Wu, who sat beside him, had helped. Then again, Wu wasn't looking so hot. Cole might have fished them both out of the swamp.

"Kimora didn't give up the enclave." That much was clear now. "Based on Sariah's half of the story, I'm guessing she spotted Kimora during an aerial patrol over the warehouse. Maybe she even followed us to find her the first time. Once she puzzled out Kimora's link to Wu and Ezra, she sicced a member of her coterie on her. Sariah wanted intel on Ezra to plan her strategy, and that was the only way they could get it."

The fact remained Kimora would have had to agree to a bargain for the Drosera to claim her skin, but she was just a kid. A few years younger than me, but lifetimes younger by any definition. They could have hurt her, scared her, God only knows what, until she gave in.

Knox kept right on ignoring me, but I don't think he was capable of processing anymore.

When my phone rang, I was tempted to ignore it. Whoever was calling couldn't have good news, and I was full up on bad. But I couldn't risk it being a call from Dad or the Rixtons, so I answered. "Boudreau."

"She ate the cat," Dad bellowed. "What do I do?"

"Back up." I rubbed my eyes with my fingertips, grimacing when

I smeared blood on my face. "Who ate the cat? A real cat, right? Not a charun cat?"

"Phoebe," he panted. "And no. I don't think so. I'm not sure."

"Phoebe," I said slowly. "She ate a cat of undetermined species?"

Cole's head shot up at the mention of his daughter, and I gave him a thumbs up to show she was okay.

"Yes." Dad grunted. "Where did — ? Oh God. Miranda. Don't run. It will make her ... " His panting voice filled the line. "Don't chase her. No. Don't — Biting is bad. No biting."

"You're telling me the pod we left with you hatched?" That Luce, always quick on the uptake.

"You've got to help me. I don't know what to do. What can she eat? Do I walk her or ... ?"

"She's a kid." I gestured Cole over so he could weigh in. "Feed her what you fed me. Walking her makes her sound like a pet. Just play with her."

A miniature prehistoric roar so tiny it could have been background noise from one of the dinosaur documentaries Dad enjoyed watching pricked my ears.

"She's a dragon?" I fisted the front of Cole's shirt when he got close enough to reach. *"Phoebe is a dragon?"*

Portia coughed into her fist. "You do understand what happens when a daddy dragon and a mommy dragon bump scales, right?"

"I thought she would be a child. A humanish child. I ... " I banged my head against his chest. "I'm an idiot. Of course she would revert to her natural form. It's instinct. This way she's got teeth and claws to defend herself."

"Put Cole on," Dad urged. "He knows what to do. Right?"

The edge of panic in his voice clinched it. "We'll be right there, Dad."

I ended the call with no clue how to make a graceful exit. Cole's daughter — *our* daughter — had woken. It was cruel to plan a reunion in front of Knox while his daughter's blood cooled on the planks. She might not have been Kimora when she died in front of him, but she had looked like her, and he would carry those images with him for the rest of his hopefully long life.

"Go." Wu stared at nothing in particular. "I'll take care of Knox."

Knox didn't respond to his name or anything else. Eyes hollow, he stared at the spot where Kimora had stood before the Drosera ripped her body to shreds as it shifted forms and obliterated any hope of him getting his child back.

Miller crossed to me, rested a hand on my shoulder. "We'll keep an eye on them."

"I'll bite them," Thom decided. "Rest will do them both good."

Rest did nothing to mend the heart or heal the soul, but sleep allowed for a temporary escape, and I was grateful for my coterie pulling together to tend our allies while Cole and I handled personal business.

Certain the bunkhouse was empty, I asked, "Any word on Rixton's whereabouts?"

"He left a note." Miller passed it over. "He's with the enclave. Says he'll catch a ride back."

"All righty then." Linking my hand with Cole's, I puffed out my cheeks. "We should hurry before she decides Dad looks tasty."

Amusement danced in his eyes. "If she ate a cat, she won't be hungry for a while."

Clearly the unexpected awakening of his kiddo had done wonders for his disposition. He might have been on the fence about waking her, but what was done was done, and it was obvious he was eager to see her again.

Worried for Dad in light of this news, I pressed Cole. "How long is *a while*?"

"An hour or two."

"Oh God."

This time I didn't wait for Cole to sprout wings and fly me. I embraced my inner dragon and let her carry me away.

CHAPTER TWENTY-THREE

Despite my head start, Cole beat me to Haven by a mile, which was a good thing considering I had no idea where I was going when I blasted off in a vague direction I hoped found my dad at the end of it. Another time, I might have wallowed in awe at the sight of the dragon gliding beside me, his majesty and grace breathtaking. Especially when I wasn't on his back. But I was too winded to do more than grunt when he called to me, and I couldn't return the tender caress of wing along wing, somehow more intimate than holding hands as humans, because any deviation in my flight pattern caused me to sink like a stone.

When Haven came into view, I hit upon another problem. The ledge entry was narrow, meant for humanoid charun with wings. Not dragons. Cole had managed the feat, but he was born in this shape. The problem registered too late for me to do anything about it but backbeat my wings and hope for the best.

My best resulted in me smashing chest-first into the side of the mountain and sliding down onto the ledge where I traded skins and just lay there, spent.

A dragon's roar bounced off the rock and rang in my ears, giving me an instant headache to go alongside the brutal aches and pains from impact.

"Luce."

Eyes closing, I groaned an answer.

A shadow fell across my face. "Anything broken?"

"Everything." I winced. "All of it's broken."

A soft laugh escaped him that irked me enough to crank open my lids. He was there to kiss my forehead, right where it hurt, and then to examine me with gentle fingers for lasting injuries.

"You're lucky. You're scraped and bruised, but you'll walk it off."

"That implies I'll be standing and moving around anytime soon."

A feminine shriek, faded from distance, reached my ears, and I shot upright, hissing through the throbbing agony. "Miranda."

Cole helped me onto my feet and got us through the door. "I'll track her down."

"You do that." I limped along, keeping a hand on the wall for balance. "I'm right behind you."

Right behind him. Right . . . a few feet behind him. Maybe several yards. How long was a mile?

The skittering of claws alerted me I had company. Given the fact other charun lived here, the source might have been one of the residents, but I didn't have that kind of luck.

A flash of silvery scales was my only warning before a bundle of baby dragon the size of a corgi plowed into me. Her front legs hit me in the dead center of my chest, right where I was bruised the worst, and I fell back, cracking my already tender head on the floor.

Oxygen whistled through my teeth as I panted through the worst pain. I couldn't draw breath to scream or speak or much of anything else, so I let my head hit the stone floor a second time and waited to see what Phoebe would do.

A pudgy face, covered in scales so thin and shimmery they showed pink skin underneath, peered down at me. Phoebe trilled a question, and I wheezed. The sound delighted her, and she ran three quick circles from my chest to my groin before butting me under the chin with her head. The fuzz masquerading as her mane tickled my nose, and I sneezed. The sound startled her, and . . . she peed on me.

With great effort, I wedged myself into a sitting position. The second I was vertical, she ran up my arm and curled her tail around my throat to anchor her as she perched on my shoulder. Black spots danced in my vision, but I inserted two fingers gently between her lithe body and my neck, forcing her to loosen her stranglehold on me.

Damp, smelly, achy, and lightheaded, I got to my feet and went in search of Cole and Dad.

The whole time, Phoebe trilled, clicked, and chirped a mile a minute. I got the feeling she was filling me in on her adventures, and I wished I could understand what she was saying. Her tiny shudders of laughter reminded me of Cole's larger ones, and I was curious what mischief had struck her funny bone.

Ahead of us, Cole turned a corner, putting him at the end of the long hall we had been wandering. "I should have stuck with you." Eyes bright on Phoebe, I don't think he was breathing. "Where did you find her?"

"She found me."

The sound of his voice caught her attention, and she puffed up her chest, flaring her wings.

"She's protecting you." His voice went soft. "I won't hurt you, Phoebe. Do you remember me?"

Her low snarl made it apparent that no, she didn't remember

him. And I could see it breaking his heart even while he kept his smile pinned in place.

"Did you find Dad?" I started closing the gap between us. "I haven't heard any more screams."

"He's calming down Miranda. She heard the commotion and went to investigate. Phoebe liked the smell, fish have always been her favorite meal, and gave chase. The others locked themselves in their rooms once they spotted the trouble. They're all nonpredatory species, so it's for the best."

The small dragon on my shoulder wasn't impressed with the hulking male who couldn't take his eyes off her. The closer we got to each other, the more vicious her growl until she was using her grip on my throat to hang forward by her tail while swiping her kittenish claws at him.

I had to admit — It was adorable having my own pint-sized defender.

While I wasn't sure how well I would mesh with a kid, a dragon was a whole different matter. She was the most precious little thing I had ever seen, and I could imagine dressing her in dog sweaters and carrying her around in a purse like a chihuahua. On second thought, seeing as how she was Cole's daughter, he would likely have an opinion on that.

Footsteps had me turning, expecting Dad to round the bend, but it was Kapoor who emerged.

"Hey." I offered him a tentative smile. "I didn't know you were here."

No emotion crossed his features. His eyes remained blank and dark, like he was seeing a stranger.

"Oh." I clutched at Phoebe when she wiggled. "Wait. No." Her tail slid through my fingers. "Cole, catch her."

There was no point in telling him. His hands were already there, his daughter cradled safely between them. For a split second.

After that, she raced up his arm to curl around his throat and rub her cheek against his while trilling, clicking, and chirping her little heart out to him.

"She didn't recognize you," I realized. "Once you got close enough to scent, she connected the dots."

Oddly enough, while most of the catlike coterie wanted to eat their avian counterparts, Kapoor sent off predator vibes rather than prey. Likely a result of his past versus his species. Either way, he made Phoebe anxious.

Scratching under her chin, I searched Cole's face. "Check on Dad for me?"

"All right," he said with reluctance. "I'll be right down the hall."

After Cole disappeared from view, Kapoor turned fever bright eyes on me.

"There's something you should know." He wet his cracked lips. "Adam is using you."

"Tell me something I don't know." I bit my tongue. Wu wasn't here to feed me random trivia, but the quip was habit. "Any particular way he's using me that I'm not aware of?"

"Has he explained what happens after you kill Ezra?" He stalked closer. "Assuming you get that far?"

"He's been vague on that part," I admitted.

"There's only one way to save this world and to protect its people, and that's for Conquest, the Seal-Breaker, to die over the breach site. Her blood will lock it. Forever."

Ice swept over my heart, but this wasn't Conquest's doing. It was fear. No, it was terror. "Why are you telling me this now?"

"I didn't think he would do it." Kapoor looked at me, through me. "He had a plan. I was onboard. But I didn't . . . " He shook his head. "I wasn't prepared for how far he was willing to go to see it through. I should have been. I agreed to his terms."

The time Kapoor spent with Ezra must have broken some vital

thing in him. Otherwise, he wouldn't be so chatty. His position as a janitor, and his job with the NSB, didn't lend itself to loose lips. His wouldn't be flapping now if his very foundation hadn't been cracked.

"Other Conquests have come before me." I grasped at straws. "They died here. Why didn't that work?"

"Sacrifice," Kapoor hissed. "For the lower terrenes to be blocked from this one forever, you must take your own life."

It wasn't enough to be willing to die, I had to be willing to kill. Myself.

"I would take Wu with me." I turned it over in my head, and I saw the pieces fitting together in a way I never expected. "That's the idea, isn't it?" A bitter taste coated the back of my throat. "My death seals the lower terrenes and his seals the upper. Together, we could place Earth in a protective bubble."

"He wasn't going to tell you until you defeated Ezra, or didn't, but I wanted you to know. When Ezra had me . . . " His voice faded to a whisper, and he had trouble finding it again. "My best friend, such as he is, knew what was coming and did nothing to stop it." He closed his eyes, fists tight at his sides. "He didn't stop it."

"He knew Ezra was coming for you." How could he not? Ezra had contacted Kapoor, given his list of demands to him. And Wu and I had blown him off, stalling as best he could while we gathered our forces. In retaliation, Ezra had apparently decided to crucify the messenger. "Wu let you get taken."

"I let myself get taken," he admitted. "I could have run. I chose to stay." He let his attention drift behind me. "I'm telling you this because you have a mate, and you have a child. I didn't think either mattered before, but now I see it's all that's important. Spend what time you have left with the ones you love." His somber gaze met mine, held. "You deserved to know the truth, the whole truth, and now you do."

"Thank you."

"I'm going to lie down now." He pivoted on his heel, eyes distant, voice rough. "I'm tired."

I watched him go then waited on Cole to join me, certain he had wandered off to give us privacy but not so far as to visit with Dad.

Sure enough, he strolled up the hall a few minutes later with Phoebe racing down his shoulders and across his back, her nails drawing pinpricks of blood he didn't appear to notice.

"Ezra broke him." I stroked Phoebe's head when she spotted me. "I didn't see it at first, the cracks were too small, or maybe Wu spackled over them, but the more time he spends doing nothing but staring at walls, the wider they get. If we're not careful, he'll fall through."

"The desired outcome determines the method used." Cole shook his head. "Ezra hurt him, physically, but it's nothing beyond a charun's ability to mend, especially with intervention from Thom. Psychologically? Those wounds take longer to heal, and they leave scars."

"I'll ask Wu if there's someone he can talk to," I decided. "Kapoor was in therapy. We can track down his therapist, get them to do more sessions with him."

And hope that was enough, that anything we did for him at this point would be enough.

"She likes your father," Cole said when Phoebe's nose started twitching in the direction of the hallway they had just exited. "He smells like you."

"That explains why she didn't terrorize him." I shrugged. "Much." She had eaten a cat, but it could have just as easily been a bite out of him. "She understands he's family." Then what he said hit me. "You can communicate with her?"

"I can't speak to her while in this form, but I understand what she's saying. For the most part. She's still a young child. Half of what comes out of her mouth is what you're hearing — happy noises."

Unable to resist the temptation, I cupped his cheek to cradle his smile in my palm.

Phoebe, unhappy to lose our attention, wound her tail around my wrist and yanked my hand down onto her back where I started scratching, as requested. "Like father, like daughter."

Cole leaned over and kissed me full on the mouth. "I love you."

"I love you too." I touched my lips. "I'm not complaining, but what did I do to earn a kiss?"

Before he could answer, Phoebe leapt from his chest to mine and rammed my mouth with her scaly muzzle hard enough to have me tasting blood. Fluttering her wings at me, I could tell she was impressed with her newfound kissing ability. I, on the other hand, wondered if I could get away with wearing a mouthguard around her.

"You exist," he answered after wiping his thumb across my tender bottom lip. "That's enough."

As much as I hated to ruin his reunion, I had no choice. "We can't stay here."

"We need to have a chat with Wu about more than Kapoor," he agreed. "Will your father mind babysitting?"

"You can shift and communicate with her that way?" I traced the tiny claws hooking my shirt. "I want her to understand she can't eat Dad, or hurt Dad, or maim anyone else. She shouldn't eat anything except what he gives her."

With the Rixtons in residence, I couldn't risk Nettie appearing too pink and plump for Phoebe to resist.

"I'll make a list," I decided, passing Phoebe back to Cole. "You two go catch up."

After they had gone, and I was alone, I backed into the wall then slid onto the floor. I tipped my head back and stared at the ceiling, seeing nothing.

I never expected to survive the war. Not really. The odds had never been in my favor.

Learning I was the sacrificial lamb on my way to the slaughter felt ... par for the course, honestly.

It didn't surprise me much. I think I ran out of that emotion a while ago. Maybe I went into shock the night they broke the news I was charun and never emerged. That might explain the numbness.

I could almost accept the role outlined for me, almost, in an academic sense, but forcing me to slit my own throat? No wonder no previous incarnation of Conquest had done the deed.

Cole would forbid me from fulfilling the role Wu had designed for me, and Dad would too. The coterie and the Rixtons would throw their weight behind them as well. But what if the cost of peace, true peace, was my life? What if the price for atonement for all Conquest's sins was my blood? Would I woman-up and sacrifice myself? One soul in exchange for billions of others?

I wasn't sure I could do it, but I wasn't convinced I wouldn't under the right circumstances.

The wiggle room in that thought terrified me, so I did what I did best. I packed it away with all the other horrors, the other maybes, the other possibilities. I stuffed it in the back of my mind to pull out and examine after we defeated Ezra, all the while telling myself there would be an after.

For now, I hauled myself onto my feet and padded to the exit, to the ledge overlooking a sheer drop-off. In the distance, a mighty dragon looped and dove while a tinier version of him bobbed and weaved on air currents that lifted hairs into my eyes. While I watched the pair play tag, I took as many mental snapshots as I had memory to save.

When Phoebe winged over to me, trilling joyously, jerking her head toward Cole, I understood I had been invited to play.

The world would still be ending tomorrow. I might as well enjoy what remained of today.

And so I stepped off the ledge, gave myself over to the feral heart that beat harder when I spotted Cole looping back for me, and I soared.

EPILOGUE

———◦◉◦———

Farhan sat on his bed in his room at Haven. The mattress was soft, his sheets fragranced with soothing lavender. The television played softly in the background. The atmosphere was tranquil, quiet. Things he once longed for but now grated on his over-sensitized nerves.

The things Ezra had done to him . . .

The things Adam had known he would do . . . and let it happen anyway.

Charun held too much power in this terrene.

Farhan had grown up believing he was human. Just a boy. Nothing special. Just like everyone else. Discovering his mother was *other* had been a wicked jolt to his system, one he never recovered from.

Not until he felt his blood draining drop by drop, his consciousness swirling down a cosmic drain. Before that, he hadn't given his mother a second thought in over a decade. She didn't deserve to occupy one ounce of headspace, but there she had been. There she still was, lurking in his memories.

As they hauled her away, screaming his name, kicking and biting, she fought to get back to her son.

As they told him the truth, showed him the truth, he wept like a child. And when he turned sixteen, they beat him half to death to trigger his inner charun.

What exploded from his skin was him and not him, and it was terrible and beautiful. They had never seen anything quite like it, which made him wonder if his mother had refused to reveal herself. Had they clubbed her? Punched her? Kicked her too? Worse? Had she kept that secret, her identity, to the last?

Farhan didn't know, and that sat heavy on his conscience. His mother was the only reason he had betrayed Adam today, even that little bit. Telling Luce the truth had been a gamble, but it was worth the risk. She was set on her path. He saw it in her eyes when she absorbed the blow, a kind of relief that the worst was known, that the other shoe had finally dropped, and she had no way to avoid its impact.

All he had done was given her a chance to make her peace. Likely, she had already begun the process, but he wanted her to understand she had to get a move-on if she wanted to mark all the names off her list.

The phone in his pocket rang, and he answered without looking at the screen. "Hello, Adam."

He wasted no time getting to the point. "Luce is there?"

"She's playing with her kid." He made a fist with his free hand. "Have you ever watched a family of dragons together? It's the most beautiful damn thing I've ever seen."

"No." He sounded wistful and yet irritated. "I haven't."

The mate bond made it hard for Adam to appreciate things like Luce having a mate or their having a child.

"I told her what's required to seal the terrenes," Farhan admitted.

The line filled with silence, and then Adam sighed. "She didn't back down, did she?"

He sounded like he wished she would fight it, fight him, but she was an arrow soaring toward its mark. She wouldn't miss. Her aim was too good.

"She'll do whatever it takes, assuming her mate doesn't stop her first."

Reminding Adam she belonged to someone else was a low blow. He might not love Luce, but he admired her. For all that he pretended otherwise, he desired her. Under different circumstances, Cole might have a fight on his hands. But under different circumstances, she wouldn't exist.

"Cole will have to be dealt with. He won't let her go easily."

The difference in how their individual mate bonds worked never ceased to amaze Farhan. Each species' biological needs echoed through that connection. Some mated for life, some for a season. Some lived on, some died. Some required it to procreate, others bred like rabbits.

Luce was caught in the middle. Adam had killed her before she had a chance to begin, and Cole would die before he lost her and faced life alone.

"The kid's awake." A distant part of Farhan couldn't believe he actually spoke the words. "That's all the leverage we'll need." A child screaming for its parents was far more convincing than the solemnity of the pod she emerged from. "They're leaving her under Edward Boudreau's supervision."

Humans were no obstacle for them, and Boudreau hadn't fully recovered from his bout with poison. He would be easily subdued, easily manipulated. An obstacle easily overcome.

"Good," Adam said, but there was too much regret there to pass as genuine sentiment. "I'll call when it's time."

"I'll be here." He ended the call, stared at the blank walls.

"Figures." He flopped back on the mattress. "Finally get some time off, and I can't sleep."

Guilt pressed too hard on his chest, regret mired him too deep in his thoughts, and the roil in his gut when he recalled with vivid clarity how far Adam was willing to go to see this through left him too close to spilling his lunch.

He hoped Luce took his advice. He hoped she said her *I love yous* and *goodbyes*.

Death was coming for her, and he didn't mean cadre.

Death, for her, would look like an angel.